PEOPLE OF THE RAIN

RAINFALL

STEVE OLDFIN

outskirts
press

People of the Rain
Rainfall
All Rights Reserved.
Copyright © 2017 Steve Oldfin
v2.0

This is a work of fiction. The events and characters described herein are imaginary and are not intended to refer to specific places or living persons. The opinions expressed in this manuscript are solely the opinions of the author and do not represent the opinions or thoughts of the publisher. The author has represented and warranted full ownership and/or legal right to publish all the materials in this book.

This book may not be reproduced, transmitted, or stored in whole or in part by any means, including graphic, electronic, or mechanical without the express written consent of the publisher except in the case of brief quotations embodied in critical articles and reviews.

Outskirts Press, Inc.
http://www.outskirtspress.com

ISBN: 978-1-4787-8745-7

Cover Photo © 2017 Steve Oldfin. All rights reserved - used with permission.

Outskirts Press and the "OP" logo are trademarks belonging to Outskirts Press, Inc.

PRINTED IN THE UNITED STATES OF AMERICA

TABLE OF CONTENTS

Journey of Self Discovery: 1

The Awakening: 12

Me and My Shadow: 36

A New World: 43

The Training Day: 60

The Fountain of Knowledge: 73

Back to the City: 87

School Days: 92

Cyrus: 115

Into the Jungle: 122

The War Begins: 145

John's Travels: 164

Laura's Watch: 172

The Council: 179

The Big Battle: 198

The Changing Tide: 218

JOURNEY OF SELF DISCOVERY:

THE RAIN FALLS in many ways and appears in many forms. Rain can gather out of thin air, condensing into small wisps of vapor, then collecting into a slow creeping fog. As your view of everything around you slowly fades into varying shades of gray, you become distinctly aware of the pervasive dampness all around. By the time you become conscious of the moisture in the air, you also realize it is not falling down, as in the form of rain, but that you are slowly being enveloped in a fine damp mist. It softly floats in every direction without making a sound. It creeps up on you slowly, saturating the air until the air can simply hold no more; eventually the moisture begins to condense onto every surface. It first collects almost undetected, like very small beads of sweat upon everything. Eventually the beads start to run together into drops, the drops trickle together into very small rivulets that, in turn, run together, until they begin to drip and drop, imitating what we normally perceive as rain that falls from the sky. This kind of rain comes quietly, usually when there is no wind at all, not even the faintest hint of a breeze. It is not recognizable as rain at all until suddenly you notice the small droplets of water, collecting, running together and dripping from everything all around you amidst the ever-thickening fog and a creeping dampness that penetrates to the bone.

Rain at the other extreme can come hard and heavy, falling in thick heavy sheets, pouring out of a dark, angry sky in such volume that it feels as if all the water of all the oceans of the world have been lifted up into the sky only to be poured back down upon you. This rain arrives with power and violence that leaves destruction in its wake. It comes like an attacking army, unleashing its full force to overwhelm all that stands before it. This rain doesn't come alone; it comes with wind, claps of thunder and blazing flashes of lightning. It brings flooding with relentless torrents of water that can undercut, overflow, sweep aside or simply destroy any human construction. It is loud, it comes hard and it comes fast. This form of rain has no mercy; it knows no boundaries and reminds us all just how powerless and small we are before the full force of nature.

The rain comes in different forms and varying frequencies around the world. Eventually the rain, in some form, touches every place on the face of this earth, from the frozen ice caps to the driest of deserts and even the vastness of the open oceans. Some places receive more rain and others less. Some places experience a greater variety of ways in which the rain presents itself to us. There are few places on this planet that are truly intimate with every form of the rain. However, there are a few places that experience the rain so frequently and with such diversity of form that it shapes not only the land but the people who live there.

In the far northwestern corner of the American continent is a place familiar with the rain like no other. It is a nexus of the ever-changing interaction of wind, water and temperature that creates frequent rain in a myriad of forms. It is a place shaped and defined by the rain as much or more than any other. In this place where the Pacific Ocean meets the North American continent, at the Canadian-American border, the vast Pacific Ocean cuts deep into the continent, forming an inland sea known today as the Puget Sound. This inland sea is dotted with islands large and small and surrounded by verdant mountain ranges on either side. The frequent rain and the temperate climate combine to paint the land with lush green growth. There are many towns and cities that have grown up in this region in the last few hundred years, the largest and most central of which is named Seattle; but it is frequently just referred to as the rain city. Indeed, there are few people in the world who know the rain as intimately as those who live in and amongst the temperate rainforests of this area.

The people who come to this place must first learn to deal with the rain as part of their everyday life. If they stay, they learn to protect themselves from the constant penetrating rain. If they stay long enough, they eventually accept as one accepts the rising and setting of the sun. If you spend your full life here, you begin to appreciate the rain for all it is and all it does. You begin to anticipate the coming and going of the rain as one anticipates the changing of the seasons or the flow of the tide. For a very few of us, those of us born into a culture of rain, there is yet another aspect to it. It is not something that even the most astute among us can see or touch; it is a quality which can only be experienced.

Long before the first European settlers found their way to these lush and ancient forests, this most intimate secret of the rain came to be known and revered by the first people to call this special place home. For many hundreds of years this secret of the rain was kept by those first few indigenous people. Even as the first wave of settlers from Europe overran them, they kept this secret. Even now, after generations of people coming to this corner of the world from every part of the globe, the secret of the rain is still known only to a very few. Like the physical form of the rain, the secret nature of rain is different for each person who experiences it.

I remember when the rain first revealed its secret to me. I was a young man and like most young men, I thought that I understood the physical world around me. I thought I had a pretty good idea, although somewhat cynical, of how things worked--where I was in this giant ant hill we called a city. I thought I knew what I was doing and where I was going in life.

I had come from a mundanely dysfunctional home. A mother and father with four children, living at the bottom end of a shrinking middle class. My father worked a mediocre job that he didn't like and was ill suited for. Just another cog in the proverbial machine. We had a roof over our heads and food on the table. Unfortunately it was a home full of the typical drama born out of the constant stress of living close enough to catch glimpses of that middle class life of status quo but not quite close enough to taste the satisfaction that was there to be had if you could just reach a little higher and a little further. In hindsight, I remember thinking my parents would have both lived much better, happier lives if they'd called it quits, given up that middle class dream and gone their separate ways early on; but they were locked into their roles like hamsters on a wheel. They could not see outside the little box in their minds that they had trapped themselves in. They chose to stay together, locked in some kind of dysfunctional relationship as co-dependent, co-enablers of each other's dysfunction and dissatisfaction, each one blaming the other for the dream that seemed to be just out of reach, each blaming the other for their own unhappiness, each driving the other to greater levels of dysfunction and self-destructive behavior--hardly engaged, model parents.

As a young person I could see the trap that my parents had locked themselves into and I knew I had to find something different. I could feel something else out there but I did not know what it was. I could feel, deep inside, there was something more than just the status quo waiting for me, something just out of my reach, just out of sight. I didn't know what I wanted but I knew what I did not. I knew there was something more than a life of mediocity, something different. It was as if I was searching for something with no idea what it was.

As soon as I got out of high school, I left that downwardly spiraling scene like a rat, I suppose, jumping from a sinking ship. Once I was on my own, I learned to shed most of the emotional baggage that I had unwittingly brought with me. Yet somehow I found myself slipping. Slowly I was starting to accept what I felt was the cold reality of the world around me. I started to see the people around me as the automatons they were. I felt myself slipping into the same behavior that leads to that darkly-tinged life. A life filled with the dull routine, the slow grind that so many people fall into because they can't see any other options. As long as I could remember, I could see past the masks that people created to hide their dull life behind. I could see everyone around me as well as I could see myself, behind the mask, as we all are, flawed individuals just trying to live our lives, find some meaning in each day to hold back the ever-encroaching fog of the grim status quo.

As a child I had struggled against the gravity of mediocrity that pulled against me, that pulls against all of us, dragging us into conformity with the world around us. I stayed out late running the streets, looking for something unique. I could not see it or describe it but sometimes late on a rainy night, I would go outside just to feel the rain on my face. As the rain washed over me, I felt I could reach out of my monotonous existence and feel the world around me. I could let loose all the frustration and anger that I absorbed day to day in random senseless ways. It was as if the rain could simply wash the anger and frustration from me. I came to understand within myself that I was searching for some meaning, some purpose that seemed to be just out of view. I knew whatever it was, I had to find it.

As I grew, I learned to wear my own mask of conformity, to conceal my weakness, my dissatisfaction with the status quo, to protect myself by burying my emotions. I learned to keep everyone at a distance with a smile, to prevent them from reading the real me. After a rocky start in life, finally I started pulling things together. I thought I had found a path out of the mist and slowly, I plodded forward. Now I had a plan. I was just putting in my time, working crappy jobs to pay for my education. That was what we were all told. Follow the herd, stay in line, move along the path reaching for the dream that is just out of reach. Get a degree, get a better job, have a better life. OK, so it was not much of a plan but it was what I had. For now, I thought it was the answer, but the reality is, I was becoming just another drone I suppose; just another hamster on a wheel, like my parents, in a city built out of wheels large and small, all turning to make the big cities go. I was young and living the mundane life of an ordinary guy, going to the university in the daytime and working a menial job to pay the bills at night. I suppressed the need to feel that strange feeling that I sensed as a young teenager, the feeling that there was something more. It was something that would figuratively wash over me when I sneaked out just to feel the rain on my face. I did not have much in the way of a social life but that was OK. After all, everything has a price. I had a plan. I didn't have time for much of anything but work and school and this was all that mattered right now. I told myself that I was not going to have my parents' life. I wanted something better, but in hindsight, I was just buying into a different version of the same thing, building my own mental box.

I remember that night was just another late night. I was on my way home from my job. After several hours of school in the morning, studying all afternoon, working a swing shift cooking over a hot grill for hours, and then cleaning up after closing, I was done. I had not slept for twenty hours and it was just another dark and rainy night, like so many others in the rain city.

I had missed my bus and at this time of night, it could be some time before the next bus so I just started walking. The rain was not a heavy rain as I recall, it was just drizzling, coming down uniformly, in steady waves as it does when the rain is here for an extended downpour. It was not really cold, just sort of clammy from the moisture that seeps in everywhere; anyway, I was no stranger to the rain so I really didn't even think much about it. I marched along the dark but familiar city streets. The street lights and the business signs reflected off the rain as it fell and off the water that collected in pools, puddles and streams across the darkened concrete landscape of the city. It was easy to find my way without much thought. I guess I was so accustomed to the rain and so familiar with the streets, even in the darkness, not to mention that I was tired, so very tired. I simply allowed myself to slip into auto pilot as I plodded along through the steady rain. I remember I was crossing one of the many long bridges we have in this city; a city that is defined by hills separated by the lakes and waterways that drain all this water from the landscape and pour it out into the Puget Sound.

My head was down and my hands in my pockets. The steady rain was occasionally punctuated by the odd car splashing past me; then I felt something. Something that is hard to explain—you see, living in the city, even when you are not really paying attention directly, part of your consciousness is always scanning the steady din of background noise. Your brain, even on a semi-conscious level is always filtering out the ordinary background noises of the city that you are accustomed to and scanning for just those noises that are out of place. I remember it was a feeling that seemed to come from a different part of my brain. You know, when you see something out of the corner of your eye but when you turn your head, it is not there; or when you think you heard something but you are not sure what exactly it was or if you really heard it at all. A strange feeling washed over me. My mind flashed but I could not tell where the feeling was coming from. It was as if, for just a moment, I was connected to every living thing. I could hear the thoughts and feel the feelings of living things all around me. I could feel the wind as it drove the rain through the leaves and branches of the trees and plants around me. I could feel the few people going about their meaningless lives late at night, slogging through the rain themselves. I could feel all the animals that lived almost invisible among us. I could feel what they all felt and heard what they thought. The closer they were, the clearer I could sense them. It was such a strange sensation and so brief that I might have dismissed it altogether as the result of long hours and too much coffee but in that overpowering flash, I had clearly felt the two people, 100 yards or so below the bridge that I was crossing. They were on a dark street that ran parallel to the waterway that flowed under the bridge. They were in the shadow of the bridge too far away to hear over the din of the city and too dark to see even if I went to the edge and looked down.

I felt the mind-shattering fear of an older woman who was struggling with an attacker. At the same time that I felt her thoughts, I also felt the fear, desperation and the exhilaration of the drug addict that was her attacker. I could feel the anger that he felt toward his intended victim driven by the pain of his addiction. He wanted that money; he needed that money to feed the monster within him that only grew hungrier each time he fed it. That need to feel the next high was consuming him. There was something else, something elusive. For just a moment, I also felt that someone else was watching, watching what was occurring on that dark street below the bridge and watching me. I don't know why or how but I knew what I felt was real and transpiring on the street far below in the blackness. I don't know why but I was consumed by the feeling, I felt like I was the one being attacked. I felt that I had to do something.

My brain was on overload. I had to fight but there was no one there on the bridge deck for me to fight. I stopped in a panic. I spun around several times, the sensations of the attack coursing through me. The attack continued and I felt it all but I could not see it. My adrenalin was racing. I pulled myself together and ran the fifty yards to a staircase on the side of the bridge. I ran down the long dark and slippery staircase. As I got to the bottom, I raced around the corner, back down the street that ran next to the waterway under the bridge.

The sensation grew stronger, only now I could see up ahead of me the faint outline of a man standing over the woman he had pushed to the ground. He was digging through her purse, throwing things on the sidewalk, searching for her wallet. I felt his desperation and the pain from his addiction even stronger as I approached. He was in the shadow of the bridge but I could see his silhouette against the streetlights behind him. His image was just a shadow but his rain-soaked outline glistened. For some reason he looked my way. He appeared to be startled and jumped back, dropping the purse and just catching himself before he fell. He paused and looked all around before he spun back my way. He must have heard the splash of my footsteps coming toward him at a run. Stumbling over the purse he had dropped, he turned to sprint the other way. By the time I got to the lady, still sprawled out on the concrete sidewalk her assailant was out of sight.

"I'm so grateful you came along," the woman said in a shaky voice as she slowly gathered herself up from the wet sidewalk.

"Are you Ok?" I asked, pulling my cell phone from my pocket and dialing 911. I offered her my hand as I spoke to the police and then I helped her collect the contents of her purse that the attacker had scattered on the wet sidewalk around us. The police arrived fairly quickly. The first officer on the scene had the woman sit in the back of his police cruiser and when the second officer showed up he went over to her to take her statement. The second officer to arrive on the scene took my statement, after which the two officers stepped to the side and spoke in hushed voices for a moment. I stood there in the rain watching them look up at the bridge deck some 100 yards over our heads in the darkness and the rain. They'd stop and look my way, then over at the lady sitting in the car. I could see there was something bothering them, something that did not appear to add up.

The woman had refused any medical attention and insisted she would be fine, so the first officer said he would drive her home. Neither I nor the woman had caught a good look at her attacker and he was long gone. I stood in the rain speaking with the second officer, reviewing what I had already told him for a few more moments after the first officer left to take the lady home. I was about to get back on my way when the police officer asked me the question. "So" ...he said, "I still can't figure this part out. If you were up there on the bridge deck, going north, what made you take the stairs down and double back under the bridge? There's no way you could see under the bridge 100 yards below in the dark even if you had gone to the edge and looked. With all the noise of the cars on the bridge deck and the rain, there's no way you heard what was going on down here. What brought you down here?"

I had not really thought about just how impossible it was until he asked, but he was right. I knew that it just wasn't possible that I heard or saw anything.

"I wish I knew," I said as I stood there for a moment, looking up at the bridge deck above me. The officer gave me a strange look. Police don't like unanswered questions but, clearly, there was not an answer that made any sense.

I turned away from the officer and headed back down the street toward the stairs that would take me back up to the bridge deck. The officer stood there in the rain, following me with his eyes. I did not have to look back to know he was still unsatisfied. I thought about that the rest of the way home. I, too, was still unsatisfied but I was also, so very tired. I was not one to buy into any kind of psychic mumbo jumbo. It had to be something like a scream I heard but did not quite register or something else like that. But even if she had screamed, at that distance, with the din of the city background noise could I have heard?

Oh well, whatever it was, it was late; I was wet, I was cold and I was tired. I still felt that creepy feeling like someone was watching me. I had just reached the top of the stairs when I paused. I stood there in the rain for a moment and slowly looked all around me. I saw nothing out of the ordinary but there were a lot of dark shadows out there. I walked on in the rain, one foot in front of the other, back on auto pilot but with just the occasional look over my shoulder.

    I got home to my little second story, walk up studio apartment in the University District well after midnight. All the street level shops of my building were dark except for the neon signs and advertisements in windows. I put my key in the knob and stepped into the small lobby. I glanced at the rows of mailboxes on one side but I was too tired to even check my mail as I headed straight up the stairs that led up to the next floor. The street level was all small businesses but the rest of the building constituted several floors of small apartments. I took off my hat and brushed the rain from my jacket as I trudged up the stairs and down the dimly lit hall. I leaned up against my apartment door exhausted, as I turned the key and stumbled into my little studio apartment. I closed the door behind me and slowly entered the dark room illuminated only by the light of the store signs and traffic lights outside, reflecting off the rain and refracting through the window glass and partially closed blinds. I hung my coat and hat to dry by the door as I came in. It was late and I was dead tired so I didn't bother turning on the lights or drawing the blinds completely. I just kicked off my shoes and pulled down the Murphy bed. I had learned long ago to tune out the background noise of a city that never really sleeps. I just threw my clothing on the floor, dove into bed and fell fast asleep as soon as my head hit the pillow.

THE AWAKENING:

I AWOKE TO the sounds of the bus at the bus stop directly in front of my building. The heavy thick rumble of the diesel engine as the bus pulled away from the curb vibrated right through my front second floor window. I didn't just hear it, as much as I felt the vibration. It was 7:00 on a Saturday morning and the street was already busy out in front of my building. Some of the store front businesses on the first floor of my apartment building were already open with people going in and out, and I could also hear a few people moving around on the two floors of apartments above me. The rain was still coming down although a bit lighter than last night. It was more like the gentle rain of spring that, in other parts of the world, could easily give way to the sun by midday but not here, not in the rain city--at least not today. I could hear the cars splashing down the street and the people chatting as they splashed along the sidewalk below my window. I could hear the sound of the water as it ran in trickles down the front of the building and the sound of the little droplets, tapping intermittently as light gusts of wind pushed them against my window.

    I slowly rolled out of bed, and stepped over my still damp clothes from last night. I kneeled on the sofa that was in front of the window and I peered through the half open blinds and surveyed the streets below for a moment. "So much for sleeping in." I turned around and plopped down on the sofa. I looked back over my shoulder, through the blinds at the pale gray sky as I thought about last night for a moment.

After a cup of coffee, I wandered to the bathroom and turned on the shower. Living in the city, there is always something going on around you, you are never really alone. Whether or not you can see them, there are always people around day and night. Even in the relative privacy of my little studio apartment, there were people just feet away from me, on the other side of those walls, just a few feet below in the shops or a few feet above in the apartments above me. I stepped into the shower and closed my eyes, leaning forward, letting the water run over my head as I lingered there in the shower. I could smell the coffee and baked goods from one of the shops downstairs.

Most people in the city simply condition themselves to ignore all the various background noises and smells without even being aware of it. Sometimes, when I felt I was becoming too complacent, I'd test myself. It was like I was afraid of losing something. I like to close my eyes and see how many of those background sounds and smells I could pull to the forefront of my consciousness and identify.

As I stood there in the shower with my eyes closed and the water running over me, I replayed last night in my mind. I still could not figure it out. How did I know what was going on so far from where I was? I could not hear it, see it or smell it. It was out of my range of normal perception. I went back to my mental exercise. I just stood there in the shower, perplexed, with my head down and the warm water running over me. Slowly in my mind I picked out each individual sound that made up the din of the background noise I was hearing there in my little apartment. I started to drift for a few seconds to become aware of those people in the adjacent apartments, in the store just below me. I was just starting to feel like I could see the individual thoughts of each person; then, like being startled awake, I snapped back to reality and looked quickly around myself in that little shower. That was weird. When I zoomed back to reality, I realized, hey, this was my day off. It was Saturday. No work, no school.

    I quickly dressed and was out the front door. The rain was coming down in a steady shower and the urban landscape around me was now muffled in a wet blanket of gray. The rain spattered off the brim of my baseball cap as I stepped onto the street. The collected rain would occasionally fall in big drops that punctuated the steady shower of small drops with big splashes that sometimes caught the occasional pedestrian by surprise. People were already hustling up and down the sidewalks, dodging the waves splashed up from the streets onto the sidewalks from the passing cars and trucks. I joined the huddle under the cover of a bus stop right in front of my building for a few minutes with several other rain city dwellers. One of the cool things about this city is that you never have to wait long before the next bus, going downtown comes along. The bus was pretty full for a Saturday morning. I filed onto the bus with my fellow travelers from this stop and flashed my bus card to the driver as I walked past. The bus is full of wet people some standing, some sitting with puddles of water collecting on the black rubber floor at their feet and then running up and down the aisle as the bus startes up and stops with the traffic. The bus pulled from the curb and my boots squeake on the wet floor as I worked my way to the back.
    The windows were halfway fogged over from the heavy moisture in the air. Some of the people chatted and others just stared, blank faced out the window or preoccupied themselves with their electronic devices. I turned to face the front as I grabbed the overhead hand rail. I zoned out a little and I felt that weird feeling wash over me again--like a hot flash and for just a moment I felt like I could hear not just the soft spoken words of the people actually talking to one another but also the random thoughts of everyone on the bus; it was all jumbled together. It felt like a massive wave that leaves you tumbling underwater before you can orient yourself as to which way is up. I had to collect myself. For just a moment I closed my eyes, holding tight to the hand rail as the bus lunged forward

and then slowed with the ebb and flow of traffic. I took a deep breath and tried to focus. I tried not to panic. I must not have gotten enough sleep last night. It felt as if everyone on the bus were all speaking at the same time. It blurred together and I felt like I was still underwater reaching for the surface. There was a strange, momentary shortness of breath. I opened my eyes and focused on just one woman who was sitting right next to where I was standing. She was actually talking out loud to the woman seated next to her. They went on about the weather, of all things, back and forth. Without looking at them, I focused on their conversation only and tuned out everything else. What was going on in my head? The other noise started to fade.

This bus was an express so it made just a few stops in the University District, then we jumped right on the freeway heading over a bridge toward downtown. I kept my focus on one conversation at a time, clearing my head. The blur of voices began to subside to just those that were actually speaking around me on the bus. The bus exited off the freeway and hit its first stop in the downtown area. We were in the city now with tall buildings all around. They did nothing to stop the rain but they filtered the light, making things just a little darker shade of gray. We finally reached my stop and I stepped off the bus into the steady rain. I was glad to be out of that confined bus so I could clear my head. I pulled my collar up against the little gusts of rain that came from odd directions. The wind channeled around and through the concrete canyons created by the tall buildings. This city has so many hills that even the downtown area, with all its tall buildings, is built on a hillside that slopes from a hilltop covered with several sprawling hospitals all the way down through a forest of concrete and glass to the waterfront.

I got off the bus in the very core of the city and I found my way down to the Public Market. It is a unique landmark in our city that overlooks the Seattle waterfront. It is a multi-leveled cornucopia of small shops and vender stalls that is well over 100 years old. It incorporates a few adjacent old but renovated buildings and also serves as an access point to an old brick paved back alley with a few hidden shops not normally sought out by the throngs of tourists that will swell the market in the summer. This is where the upper middle class of eco-friendly engineer types come to buy their organically grown, all natural fruits and vegetables direct from the local growers. It is interesting to watch them with their ergonomically designed child carriers as they mingle with the tourists, picking out their fresh produce, latte in hand, and blue tooth in their ear. They like to think that their success hasn't changed them but they worry about parking their new Land Rover too close to this area just the same. They try extra hard to be personable with the local artists and venders at the same time they also try to avoid eye contact with the occasional cadre of urban panhandlers. Like all cities, there is a segment of the population who has fallen. Some have made bad choices that have led them to this life on the street, living day to day. Some have been run over by the machinery of society and some never had a chance from the beginning. It is hard to say, at a glance, how some of them got to be where they are. They are the alcohol or drug addicts, mentally ill or other misfits and castoffs of our society that intermingle with the droves of tourists that come just to watch the fishmonger toss their fresh caught salmon and sell other Puget Sound delicacies. They pitch the fish high and long from one end of their stall, and never miss a catch. The tourists love the showmanship. The market is packed with small venders selling handmade jewelry, stall after stall of locally grown produce, exotic teas from around the world, second hand books and every kind of pastry imaginable.

    There are three levels to the public market. The top level is open at street level toward the city and on the other side, the market offers windowed views of the Puget Sound on the top and the two levels below it. The original cobblestone streets have been maintained around the market and into the adjoining alleyways that disappear into shadowed back streets of a much older part of the city. The air is filled with the smell of fresh made foods of all sorts, locally grown fruits, vegetables and cut flowers, fresh fish and other local sea food. The two lower levels are below the street level on the city side but face outward, overlooking the waterfront on the other as the hillside slopes down to the waterfront. The lower levels have restaurants, gift and antique stores of all sorts and its antiquated construction only adds to the overall character of the place.

I headed to my favorite spot, a diner-style restaurant on one of the lower levels of the market that serves breakfast American all day. I like to sit near the window and look out over the waterfront. If I get a window seat, even in the rain I can eat my breakfast and watch the ferry boats coming and going from the city across the Puget Sound to the heavily forested Olympic Peninsula or to one of the many, rocky tree-blanketed islands that litter this inland sea.

After a long relaxing breakfast, I worked my way back up to the main level through the throngs. My head had cleared and I was just enjoying the ambiance as I wandered through the covered market area, taking in the exotic mix of sights, sounds and smells that make the market so interesting and unique. I walked out the open end of the building that faced back toward the gray city and away from the waterfront. Pausing, I looked down the dark cobblestone alley and I realized I had never looked in on the few shops down this way. There was something intriguing to me down there. I started to turn that way but no, not today. I put up my collar, pulled down the front of my hat, and crossed the street, glancing up the street to the far end of the market. There was a very small park just outside the covered market area at that end with a totem pole in the middle and a circle of park benches. It offered a great view of the Puget Sound. It was also where the street people like to congregate when it wasn't raining. Across the cobblestone street stood a few old buildings of the same vintage as the Market itself but redesigned to more modern standards. It houses more food shops, fresh made bread, famous coffee and some other international food of the on-the-go type. I put my head down as I splashed my way across the street through all the purpose-driven pedestrians coming and going from the market and all the chic coffee shops and bakeries that lined the street across from the market. The smell of fresh brewed coffee and baked goods mingled with the smell of the garbage bins in front of the market. As I strode across the street, the sounds of the city were put to a melody by an a cappella group, just down the block, huddled under a store front awning, singing blues songs for tips from the rain soaked passers-by.

    The steady rain drove most of the foot traffic to the covered walkways in front of the buildings just across from the market. These storefront bakeries, sandwich shops and coffee shops are all pretty new, upscale and inviting to the cell phone chatting, laptop browsing, tech savvy sort. There are always a few street performers working for tips from the tourists as well as a few of the local alcoholics and other street people panhandling in this area. Over time, most of us city dwellers developed a blind spot for these people. They became just part of the urban landscape. I guess I was no different in that respect because I walked obliviously past one of the local street people; he was just sitting on the concrete sidewalk in the rain with his back to one of the heavy city garbage cans that line the streets. I did not even take note of what it said on the cardboard sign that he held up or the few small wood carvings he had laid out that he was apparently trying to sell there on the street, in the rain. I would not have even looked at him had he not spoken to me as I passed. Granted these guys always have some line and usually I'd just walk on like I didn't hear him but this guy said something that caught my attention. He did not ask for spare change or food. He said, "Good job helping that lady last night."

It took a moment and a few steps to register because it was as if his voice was inside my head. I heard it clearly, though, as if it was the only sound that existed for that moment yet he never looked up. I was stunned so I stopped there in the rain. I thought for a moment that there must be something wrong in my head. After all, I had been having these strange experiences all morning. I turned around. "What did you say?"

He looked up at me and the rain was running down his face as he spoke. "Some folks would have just gone on their way, even once they realized what was going on. Even with all your personal baggage cluttering up your head, you still went to help. You got involved. Good for you. Not always the smartest thing to do, but good for you just the same," he said with a quick forced smile.

I looked at this man sitting on the sidewalk, water running off his hat in a small stream. He smelled, even in the rain, like you would expect from someone who appeared to be an alcoholic living on the street. I could tell from his face, he was Native American, in his fifties probably, but appearing older. Life had clearly been hard on him and he looked like he had not had a good meal or a bath for some time. He wore an Army surplus jacket that had seen better days and his black unwashed hair was pulled back into a wet ponytail, highlighted by the gray that showed itself around the edges of his hat.

"How do you know what I did? Were you sleeping under the Ballard Bridge last night?" I asked.

He looked up at me with bloodshot eyes. "No, but I was close enough and not yet drunk enough so yeah, I could feel it too, what you felt, but unlike you, I did nothing—so good for you." He slowly gathered up his few wood carvings and stuffed them into a raggedy shoulder bag. I was still stunned. I stood there in the rain with my mouth open but without a word coming out. I watched as the man struggled to get to his feet. Without looking back at me he turned to walk away. "Feel it," he had said, and that is what it was. It just clicked in my mind when he used those words. I had not heard or seen it, I felt it.

The man was slowly wandering through the rain soaked people, down the street. He'd just stepped out from under the covered sidewalk, into the crosswalk and the rain. I ran after him. "Hey, what do you mean felt it?" I yelled at him as I dodged past a few people on the sidewalk and stepped out into the rain after him. "What exactly did you mean?" I repeated as I reached out and caught his shoulder.

He turned to face me and all of sudden I felt it again. I felt him. We were connected—only this was way more intense. I felt the pain in his body and mind like it was my own. I felt the stiffness in my hips and shoulders that he felt from sleeping on the hard asphalt of the alley where he'd been with nothing but a piece of cardboard as a mattress. I felt the hangover headache pounding in his head like it was my own. My knees started to fold under me from the pain of his arthritis. It was so intense. I could feel his thoughts, his desire to drink something, anything strong enough to numb his mind.

He reached out and caught me by the arm. "Sorry," he said. "You will need to learn to control that. You can't just be open all the time. I didn't mean to dump all that on you. It could drive you to drink." He laughed to himself. I grabbed the street post as he let go of me and turned to walk away again.

I could not believe this sensation; this feeling of other thoughts and more, was so intense but it couldn't be. I peered down the street as my head cleared and the pain in my body subsided. He had disappeared into the crowd. I started down the street to look for him and had only taken a few steps when I felt him in my head. He was coming back my way. I just felt it. I looked up and now I could see him.

As he got close to me he said, "Ok, new guy, this is all new to you. I get it. Come on with me."

"What is this thing? What is going on with me? How are you in my head?" I asked.

He reached out and took me gently by the arm, I started to feel his aches and pains again, then he glanced at me and it stopped. "Look I know you're a beginner so I'll block you for now but we need to get out of this rain before it gets out of control. Besides, I need a drink."

We went back into the covered market. He paused and looked me up and down as if he were sizing me up. Then he said in a soft and strangely comforting voice, "Come with me. It is going to be Ok."

I was in a daze, was I going crazy?

"No, you're not crazy," he said out loud. We worked our way down two levels, out the back side and down the long stairs toward the waterfront. The hillside stairs start with a pedestrian bridge that connects with the lower level of the market and passes over a street that traverses the hillside just under the market on the waterfront side. There are several landings for the tourists to rest along the way down to the waterfront. This long staircase connects the Public Market, a tourist hot spot, to the waterfront below. The waterfront is another favorite of the tourists with a large waterfront park at the north end, and a number of piers, including one where the cruise ships dock, a waterfront hotel, piers with tourist shops and restaurants, a waterfront aquarium, tour boat docks and a massive ferry boat terminal. The waterfront was always busy with tourists.

As we stumbled down the stairs, my head started to clear. I didn't plan to spend my afternoon hanging out with an alcoholic, street person but I needed to know what was going on with me and, somehow, I felt I could trust this guy. I don't know why but I knew he genuinely wanted to help me. I still did not know what was going on in my head, but it was real and this guy knew something about it. I had to get my head around all this.

We reached the bottom of the broad staircase and wandered south through a sea of parked cars. We approached a large brick building that appeared to be almost the same age as the market. It was just down the way from the foot of the hillside stairs. It was an old warehouse building with a covered loading area across the front. It had a big sign, Antique

Furniture, across the front that faced out across a parking lot and busy street toward the waterfront.

"Come on," my new friend told me as he took me under the arm again and pulled me in the front doorway. It was a large musty smelling place with a high ceiling. It was filled with all kinds of old cabinets, bar appointments and other antique oddities and fixtures salvaged from old buildings before their demolition.

We went down an aisle of old canopy beds and dark wood chests to the back of the store. My companion opened the door that was labeled "employees only" and motioned to me with one hand as he held the door open with the other. "Come on," he said.

I followed him with some trepidation into a cluttered hallway not nearly as well lighted as the rest of the store. Down at the end of the hallway was a small office with the door open. I could see a man sitting at an old rolltop desk with his back to us. The office had a tall antique display cabinet with glass doors packed full of other antique trinkets. The man at the desk never turned to look at us but he had to hear us shuffling down the hallway, dodging the odd stack of boxes and stray bits of furniture. He did not bother to turn around as he called out, "John! It's been a long time. I thought maybe you were off somewhere drinking yourself into oblivion. What have you dragged in from the rain this time?" He swiveled around in his chair and looked first at my alcoholic friend then at me. "So who's your friend, John?" he said with a little hesitation in his voice as he had now turned all his attention to me.

He seemed a little apprehensive as he stared intently at me. He removed his small half size glasses and laid them casually off to one side of the desk; at the same time he slowly looked me up and down as if he was sizing me up. The next thing I knew I felt him creeping into my head like John had done earlier. This was different in some way. I did not like the feeling at all as his manner was much more forceful.

"Hey," I said. I was trying so hard to keep him out that my head was starting to pound. I could see a look of surprise on his face as I tried to resist him. We struggled mentally as he held me frozen with his gaze. As I proved more challenging than he had anticipated, he started to slowly reach his right hand across in front of his chest and under his well-worn, brown leather jacket for something concealed just under his left arm. Being a city guy, I knew there was just one thing he would have tucked up under his jacket.

His mental grip loosened on me just enough for me to speak. "Hey, easy, I don't want any trouble. I don't know why he brought me here. And now, if it's all the same to you, I'll just be leaving." I put my hands part way up so he could see that I was not concealing any sort of weapon. I started backing slowly toward the doorway where we had entered his little office from the hallway. I could still feel his presence in my head, reading my thoughts and I could feel his apprehension with me. He was afraid. I knew what he was reaching for under his jacket and I didn't need to see it.

"Damn, Art, will you settle down?" my new friend said.

The man at the desk slowly stood and looked hard at me. He dropped his right hand back down to his side. He was about what you would expect at an antique warehouse I guess. He looked to be about 60ish, an average looking guy with a receding hairline. What hair he did have was drawn back into a thin salt and pepper ponytail. He had a medium length, salt and pepper beard with a bit more salt than pepper and he was carrying at least an extra thirty pounds around the middle. He wore blue jeans and a Grateful Dead T-shirt under the brown, leather baseball style jacket. As he moved toward me, I could just see the back end of the handgun he had slung in a holster under his left arm. That confirmed for me what he had been reaching for earlier. He looked me up and down again as if he was still taking some kind of mental measurements. He clearly had the same ability as my new friend as far as getting into my head, but at least he had stopped trying for the moment.

I'd spent some years learning to suppress my emotions, to hide my true feelings. I never did like the idea of people getting that close to the real me, let alone getting into my head literally. "Art, he's new," my friend said with a tone of explanation in his voice.

"What?" Art said as he continued to walk around me, looking me up and down.

"Hey, like I said, I don't know what is going on here and I don't want any trouble. I'll just see myself out." I started to step backward again. I was really feeling in over my head now and I could not figure out how I was going to get myself out.

"Hang on, Hang on, No worries," Art said as he looked at me and gave me a half smile. He had stopped pacing around me now. "Let's all just take a walk outside shall we," he said and he motioned with his left hand toward a side door at the back of his cluttered little office.

"It'll be OK," my new friend reassured me as he also motioned toward the door. "Say, Art, you don't have anything to drink around, do you?" he asked as he glanced around the cluttered little room.

"Outside," Art replied with a tone more an order than a request, as he gave a slightly cross glance at my companion.

"Look guys, I think this is all just some kind of big misunderstanding. I'm not really sure why he brought me here or what is going on anyway," I said.

Art looked at me. "Relax," he said with a forced smile. "I understand this is all a little confusing right now but I think I can help you out. Everything will be clear in a few minutes but you will have to excuse me. You can't be too careful so, how about you just go along with us for another moment. Now, can we simply step outside for a quick moment where we can talk more freely?" With that, Art motioned again toward the door.

We all stepped out a single side door from Art's little office, down a few concrete steps on the side of the building, into a parking lot and back into the rain. I was already wet so it didn't make much difference that we were back out in the steadily falling rain. The rain washed over us in gentle waves as we walked together just a few steps from the building. We paused and just stood there looking at each other for a moment as the rain soaked in. I could feel it running down inside my collar. There was a moment of silent tension as we just stood there looking at one another. John looked a bit worried and Art just had a kind of creepy half smile. At just that moment Art reached over and pulled the baseball hat off my head.

"Hey!" I started to reach for it back when I felt Art in my head again. This time he was going for it; it felt like he had hit me with both fists, hard in my chest but he was just standing there, with one hand in his jacket pocket and the other holding my baseball cap at his side. He was staring at me with no expression at all on his face. I doubled over and grabbed my head with both hands like I might squeeze him out of there. I could hear him in my head, asking me questions and then finding the answers for himself inside my mind. He was rummaging through my mind like a burglar ransacking a room, looking for something, pulling out drawers and throwing things on the floor. He pulled a memory from my childhood that I had forgotten, then, out of nowhere he asked me why I eat my breakfast at the market. Without moving his lips, he asked me in my head. I was powerless to stop him. My head hurt, my heart was pounding and I felt short of breath. I could barely stand up but I could not move my feet.

"Take it easy, Art," John said but Art was not done. I felt like I had in my childhood, powerless in the face of mental violence. I was frozen like I was held still by some unseen grip. I screamed perhaps only in my mind and when I did, I felt Art's grip loosen on my mind and body for just a moment. Art stumbled back like someone had just pushed him off balance. I felt like a giant, that had been holding me clenched in his fist, had just released me.

"What the hell!" I gasped as I tried to catch my breath. "What the hell are you guys? What are you doing to me?" I stumbled back a few steps then I turned and ran.

I pushed past John and ran as fast as I could across the open parking lot. I stumbled and gasped to catch my breath but I had to get away from them before someone jumped into my head again.

"Wait," Art called after me. I was on the street now and running down the sidewalk dodging past the few people walking by. "Wait," Art called out again but this time in my head. All of a sudden I was frozen again. Damn, he was in my head again. It was as if I was completely paralyzed this time. Art was talking to me but he was not speaking aloud, he was talking in my head. "I'm sorry but I am just too old to chase you down and you really do need my help," he said in my head. I was frozen. I could not move. I just stood there like a statue in the rain. People were walking past me like I was not even there.

Art and John walked up from behind me and stepped around in front of me.

"Look, I get it." Art said. "I was in your head and I know exactly how you feel right now. Really, I do know exactly how you feel," he repeated." Art paused and he and John both looked around nervously at all the passing people on the street. Not one person looked our way. They walked past like we were not even there. He started speaking to me now like a normal person, with words coming out of his mouth.

"You didn't have to be so rough," John scolded him.

"Yah, yah, I know and I'm sorry but we have to be sure. We also have to be sure that nobody else is onto him yet." Art paused and looked around real slow again. I could feel him reaching out, searching the thoughts of all those around us. He put one hand on my arm and with a nervous, uneasy look on his face, he continued in a soft voice, "We need to know that we have time to help you before anyone else finds you.

Look, I'm going to let you go," Art said to me as he stepped directly in front of me and looked me in the eyes. I was freaking out inside but I was still frozen. I could not move or speak. "I'm going to let you go and I want you to relax and take a deep breath. Just hear me out. That is all I ask, OK?" Then I was free.

I almost fell forward as I gasped for air, "What the Hell! What kind of mind games are you pulling on me? What is all this and why me?"

"OK, OK," Art said nervously, looking around again. "I'm really sorry. I have let you go and I will not go into your head again without your permission but you've got to agree to just hear us out, I promise." With that, Art let go of my shoulder and I almost collapsed right there. Art continued, "I just need you to calm down and take a couple nice, slow, deep breaths and then, just listen. We need to tell you some stuff. Believe it or not, you are just like us only you just discovered this part of yourself. You need time to get your head around all this. I get it but right now, you're in danger. You're lucky that John found you and brought you to see me."

"Yeah, I'm in freaking danger if you can jump into my head like that whenever you want. No shit!" I said still hunched over with my hands on my knees, trying to catch my breath. "Look, just hear the man out," John pleaded. At least these guys were talking to me like normal now and not in my head. "OK, fine but stay the hell out of my head."

I had a million questions but I wanted see what else they had to say first.

"I'll stay out of your head but you will need to try to stay out of ours," Art said. "Right now you are broadcasting. It is like you're standing here yelling at the top of your lungs for anyone else like us to hear and we really don't want to attract any attention." Art paused and looked around again. "At least not from some of the other folks out there that might be able to receive your broadcast. So right now I need you to take another deep breath. I will stay out of your head. Now look at me."

I slowly met his gaze, albeit with some trepidation. Art stood directly in front of me and looked squarely in my eyes. He put his hand on my shoulder again. He spoke softly, "Now focus in your mind. You need to be able to shield your thoughts, to keep them in your own head. Now breathe and turn your thoughts back inward, don't just let things fly around in your head, think softer, quieter."

I tried to calm myself. "Good. I'm going to help you a little but from the outside. I won't go back in your head I promise. Now let's get out of the rain," Art said as he turned to walk back toward his shop, still keeping one hand on my arm as we walked.

We headed back for the building. I was uneasy about being around these guys, particularly Art, but there was something going on that was so far outside my idea of reality. I had to find out what it was. My life had just been turned upside down. My plan for my life was being rewritten and I needed to see where it was going to take me; besides, somehow I trusted John. I do not know why, I'd always been good at reading people and despite his appearance there was something far more to this man, I could feel it. I sensed he genuinely wanted to help me. Which is strange in and of itself, as he looked like he could use some help. As we stepped inside, John turned back and looked around outside nervously before he closed the door behind us.

Back in Art's cluttered little office at the back of the antique store again, we brushed the rain from our jackets and glanced uneasily at one another. Art took some books off one chair and a stack of papers off another. "You did good, John," he said as he motioned for us to sit. He glanced over at John. John was rubbing his head, now in a full on hangover.

"Sit down. Let me get you guys some coffee," Art said as he stepped around the corner to a strange little kitchenette area. I could hear him fill a pot with water and pour it into a coffee machine. He flipped it on and looked back around the corner into the office at us. "I turned the heat up," he said. Then Art stepped back around the corner and grabbed a couple of towels from a wall hanger and tossed one to John and one to myself. "Take off your wet jackets and I'll hang them to dry here by the heater. Then dry yourself as best you can."

I nervously passed him my coat and so did John. Art hung them on an antique coat rack next to his cluttered rolltop desk, just in front of a small electrical space heater on the floor, then he reached back into the kitchenette area and grabbed a pot of fresh coffee and several cups. He set the coffee pot on a couple books stacked on one side of his desk and then reached into a small refrigerator in the kitchenette and pulled out some cream in a small carton. He sniffed it, nodded approvingly and then set it next to the coffee pot. He turned back toward his desk and pulled out one small drawer, then another until he found what he was looking for. He tossed John a small bottle of aspirin that he pulled from the drawer, then he cleared himself a place to sit on a small leather sofa. "There now, we are just three regular guys having a nice chat," he said with half a smile.

Art glanced at me and said, "I can't hear your thoughts without trying anymore and you can't hear mine that much better. Have some coffee," he said as he gestured toward the cup he'd just handed me. "I know you are wondering if you're going crazy or if someone slipped you a hit of acid right about now but trust me, it gets weirder before it gets better."

Art paused as he poured himself a cup of coffee and leaned back into the sofa across from me. He added a little creamer and stirred it around with a pencil he pulled off the top of his desk. He tapped the pencil on the side of his cup then set it down on a stack of papers. He sipped the coffee as if he were sampling a fine wine before he finally looked up at me again "It's the water," he said. "The water, it's like a conductor. We humans are more than eighty percent water ourselves and our nervous system is constantly sending and receiving incredibly small electrical impulses that travel around inside our water filled bodies. Some of us are just wired a little different and when the conditions are right, our ability to send and receive these little signals is, to put it simply, not limited to inside our own bodies. Water is a conductor. There's a small percentage of people who are wired in such a way that, to varying degrees, they can send and receive these little electrical signals outside their own bodies. Of that small percentage, only a portion of us ever figure it out to any degree. Just like some metals are better conductors of electrical impulses, some of us are better conductors of these little electrical impulses. I would guess that you have had experiences in the past where you felt like you were really in tune with someone, really connected. You have generally had a good sense of people and sometimes you felt like you could read them like a book. Well, last night your mind was opened, the air was saturated and the strong emotions of the assailant and the victim forced their way into your consciousness. If the conditions were not so optimal you would have felt something but it would have been vague and your conscious mind would have suppressed it because there was no stimulus that you recognize like a sound or a sight that corresponds to a vague feeling or perception. Now things are different. The gate has been opened, so to speak, and your mind is more perceptive now. I know you still have your doubts but you have now experienced the connection and there is no going back. In time you can learn to connect to the world outside your body in ways that you cannot imagine even now."

    Art paused and took another sip of his coffee. Then he looked back at me, over to John and back at me. He was silent for a moment with a contemplative look on his face, then he continued. "It is different for each of us. There is no telling how your abilities will manifest themselves in you or how strong your particular gift will be right now. You have only just dipped your toe in at the shallow end of this swimming pool. It will take some time for you to sort all this out; but now for the bad news. This gift can also be a curse. You see my friend John here? His gift is a powerful one, far more powerful than mine without a doubt, but you see the toll it has taken on him and how he struggles with it? You cannot imagine the price he has paid, that he continues to pay every day. Don't misunderstand me; I do not say this to be mean to John. He uses alcohol to try to numb his mind, to escape from this gift." Art paused again. He had taken on a subdued tone and looked down at the floor then back up at John.

John did not look up from his coffee, he just muttered, "I do what I have to do to get through the day."

"I know, my friend, I know," Art said as he reached out his hand and put it on John's shoulder. John looked him in the eyes for just an instant and then looked back down at his own coffee. "You better tell him the rest." John said without looking up.

"Well yah, I was getting to that part," Art said. "John and I are old friends, we go way back. He is the one who found me, just like he found you. I was just as confused as you are right now. I suppose he saved me the way he is trying to save you now." Art paused, he looked again at each of us in turn, then continued, "I have not seen my friend, John, for a bit. He, ah, He has been through some terrible stuff lately and as much as I would do anything for this man, I know that there is nothing I can do for him until he is ready. I know he is around and I keep tabs on him the best I can but have not been able to reach him until now. For some reason he felt you were worth pulling out of his downward spiral for." Art paused. "To get to the point, well, the reason that John felt that he needed to drag you down here to see me right away, um, yah see, we are not the only folks around who have figured all this out. There's a good number of folks like us around, some more powerful than others and some with, shall we say, a very different outlook on where we fit into the fabric of society. Some folks out there do not think that people like us should be just left to find our own place in the world. This is why we who have this ability have had to keep a low profile, even from each other, for some time now. Now you know John and you know me. If one of these others gets a hold of you and gets in your head, they will know what you know. Ya see my point? These guys hunt people like us and, if they find you, you will disappear and then they will come looking for us. So now you see the risk that John has taken for himself and for me--you see our dilemma? These guys will get into you head and then they will be knocking on my door, you see what I mean? John may have saved your life by bringing you in but he has bet both his and my life that you are worth saving."

Art took on a contemplative look as he stared at John. He continued speaking to me but now his gaze was fixed on John. "These guys can and will get into your head, brainwashing you and making use of your abilities not just to help find others like us but worse. From their prospective you are something that they can use or you are a threat that they need to eliminate. As best we can tell, there is no middle ground with those guys so, my suggestion to you, is to keep a low profile for now. Don't tell anyone and try not to be in a vulnerable position until you get this figured out a little. Stay dry and try to keep your thoughts in your head. Maybe take a vacation to place that is warm and very dry. Well that's it, kid. Good luck," and with that, Art abruptly stood up and took his coffee cup back into the little kitchenette area.

I was stunned but instinctively I tried not to show it. I just sat there and took another sip of my coffee. "So that's it?" I asked.

"No there's more but that is enough for now," Art answered without turning around.

John looked up from his coffee at Art. "You got to take him on, Art. You could coach him some. I have a feeling about this kid. You can't just turn him loose on his own, not now, not yet..." John's voice took on a slightly desperate tone as he stood up looking straight at Art who was now avoiding John's gaze by turning his back to him to rinse his coffee cup out in a small sink. There was an awkward moment of silence "It's OK, fellas, I'm grown. I can take care of myself," I said with a somewhat cavalier tone. They did not need to read my mind to know that I was trying to conceal my insecurities but what else could I do? I had learned long ago to rely on myself and not to expect much from others.

    I stood up and set my coffee cup down with one hand as I reached for my coat with the other. John turned and looked right at me for just a moment. His bloodshot eyes seemed truly focused on me for perhaps the first time. Then he looked at Art who was standing in the kitchenette, avoiding his gaze, still washing out his coffee cup. "Hold up, kid," John said. He stood up and stepped toward Art, who still pretended not to notice.

    "That's crazy Art; he doesn't even know how to protect himself yet. Come on, man," John demanded.

    "No, thanks for the heads up guys, I'll be OK. I can take care of myself," I said, with a little less conviction as it all started to sink in. " I've been around the block." I put my cap on and turned for the door. John grabbed my wrist and instantly I was frozen. I could hear him in my head say, "Sorry, kid, you haven't been around this block." He then turned back to Art and pleaded, "Come on, Art. Can't we hook him up with someone who can at least show him the basics?"

    Art glanced over his shoulder toward John. He hesitated for just a moment then he coyly said, "Why don't you show him the ropes, John?" He slowly turned and met John's gaze. "This might be the best thing for both of you," Art said as he forced a small fraction of a smile.

    "Are you nuts, Art. He needs someone; you know, well, sober for one thing. He don't need no drunken Indian to hang around with." John let my wrist slip from his grasp.

    "God damn it! That is really starting to piss me off," I said as I stepped away from John and pulled my arm back.

"Sorry, sorry bro, look, now that your nervous system knows you can send and receive signals outside the limits of your skin, it will be more and more open to signals from the outside and you may let things out by accident, if you do not learn how to control it. You need to learn to close yourself off from the outside. Be conscious of your thoughts and keep them in your own head. It is like, you know, if someone is going to sock you, how you tense up? Just try this, I'm going to grab your wrist again only this time, don't let me in your head," John said as he slowly reached out to me again.

"Oh, hell no!" I said as I stepped back.

"Trust me," John said. "I'll go easy. Just try this. Focus on closing off anything from the outside. Just let all the pores in your skin close like bracing for a cold wind," John said, as he reached out and touched the back of my exposed hand. I focused on his voice. As he touched me I could feel his mind trying to force its way into mine again but this time I was pushing back against it. I was not going to have these guys in my head whenever they wanted. I felt him push harder but I pushed back harder. The last thing I wanted was someone in my head again.

We stood there motionless, mentally pushing back and forth for a few moments. Finally John released me from our mental Sumo match. "Wow, I told you Art, you see that?" John said. "I had a feeling about this kid. He has got something." John looked back at Art with a smile on his face. Art never returned the look but I could see him nodding to himself as he said, "Good, you already have given him his first lesson. Keep me posted on how things work out with this one."

"No Art, come on, give this kid a break." John looked back at me. I could feel the frustration building in John. "I'm sorry, kid, I'll look out for you, you know, until I find you someone." Then he looked back at Art. "Asshole," he muttered. "OK, let's go kid, I definitely need a drink." John turned and opened the side door. He paused and looked back at me. I'd just been standing there listening to their banter. "Well, come on." John said to me.

"The last thing you need right now, John, is a drink," Art yelled after us.

ME AND MY SHADOW:

AS WE STEPPED outside I hesitated for a moment and realized it was still raining, gently but steady. I felt uncertain for a moment. "Remember what I said about closing yourself off to the outside," John reminded me. "I'll help you but you will need to always be alert from now on. Keep your thoughts in your own head."

I took a deep breath as I stepped out into the rain. I gathered my thoughts and focused on closing them off to the outside world. "Good," John said, "just like that. I can't hear any of that crap that you have rattling around in your head at all."

I looked at him quizzically, "Crap?" I asked.

John did not answer. We started working our way back up the long stairway up the hillside from the waterfront. John would stop out of breath at the top of each flight of stairs, all the way back up to the public market. When we got to the bottom level of the market itself, John, in between catching his breath, said, "Hey, check this out. The lady that runs the bead shop on the lower level of the market here is like us but just barely. She is only mildly perceptive. She thinks she is some kind of psychic because she gets these feelings," he said and he waved his hands in the air. "Folks like her can get just the very slightest bit of a sensation. She is like us but the impressions she gets are much foggier, much fainter. She thinks she is getting messages from beyond," John said as he rolled his eyes. "She doesn't know it is only just beyond the walls of her shop." John laughed to himself. We stopped at the entrance to the lower level of the market. "Close your eyes and try to just reach out a little with your mind, search for something or someone different," John said. "Focus on her, just a few feet that way, that direction. She should be easy to find and read with all this moisture in the air. She will stand out from the rest—you'll see."

I looked at John and he motioned with a head nod in her shop's direction. "Try, you'll see," he said again. I stood still and closed my eyes. It felt hazy at first, like being in a thick fog but I could hear what sounded like people talking softly all around me. Then I felt one voice that was louder, clearer than the rest. Once I focused on her it was clear; it was like I could see what she saw, hear what she thought. I moved closer in, and the mist and the fog started to clear. Her thoughts grew louder and clearer in my head and the rest faded.

"Keep your own thoughts quiet," John reminded me. "Fortunately, she is not sensitive enough to even tell where the sensations are coming from on her own if she picks up on anything at all. But she can pick up on you. If you're not careful you can be much louder and stronger in her mind. If she detects you at all she can't pinpoint where the thoughts she is receiving are coming from but you need to understand that there are many people like her with varying degrees of sensitivity and capability. They always stand out from the other voices you will hear unless they know how to hide their thoughts." John paused and took on a serious tone. "Someone like her, you could easily twist around if you wanted to right now, just like any other regular person. You could have her say or do whatever you want. You could walk in there and have her hand over every dollar in her cash register and make her think she was just making change. Just like if someone stronger or more skilled discovered you, someone who wanted to make use of your abilities for their own purposes, you could be the one getting twisted. The difference is that the worst she could do is pick up on very basic stuff: is someone telling the truth or not? more like a vague feeling. She could not tell you word for word what is in their head.

"As a rule people like us, we have always tried to keep our talents on the down low. Especially with the air so full of moisture, the wetter everything gets, the harder it is to hide your thoughts. This is for your own protection. Got it?" John said.

"Where are we going now?" I asked.

"I don't know," said John, "but wherever you're going, I'm going, at least for now, until we get you a proper trainer. I'm sorry, kid, but you have something unique and special. I spotted that much right away but you kind of popped up at a bad time for me. I just need to make sure you get a chance to see what you have before…before any bad guys get a line on you."

We wandered up through the market, people bustling all around us and out the top level on the other side that faced the city. I was starting to relax, at least to a degree now, and I could hear the random thoughts all around me as we walked through the crowd, like they were all softly speaking. Whatever was on their minds was just flowing out and they had no idea John and I could hear every word. I paused for a moment, just standing there in the rain. I looked around at all the people coming and going, astounded by the sensation. I stood there for a moment in front of the market. I looked to the south, down the cobblestone alleyway. I felt a strange sensation coming from that direction. John saw me pause and look down the alley. "Never mind that now," he said. "I know what you feel but we will have to cover that some other time. For now we need to move along."

We walked across the busy city street. I didn't know how being joined at the hip with a wino was going to work out, and then I looked at John walking next to me in the rain. "Sorry, I didn't mean…" I started to say aloud, but John cut me off. "Look, I understand. You forget, I hear what people think about me all the time. I know what I look like. Look, I promised Art that I wouldn't drink on the job and besides, you won't have to put up with me for long. We'll find you someone better able to train you up soon enough. It's just that you..." John paused. "I have a feeling about you and, we can't afford for you to fall in with the wrong crowd."

I tried to read John's thoughts but he was closed off to me. "Hey, come on rookie," John said with a chuckle. "You'll need a little more practice before you can peek into my head without me noticing. Just put up with me for a little bit and I will show you how to sneak in the back door and look around in the thoughts of even some fairly skilled people, without them even noticing that you were there. For now, we should probably get out of the rain. At least until you are better at keeping your mind closed, Ok?" John said.

I laughed. "I was always told to keep an open mind," I said aloud. I laughed again. "I guess I'll have to rethink that now. How about we get something to eat?" I said as I looked over at John. He was not looking so good and I did not need to read his mind to see that living on the streets had taken a toll on him.

"Great! The last thing I ate was, well, I don't know what it was but I threw it up this morning so I'm pretty hungry right about now. I could also really use some aspirin if you got any..." John paused and patted down his pockets, looking for something. He pulled out the bottle of aspirin Art had given him earlier. "Oh yeah," he said. He dropped a couple in his hand and stuffed the bottle back in his pocket with one hand tossing the aspirin into his mouth with the other. "My head's pounding and I really could use a drink but...some food sounds great," John said as he winced from the headache. "Ok, I'm good for now, I guess," he said as he put on a fake smile.

"Wonderful, this sounds like the beginning of a great weekend," I said, aware of the cacophony of thoughts pouring out all around us, like a never-ending background din of chatter in my head.

The two of us wandered into a small little pizza place half-filled with people of all kinds. I stared up at the menu on the back wall. The guy behind the counter glanced at me then looked over at John.

"Get the hell out of here," he yelled at John. Then he turned back to me and without missing a beat, he smiled and said, "What can I get you, sir?"

"What?" I said, with a quizzical look. "Not you, sorry, I was talking to the bum over there. We get those guys wandering in looking for table scraps all the time." He turned back to John who was just standing there. "Hey, did you hear me? Get out," he said sternly as he now leaned over the counter in John's direction. I looked at John, then back at the guy. "Take it easy, he's with me" I said with a bit of tone in my voice.

A few days ago I might have dismissed John the same way where I worked, but now, I was a little upset to see him treated that way. I was also a bit embarrassed as I knew that John realized I would have been that guy just a few days ago.

The guy behind the counter looked at John, then back at me with a frustrated look on his face. "Suit yourself. So what can I get you two fine gentlemen?" he said in a somewhat condescending tone.

"Just give us a large supreme to go," I said. I looked back at John and took a deep breath. How did a guy with his abilities end up living on the street? Then I realized I might as well have said that out loud as well.

John just looked back at me. "Everyone has a sob story, kid. I'll tell you mine some other time," he said in my mind. I paid the man with a twenty, he gave me twenty dollars back in change and then smiled at me. I looked at the change and was about to say something but as I started to speak, John cut me off and said, "Come on. We don't want to miss the bus." John smiled a big smile at me.

I took the change and the pizza and we wandered out the door. I was looking at John with a somewhat quizzical look waiting for him to explain.

"Asshole," John muttered under his breath.

"Aren't there some kind of rules about stuff like that," I asked as we went out the door.

John stopped and looked at me with a bewildered look on his face. "Who would make these rules and who would enforce them? This isn't the comic books, kid." He then turned, not waiting for an answer that he knew I did not have. I stood there with my mouth open for a moment pondering what he had just said, and then I stepped quickly to catch up with him as he shuffled along the street.

We got on the next bus back to the University District. The bus ride back was interesting. Getting on the bus was like merging into a mild sauna. The heat was cranked up and the bus was packed. The humidity was high and it was standing room only, surrounded by all the soaked bus riders. I could hear the chorus of thoughts all around me. John took the opportunity to give me another lesson. He would block then unblock all bus riders' thoughts from running into my head. I heard him talking in my head, telling me, "This is how we control the flow. Sometimes you need to be able to close your own mind so nobody can hear your thoughts or get into your head but you also need to be able to reach out and close off someone who may be like you, so that they can't hear you or anyone else. Now you try."

I could close my own mind but trying to reach out was harder. "First, focus on just that person. Hear just their thoughts," John said. "Now think of reaching out with your mind, throwing your focus over and around them like a blanket around their head."

By the time we got to our stop, John was jumping from one person's head to the next and I was trying to get my thoughts around their head to block him from reading them. It was like mental Kung Fu. On the outside we were both just standing there, holding the hand rail as the bus lurched along, but on the inside, John would reach out for one person's thoughts,

I would move to block, he would reach around to another person and I would spin the daydreams of another sleepy bus rider into his way. Thrust, parry, block and attack, all the way home.

A NEW WORLD:

WE JUMPED OFF the bus at the bus stop only feet from the entrance to my apartment building. I fumbled for my keys and opened the front door. As John and I trudged up the poorly lit stairs and down the dingy hall to my little studio apartment I could feel the heavy weight of some deep anguish that John carried. He quickly closed me out as soon as he realized I was sensing something but he knew I had felt some small part of something very deep and painful to him.

There was a deafening silence there for a moment as I unlocked the door and we wandered into my small apartment. I threw the pizza on the table, opened the refrigerator and grabbed a couple of sodas.

"No beer?" John asked.

"Sorry man, I'm not much of a drinker," I said.

"Just my luck," John muttered to himself as he sat down at my little table and grabbed a slice of pizza. I sat down across from him and picked up a slice. I had already taken a bite when I noticed that over the smell of the still warm pizza, I was picking up another smell. It was the smell of a guy who had been sleeping in the same clothes without a shower for some time. Not a good smell. I took a drink of my soda. I was consciously shielding my thoughts as I worked out a diplomatic way to say what needed to be said. "Look, man, this is a small apartment," I started.

"No worries, bro," John said as he wolfed down the rest of his first slice. "I can sleep on your sofa there and you won't have to put up with me for long, just until we get you hooked up with a real trainer. I won't cramp your style for too long."

"No man, you're cool and all… I don't want to hurt your feelings but…this is a small apartment and so … Look, don't take this personal but you might want to think about taking a shower and letting me run your clothes through the wash one time."

"Wow, I wasn't going to say nothing, cause I thought that was you I was smelling," John said as he grabbed the front of his sweat shirt and pulled it up to his nose for a sniff. "Yeah, I guess it has been a few days," he added as he grabbed a second slice.

John jumped into the shower and I quickly hurried his clothing down to the laundry room in the basement, and ran them through the wash. I came back to find him sitting on the sofa by the window, wearing a baggy set of my old sweats that I'd thrown in the bathroom for him. I was about 6'2 and John was only about 5'9 so he had plenty of extra room in those sweats. He sat looking out the window at all the people on the street below, going about their lives under the gray canopy of clouds, the rain washing over them in subtle yet relentless waves. They had no idea that people like us could hear their every thought or pry into their minds. John had his hand on the moist glass of the window.

"What are you doing?" I asked.

"Scanning," he replied. I was dry but I could still pick up on his mind reaching out as I entered the room. "What are you looking for?" I asked.

"OK, bro, I'm just going to give you the straight skinny here," he said as he turned around and settled back into the sofa. He pulled his silky black and gray hair straight back from his forehead, slipping a rubber band on to hold it back in a ponytail. "I will get you a better teacher than me soon enough but I'm just going to lay this out for you as best I can." John sat back on the sofa and his eyes sort of glazed over. "About one out of every thousand people may have some small degree of what they might call psychic ability. Of those people, few ever realize it. Most people just think they have good instincts or some sort of special ability to read or understand other people but they never really get it. They do not understand how or why it works. They do not know why sometimes it works and sometimes not. The few that do get it, that know they have something more than normal people, few of them make the connection and figure out the mechanics of it all, like Art said. They don't realize the link is water.

Up until that moment, the other night on the bridge, you had probably had a few minor situations that you never really understood. You thought you just got a vibe off someone or you felt a strange connection but you never thought much about it. Now that the veil has been lifted, so to speak, you can focus and fully understand those signals that you are able to receive. Now you will recognize them for what they are. Now you must also learn to be aware of the signals you send and who might be out there to receive them. Like Art told you, there are others out there with the same ability—only some of them...well, let's just say, like in the world of normal, non-psychic folks, some are good, some are bad and some are just ugly. You will find that the less moisture is in the air and on you, the less you can clearly feel or be felt. The more moisture, the more connected you are." John turned and looked back out the window. He put his hand back on the window that was moist with condensation. "You got any coffee?" he said without turning to look back at me.

"Yeah sure," I said as I stepped into the kitchenette to put some water on to boil.

"So who are these other folks that you and Art are so worried about?" I asked.

John continued, "I'll get to that in a minute but first let me give you a little history. There are only a few places in the world where a person who is predisposed to this type of connection is really likely to experience their ability to its fullest. This is the best spot on the planet, because of the geography, the weather and the climate, to find your connection, if you are predisposed. My ancestors have known about this for some time. We called those with the gift shaman or medicine men. As more white folks started moving out here, we discovered that there were some of your kind that also had the connection. My ancestors always just assumed that anyone with this rare gift was special and those few of us that possessed the rare gift were bound by our culture to use these abilities to help our people and others, and so we just assumed you guys would honor this gift as we did. The first few white folks we discovered with the gift were good people and they did just that. It never crossed our minds that one of our kind with this special ability, would ever use the rare gift to do harm to others. The first settlers that we found with the gift understood my people on a deeper level through this connection. They shared our reverence for this power, this gift. This is why the Duwamish people who once lived right where the city of Seattle now stands helped the first white settlers. The great chief of the Duwamish taught them about the land and warned them when other tribes came from the East and the South to drive the white man from this place." John paused. "Boy, I wish we could get a do-over on that one. Just kidding," he said as he flashed a half smile.

"OK, now I got to tell you the bad news. You may think that you have fallen down the rabbit hole like Alice in Wonderland but I got news for you. You have only just found the rabbit hole."

I sat down next to John on the sofa and handed him a cup of coffee. He looked at me for a moment. I could tell he was passively trying to hear my thoughts but I kept my guard up, kept him out.

Then he started again, "You still don't understand what it means to be connected. Not every person who is connected is the same. Most just learn to hear the thoughts of another and, to some degree, place their thoughts in the mind of another. You have experienced what it is to be able to hear the thoughts of another person and you are a natural when it comes to reaching out with your thoughts. You have also felt what it's like to have your deepest thoughts pulled from you against your will. You remember what it felt like to have Art stop you on the street and take physical control over you? All these things are still only a small part of what you will soon be able to do. Your connection is strong. I don't know how strong yet. This is part of why I took a chance. I had to get to you first, before…, Ok, I don't know how to say this so I will just lay it out. Most of us that are connected try to keep our abilities on the down low. We rarely expose ourselves even to others with the gift. We try not to do anything that will draw attention. There is the obvious reason, that normal folks just don't like the idea that someone can see what we all try to keep hidden in our heads but there is a bigger reason. People like us are being hunted--hunted by some of our own kind, well kind of. There is a group out there that is attempting to find anyone like us. Only if they find you, if they get into your head, you're done. You will just disappear and if you are seen again you will be just a zombie, a shell with your connection being used to find others like us. I do not know who they are or how many of them there are. I don't know much about them except that when they find you, you will cease to exist as you are now. These guys see someone like you and me as one of two things. You're a threat or a weapon for them to use. This is why I had to bring you in once you became aware of your connection, once we became aware that you had this connection. If I didn't find you soon enough, they would have found you and either made you disappear or turned you into what we call a scanner. Don't get me wrong. I like you and all, I think you have a lot of potential but I am helping you now so I don't have to hide from you or kill you later." He paused and looked right at me, then glanced back at his coffee. He took a sip and then carried on with eyes averted.

"It's just easier for me this way. People like us, we generally try to keep a low profile and avoid contact with others that are connected. Good or bad, if someone who knows you gets taken by one of these bad guys, they could extract information about you from them and use it to track back to you. I know you didn't ask for any of this but here you are, in the middle of a war, well not really a war or maybe it's just my personal war. I don't know anymore. Anyway, not to worry, I'll hook you up with someone who can help you develop your skills soon enough and then you'll be fine and I can get back to...my, what I was doing."

John stood up and walked across the room, away from the window. He looked around. "This is good," he said. "You are undetectable in here, as long as you stay dry. Just remember to be always conscious of your thoughts. They can betray you. As long as you contain your thoughts they can't detect you. One more tip, just so you know, I have also found that a good alcohol buzz is an easy way to contain your thoughts. I'm just saying..." John said with a grin.

"With your capabilities, if they are out there somewhere just scanning, you will feel them long before they can detect you. You will know that they're around long before they can detect you. As long as you contain your thoughts they will not be able to find you. Hell, you could stand directly in front of them and they would look right past you. We'll work on all this later. Living in the University District like this with so many people, there are always scanners passing through this area. Sooner or later you will sense one of them but you will be fine as long as you keep cool. All these people will give you lots of cover. We will worry about all that tomorrow."

"Come on now, you gotta tell me more. You can't just tell me 'hey guy, you now have this great fantastic gift and, by the way, there are some guys out there who want to kill you for it,' I said. "I want to know how many are out there, who are they, where are they, and how am I going to tell the good guys from the bad?"

John looked at me and gave me a kind of half smile. "I want to tell you everything but I can't risk too much just yet. The good news is that I don't think that these scanners, at least the ones I have run into, know very much or have a great deal of skill or abilities, but just in case you don't make it and they get into your head before we get you trained, well, for now kid, I'll tell you what you need to know. Tonight we need to go see if we can get you hooked up with someone who can train you up right. I think I know just the person who can help you." John then turned back to the window, placed his hand on the moist cool glass and cast his consciousness like a far reaching net out into the wet, gray afternoon.

We spent the afternoon hanging around my apartment. Every so often John would turn back to the window, placing his hand on the glass. I could feel what he was doing. He was searching, but for what he did not say. He would pause, chew a few aspirin and share a story or two about his life on the street. I had seen people go through withdrawal of various types before but for a guy that, at first glance had looked like a hard core alcoholic, he seemed to be managing pretty well, so I didn't want to make it any harder on him by bringing it up. He seemed to be almost back to normal in a matter of hours for what should normally take days or even weeks. We were just sitting on the sofa watching some news on the TV when John looked over at me and said, "Don't worry about me. It's just that it has been a long time since I went on the wagon but as you can see, even that is easier for people like us. I'll get straight long enough to get you situated. No worries."

Evening came early as the heavy laden skies turned to black. The unrelenting rain increased with a growing, steady rhythm. "You are doing a great job at keeping your mind closed in here where we're both dry but we're about to get wet again so remember what I told you, " John said as he stood up from the sofa. "I appreciate you letting me crash here for the day and the pizza and all but it is time to get you hooked up." John grabbed his freshly washed clothes from where I had placed them and stepped into the bathroom to change. I walked to the window and looked outside. I slowly put my hand on the glass the way that John had. I listened in my head to the tapestry of voices out on the street. I could feel them all. The chorus of voices started to swell. I tried to restrict the volume as it got louder still in my head. My head started to pound. John stepped out of the bathroom and grabbed the freshly washed, army surplus jacket from the chair. He glanced over at me and observed as I copied his scanning technique. He smiled to himself as he started to slip one arm into the sleeve then he stopped and held it up in front of himself to look at it. He gave it a sniff, he shook his head to himself and put the jacket on. Then without a word he stretched out his arm in my direction. I felt his presence in my mind. "Easy, young man," I heard him say. Then like a fencing master he directed my mind, showed me how to focus, pull back or reach out but with control. I took my hand from the glass and took a big, deep breath. "Wow, that was intense," I said. John just turned back to the door and put the few belongings he had with him into his raggedy shoulder bag.

I walked over to my little closet by the door and grabbed my jacket and a baseball cap. "I can't read you either so you want to tell me where we're going?" I asked as we stepped into the hall. I turned and locked the door to my apartment behind us. John didn't look back at first. He just took a few steps down the hall, smiled at me, then turned away again. As he walked down the hall he said. "Where else would two cools guys like us go on a Saturday night? Oh, by the way that hot chick that lives upstairs, that you have been thinking about for the last six months: bad news, it's never going to happen for you. Let's just say you are not her type, sorry. But the good news is, I'm going to introduce you to a girl I know. She's a little older but she is kind of a cougar if you know what I mean," John stopped again and looked back over his shoulder at me and gave me a wink. "What? You never had a wino for a wingman before?" He said with a chuckle. "Come on. I'll hook you up, bro. It will be fun. Just remember to keep your thoughts in your head until we are sure it's all clear."

"Great, I got a homeless guy who lives in an alley hooking me up with a date. I can hardly wait to meet her, John," I said sarcastically.

We went down the stairs, out the front door and onto the busy street. The rain was not bad now it was just a little more than a heavy mist. I could hear the thoughts of everyone walking up and down the street like they were talking out loud. It was kind of cool. John showed me a new trick. As we walked, he blocked out every thought of recognition in the minds of the passing pedestrians. Anyone who glanced at us as they walked by or looked in our direction from a passing car that had even the faintest thought that included us was blacked out. We were seen but not seen. This was a cool trick. People could see us, walk around us, but we were, at the same time invisible to them. They had not even the faintest impression of us.

University Avenue is mostly cheap restaurants of all kinds, some regular clothing stores that cater to the college crowd, a few used bookstores, a lot of coffee shops, a couple movie theaters, a tattoo parlor or two, several music stores, not to mention the odd pub and head shop. The strip was full of people, mostly students but with a sprinkling of street kids, homeless people of various sorts, a thug or two, some ordinary folks that just happen to live in the area and of course a few street people with serious mental illness, all attracted by the lights and the crowds.

As we walked down the street, we blended with the throngs of pedestrians that you always find in the University District. We walked past a street musician strumming his guitar, standing behind his open guitar case under a store awning with a sign asking for spare change. The chorus of people's random thoughts blended with the music. Actually the music made it a little less disturbing to listen to people's random, unfiltered thoughts. The most ordinary-looking woman might be contemplating her secret desire to strangle her husband and the Emo guy with the multiple face piercings is reworking a calculus problem in his head. I was beginning to understand just how different some people can be, when you hear their thoughts, from how they appear from the outside.

I think what I loved the most about living in the University District was that you get a little bit of every segment of society. You could walk one block and see people from every corner of the globe and hear at least ten different languages spoken. Where else in the world could you find a copy shop next to a tattoo parlor, next to a dentist office on a street lined with restaurants displaying every type of cheap food imaginable, from Algerian to Vietnamese.

We stopped our stroll down the avenue in front of a coffee shop. John turned to me and looked me up and down as if he were measuring me. "You look Ok; how do I look?" he asked with the slightest nervous tone in his voice. I gave him a blank look. I probably would not have said what I thought but the first thing that came into my head was, "You can't be asking me that. You've been sleeping in the streets for I don't know how long. I mean you look better now than when I met you this morning... I mean,...crap,... It is hard to be politically correct if you are in my head before I get a chance to filter my response." John took a deep breath and turned to grab the door. I could hear his thoughts as we walked into the dimly lit coffee shop. The place was full, mostly with college kids. The glow from all their laptops and handheld devices in the dimly lit coffee shop, added to the ambiance. The walls were covered with student art work for sale. It looked like more of a hangout than a business and it definitely was not Starbuck's. John was not blocking me out of his thoughts. He was surprised, I guess, but I did not yet know why. He was letting me see an image of the woman we were looking for. The woman he was looking for was here but there was someone else--someone he had not expected to find. This other person was someone he had strong feelings for. She was special to him. She was family of some sort. His feelings were all a jumble of good and bad, happy and sad. He kept the details to himself and I did not push in any deeper than he was letting me see.

Just then, I heard a voice in my head and so did John. "Over here by the window, guys." I knew instantly this was not who John expected to find; this was his daughter. John immediately closed off. He was not going to have anyone in his head right now. I could see the trepidation on his face, so I did the same just because he did. I didn't know what was going on and I did not want to take any chances, not after the way I was slapped around by Art.

We walked over to a table by the window. There was a John's daughter, a beautiful young girl about my age and sitting across from her was the woman we had come to see. She was clearly no relation. John looked at his daughter and over to the other woman, then back at his daughter. He had a look of concern on his face. "Sparrow, what are you doing here with Laura?" he asked.

"Come on, Pop, don't start," she said. Then she turned to me and smiled. She tried to get into my head but I kept her out. "Hey, you're as closed as Fort Knox," she said to me and smiled again.

"I never let a girl into my head on the first date," I responded with a smile."

John turned and gave me a cross look, then he punched my arm hard. "First date?" he said. "Hey, that hurt," I replied as I clutched my arm.

John turned to Laura. She was older, 50ish, and had a serious look about her. Her appearance was like that of a librarian with just a hint more style. The entire time she'd been looking me up and down in a way that made me uneasy but I could not yet say why.

"Sit down, gentlemen," she said in a rather businesslike tone as she brushed her long gray hair back behind her shoulder with one hand.

Just then the barista came over with four coffees. "OK, two Americanos, both with cream, one with sugar, one tea, Earl Gray and one Caramel Delight for the young lady," he said with the kind of smile that young men get when gazing at a beautiful young lady.

As he handed me my coffee just the way I like it I started to ask, "How did you?...never mind."

Laura looked at me over the top of her half glasses as she paid the barista. She looked at John and gave him a forced smile. "Long time, John," she said.

"You know why I'm here, Laura," John replied in an equally businesslike tone. "I don't like the look of this... dragging Sparrow into your line of work," John added as he glared at Laura.

"Come now, let's take things one at a time, shall we? First, the young man," Laura replied, then she turned and looked back at me across the table. She took her glasses off her face and let them hang in front of her on a silver chain she wore around her neck. She gave me her full attention now, staring at me with penetrating gaze. "I know you went through all this with Art earlier and it appears you have learned a thing or two today. To make things easy, I am going to have to ask you to let me into your head. I promise you, I will not be so ham-handed as Art was. Subtlety is not a word I would ever use to describe him," she added with a slightly disapproving tone. "I don't know if you are aware but I have been trying to slip quietly into your thoughts from the moment you walked in here and I am actually quite impressed that you have managed to keep me out thus far. You see, actually," she paused for a moment, looking me over again, before continuing, "this is somewhat of a specialty of mine. As it is apparent now that I will not be able to sneak in, before I can tell you more, I really must ask that you allow me to have a look inside, if you please."

I looked over at John and he nodded approvingly. I took a sip of coffee and set down my cup. I set aside my misgivings, leaned back in my chair and let down my guard. "May I look too?" Sparrow asked. "Nothing in there you need to see..." John said before Laura cut him off.

"Nonsense, come with me, Sparrow." She cast a stern look at John, then she looked back at me and reached across the table and put her hand on top of mine. I tried to be as relaxed as I could under the circumstances. My guard was completely down now. I took a deep breath, I closed my eyes and I slowed my breathing. "Ok, have your way with me," I said with a chuckle. She slipped slowly into my head like a descending fog. It was not brutal at all like with Art but soft and comforting. I was aware of her presence but only because she was speaking to me as she floated through my mind like a soft melody of some forgotten song—it was almost like a butterfly in an open meadow. Then I felt as if I was wrapped in a warm blanket that lulled me into a sort of half sleep. Her being present in my mind was like a drug that was relaxing me, soothing me. The sound of her voice floated gently all around me, talking in soft whispers. I could also sense Sparrow's consciousness as it trailed Laura's, floating softly around in my head, shadowing Laura, but she had a different presence. She was also soft and soothing; she did not say anything but I could swear I smelled lavender. I tried to connect with Laura but she was not going to allow me into her thoughts willingly. I found Sparrow's thought stream and I found that I could easily follow it back and slip into her thoughts. She was thinking that I looked rather well put together. She was concerned for her dad and she was pleased to see that he had seen something that motivated him to get himself off the booze and distract him from this obsessive path that had been consuming him. She did not share the specifics but she was hopeful things would go different for her dad this time. She hoped she would see me again and...

"Wake up, wake up." John was shaking my shoulder. I awoke with a start and almost spilled my coffee. "This is what she does," John said as he looked over at Laura. "There is nobody better at creeping into even the most guarded minds out there. Those guys I told you we don't want to run into? Well, she is the one that they don't want to run into. By the way, I did not bring you here to hook up with my daughter. I brought you to see Laura, because if anyone can train you to use all the skills of the mind, she is the one," John said as he smiled at Laura.

Laura looked at John and smiled a genuinely warm smile. "Why, John, I am flattered. I had no idea that you thought so highly of me but, well, as you can see, I am otherwise engaged with a very talented apprentice and well, you wouldn't want to place him in the care of a cougar who might take advantage of him, now would you?"

John looked at Laura then over at his daughter. "No, Laura, come on, I was just kidding and …hey, you're not dragging her into your…" Just then, Sparrow reached across the table and touched his hand. I could see frustration fade from John's face and in its place I could see the concern he felt for her.

"Pop, you know I can take care of myself and besides…"

John cut her off. "I know. I kind of gave up my right to tell you anything some time back didn't I, but just tell me why you?" John looked at Sparrow then over to Laura. He did not say anything more.

Laura met his stare for a moment, then she said, "As long as I live, no harm will come to her, I promise you that. She has the skills, John." Laura paused for a moment and put her glasses back on. "Art seems to think that you should be the one to bring this young man along and after seeing how he was able to hold me out of his head already, I would have to agree with Art. By the way, don't you dare tell him I said that," she added quickly. Then she paused and looked deep into John's eyes. "John, give this young man a chance; give yourself a chance."

John looked at her. "I thought I was the one who had a problem with alcohol," he said with a half laugh. "You see the potential he has. He needs someone with the highest level of skills to help him reach his full potential."

"Exactly, then we are in agreement?" Laura replied. She kept her gaze directly fixed on him and she reached out and placed her hand on top of his. "If you are with him, he could have no better teacher."

John stood. He looked at his daughter. "I'll be checking in on you from time to time, if you don't mind."

She got up and touched his hand again. Stepping close, she wrapped her arms around his neck and hugged him the way a daughter does, placing her head on his chest. They shared some private thoughts and I could see the sadness overcome John's face for just a moment. "Sorry, kid, it looks like you're stuck with me for a little longer," John stood up and started for the door. I got up, put my hat on and followed him. I could not help but look back if only to see the beautiful smile on Sparrow's face.

John did not even look back as we went out the door. "Wipe that stupid grin off your face; she was smiling at her old dad, not you," he said in my mind. John closed the door behind him and, still looking back. I walked right into the closing door with a bang. All the people sitting close to the door looked up at me as I collected myself and struggled to get out the door. John laughed to himself. "Watch the door," he said as I finally made it outside.

Out on the street the rain was falling in light sprinkles. We walked slowly up the avenue, swimming in the stream of thoughts that flowed all around us. Each person's thoughts would get individually louder as they approached us and then subside as they got farther away. John was closed off to me but I could tell that he was thinking about his daughter. "So do you want to tell me a little more about Laura?" I asked John. I really wanted to ask him about Sparrow but I thought, better not go there.

"Normally, as new as you are, I would say no," John said aloud. "Remember this, as long as we speak and think like everyone else, no scanner can sort us out from everyone else around, unless they just happen to overhear our conversation or be reading our thoughts directly, which they can't do, as long as your mind is closed. When you use the connection to reach out it is like sending up a signal flair that any scanner in the area can pick up.

"If they find you or anyone that is connected to you in their memory, they will track you, capture or kill you and if you are ever seen again, you are working for them. We do not know where they take the ones they catch. We do not know how they twist the minds of their victims. We do know that they have some special way to pull every thought and every memory from your consciousness and then rewire you into one of their goons. Laura finds these scanners and ...well... the few that she's captured, we take them to see if we can restore them; so far we have not found a way. Lately they have also been programmed to kill themselves rather than be captured and there have been a few she just has to kill outright. Don't be fooled by her physical appearance, her connection is one of the strongest you will ever see and she is ruthless. She has to be. I thought with your connection as strong as it is and...well... you're nobody's punk. I know that from being in your head. You could be a big help once you learn to manage the full scope of your skills. Oh, and to satisfy your curiosity, I have not been around for my daughter as I should have been but I don't like the idea that Sparrow is going down that path with Laura. What Laura does is dangerous work but that is her choice. She has her reasons for what she does. There was something they were not telling me, but nothing I can do about that right now, anyway." With that John paused and thought for a moment. "I'm hungry and my head is starting to hurt again," John continued. "Come on, I know a good noodle shop just up the way," I said. We walked on, up the street.

The rain was falling steadily now and we let the waves of rainfall wash over us. John linked my mind and showed me again how he could make us invisible to those around us as we strolled among them. We passed through waves of thoughts from everyone whowalked by. The blend of random thoughts from passers by and the aromas from all the small restaurants, tobacco shops, and pubs, swirled around us in the rain. It was well into the night but the lights from all the small shops reflected off the shimmery street. "Ok, so if these scanners are such a threat, how come you and Laura don't just hook up with Art and a few other bad asses like yourselves and kick all their asses?" I asked as we strolled along in the steady rain.

"Yeah, why don't we?" John said, without looking over at me. He stopped and turned to look me in the eyes, "Up to now, we have all just lived the quiet life and kept a low profile because nobody wanted to risk the general public or worse, the government, getting on to us. No one wants to risk being exposed. It would put us all at great risk." With that he turned and walked on and I did a quick step to catch up. What had I gotten myself into?

"Exactly," John said.

THE TRAINING DAY:

THE NEXT MORNING I awoke to the sound of John rattling around in my little kitchen. I could smell the coffee. "About time you got up," he called out from around the corner. I dragged myself out of bed and ran my fingers through my hair as I walked into the kitchen and sat down at the small table. John brought over some coffee and some scrambled eggs for me. "You seem in pretty good shape for a hard core alcoholic, who hasn't had a drink for almost two days now," I said. He did look remarkably well, almost as if he was two weeks into his rehab, not just a little over 24 hours.

"Don't hate me cause I am so handsome," he replied with a grin. "One of the benefits of spending your life learning to control your mind and using your mind in ways that others can't," he responded. He changed the subject. "Look, I got a problem. Now that you are connected, there is a ton of stuff you need to know. You're in the mix now and you have all the tools to be very good at this stuff. I have an obligation to the rest of the folks that are connected, as well as to you, to make sure you can't be used by the scanners. The best way to do that is for you to discover your full potential. I'll be honest with you; usually it takes a lot of time to learn what you need to know to get by undetected by those that would seek you out and cause you harm, let alone to develop your skills to your fullest potential. I had hoped to get you hooked up with someone with skill and experience, who could take the time to help you build your skills. You have a great deal of potential. After the pep talk from Art and Laura, I thought for a minute that I could be the one to help you. I thought that if I could help you, I could in some way get myself back on track. I guess it's about time I level with you.

"I wasn't just hanging out, drinking myself into a stupor every day for kicks. I mean, I wasn't always like that but things kind of just fell apart for me I guess. See, I lost,...well, I lost track of things. It doesn't matter now why, but I failed everyone around me and, um, I just met you and I don't want to let you down too. The trouble is last night I picked up a bad vibe from Sparrow. You see, I have been sort of M.I.A. from her life for some time now but I never meant it to be that way. I set out to do something and I kind of lost myself. She is still my daughter. Sparrow and Laura were keeping something from me, something, I don't know what, but it was not good. I'll be the first to admit that I'm probably the worst father in the world for a kid like Sparrow to get stuck with. I should have been there but I wasn't so I can't really just start telling her what to do now. I couldn't really ask her or pry the thoughts from her head without someone noticing but there is something going on and Sparrow is not just tagging along, she is in the middle of it. She was not lying when she said she could take care of herself, I know, but I need to be assured she is safe. That Laura is dangerous business and if she is planning on going on the offensive with these scanners, well, you have to understand there is no special set of rules for people like us, no judge or courtroom. If one of us does wrong, I suppose if there was a sheriff for folks like us, it would be Laura. I don't know what Sparrow is doing with her but I've got to find out. You know what I mean?"

I took a bite of my eggs and looked at John. "It's too bad that you can't just download the files I need like on a computer."

John stared at me for a minute, took a sip of coffee then said, "Funny you should mention that because I was thinking of just that. There is a way." He paused, took another gulp of his coffee then started again. "The trouble is, it's a little dangerous and I can't do it without some help."

"What are we talking about here?" I asked.

"It's hard to explain but it's pretty much like what you said. I can just, ah, download all my information to you, all my years of training and experiences. The trouble is I can't filter it, so you'll get all the other crap too. You would see it all." John paused for a moment and took a sip of coffee. "I'll just say my life story is not pretty but you should get everything I have to offer. I have been in your head and I know what kind of person you are. You may feel like you know a lot about me for the short time we have known each other but I know you, from going through your head, as if I watched you from the day you were born to this day. If we do this, you will gain in moments what took me a lifetime to understand. I just can't be in two places at the same time. I can't get you involved in what I have to do and I can't leave you on your own--not now. If you're not ready, it's dangerous for you either way. Whatever it is that is going on with Laura and Sparrow, well, I owe her better. You deserve better," John said.

I looked at John searchingly, trying to make sense of what he was saying. "Well, I don't much relish the idea of walking around just waiting for one of these scanners to jump me so I guess I'm in," I responded.

John paused for a few moments, his fingers wrapped around his coffee mug, thinking before he asked, "I hope you don't mind taking a little trip with me?

"Hey, I have class today and midterms coming," I said.

"Don't sweat blowing off school today," John said. "You will find studying much less time-consuming now that you can just absorb the information directly from your teacher or anyone else around you. You'll be just fine. If you're in, well, then today we should take a ferry ride across to the peninsula. There is just one place we can go to get the help we need to make this happen." John still had a look of trepidation on his face but it appeared our plans was set.

We finished our breakfast and John borrowed my cell phone to make a quick phone call. We grabbed our jackets and headed out the door. We took the bus back downtown, this time to the middle of town. It was just a short walk down to the waterfront.

Seattle's waterfront was once the transit station for travel to Alaska and Asia, now it is a busy container ship hub at the south end. There is a Coast Guard pier, a Cross Sound car ferry terminal with a pedestrian overpass that takes the Cross Sound commuters from the terminal building over the busy waterfront street and the train tracks, directly into the city. Today we were headed for the Cross Sound ferry terminal. We blended into the crowd of commuters as they crossed the overpass, over the multilane street that ran along the waterfront and into the crowed passenger terminal, full of commuters that work in the city and live across the sound. We approached the ticket window and as I reached for my wallet, the agent just passed us our tickets and said, "Thank you, next please."

I looked at John and he just gave me a wink and said, "Come on, let's go."

I was not sure how I felt yet about taking free stuff like that. We walked through the seating area and handed our tickets to the ticket taker as we boarded one of the big multi-deck car ferries that cross the Puget Sound to the Olympic Peninsula.

The sky was a maudlin gray but it was not raining as we boarded. We walked through the crowd of people milling around, looking for seats where they could plug in their laptop or get the best signal for their tablets' Wi-Fi. We stood there on the back end of the boat, on the top passenger deck watching the city skyline of tall buildings framed by the space needle on one end and the sports stadiums on the other, fade into the mist as we pulled away from the city. The ferry had two full decks of cars, trucks, campers and motorcycles covered with another two enclosed decks filled with passengers. The massive diesel engines rumbled into action, churning up the water and pushing us away from the nest of wooden pilings that had been the boat's resting place earlier as the decks filled with vehicles.

As the heavy vessel slowly lumbered up to speed on its course to traverse the Puget Sound, we walked through the protected cabin area and down to the other end of the boat. We opened the doors and stepped out of the protected cabin area onto the open deck. I could feel the cool wind against my face. I took in the smell of the sea and listened to the heckling of the seagulls that followed the boat, floating in the air above us as we watched the Olympic forest, shrouded in mist and crested by the snow-capped Olympic mountains, come into view. The vast Olympic Peninsula is far less developed than the mainland. Mostly small towns and a few tribal reservations ring the coastal edges. The middle is a large, protected, national forestland holding some of the oldest trees in the country. A dense, old growth, temperate rain forest just a one-hour boat ride from the urban jungle of the big city.

The cool misty sea air felt good against my face as I visually scanned the open water to see if I could catch a glimpse of any of the Orca whales that call the Puget Sound their home.

"They are out there," John said. "About a mile off to the north, can you feel them?" I don't know why I was surprised to find that I could sense them, and what's more they could sense me. I looked at John with wide-eyed excitement. "This is amazing," I said aloud. These creatures were communicating with each other and with John. They shared greetings and then the leader of the pod of Orcas turned the group to pursue a school of fish. They were training their young in their hunting methods. I could hear them calling out instructions, then, without warning, they all closed off their thoughts and disappeared. I turned to John, still astounded. "Can all of them do that?"

John looked at me and said, "Sure. You know my ancestors coexisted with the Orca for a great many years. We respected one another as hunters. They live much as we did before the settlers came. In the water they are the masters of their domain. They are the top of the food chain just as we were on land. Did you ever wonder why you never heard of an Orca killing a man? How many stories have you heard about people being saved by dolphins from drowning or from sharks? Orcas are simply the largest species in the same family with dolphins, porpoises and the like. They can all feel us."

I looked at John. "There was that one Orca in a big aquarium that drowned a trainer." John replied without hesitation. "Well, if you were taken from your home and family and locked up in a small cage, then forced to perform tricks for your food, how safe would your captors be from you? They are smart, in some ways smarter than us. We humans would be easy prey for them. Sharks attack people when they happen to run into us and sharks are just basic animals that have a primitive mind. The Orca knows that we are higher thinking creatures like them. They do not want war between us, so the basic deal is 'we don't eat them and they don't eat us.' Just the same, they are not too happy with us humans as you might imagine. Can you blame them?" John said as he looked out at the open water.

When we arrived and the boat docked, the cars started driving off the ferry, two by two. We walked across the passenger bridge down a long covered walkway and into the parking area. A new expensive looking sport SUV pulled up and the electric tinted windows on our side went down. The driver was a young Native American man, about my age, "Hey, Uncle John," he yelled over the heavy bass beat of the rap music he was blasting. "Oh sorry," he said as he shut off the music. "Jump in, guys."

I was surprised that someone was there to meet us but John was not. John just opened the door and jumped in. I ran around to the other side and did the same. The driver looked back over his shoulder at John and reached around to grab his hand. He had a big smile across his face. "It is really great to see you, and even better to see you sober, Uncle John. Welcome."

John looked at me with a little smile. "This is one of my sister's boys, Raymond."

"So, Uncle John, I was surprised to hear that you were... ah...back in action again but it was a happy surprise, you know," Raymond said as he glanced over at me. "So what is your story, pale face? I don't have the connection so I can't read your mind in case you were wondering but I guess if you got the mojo, then you already knew that, so I guess I'm just talking for no reason. Whatever your story, my uncle thinks you got something. Whatever it is, it is special enough that he gave up the booze, for now anyway. That makes you Ok by me." Raymond offered me his hand.

I shook his hand. "Nice to meet you, Raymond. My name is Alex. I'm still kind of new at this so it is a lot to process."

"Say man, you ever been to a Rez before? If not you're about to find out what it's like to be a minority, dude," Raymond said with a laugh as we pulled out of the parking lot and headed down the road. "So you know all about this stuff and you don't even have the connection?" I asked. Raymond just laughed and drove on. "You must have missed that memo, huh city boy," he said with a grin. He stopped talking but his mind was still going. He was genuine in his welcome I could feel the honesty in him. I was impressed that someone who did not even know me would welcome me so openly and without pretense.

I leaned my head back and closed my eyes. I was thinking about how my perception of the world had changed over the last few days. I started thinking about John; what was his story? He was obviously not your average, sleeping-in-the-alley type of wino. I opened my eyes for a moment and watched the deep green of the moss-heavy forest envelop the road as we traveled along, deeper into the forest. The cars around us on the road were fewer and fewer. I was trying to be careful to shield my thoughts as I wondered, what did Laura say to John when he told her I needed a highly skilled trainer? She seemed to think a great deal of John's ability, just like Art and these guys seemed like heavy hitters to me. Clearly there was a lot more to this guy than meets the eye. My mind wandered on.

What about Sparrow? She was cute and when she was in my head her presence was nice, comforting and warm. I hoped I would see her again because ...Smack! John hit me in arm. "That's my daughter you were about to start daydreaming about," he said.

"So you met my cousin?" Raymond interrupted. "She *is* pretty hot, Uncle John," he said. John slapped him in the back of the head.

"My sister has four sons so I don't think she would be too mad if she lost just one," John said. "I'm just saying, Uncle John," Raymond replied.

After a few hours of driving through smaller and smaller towns and a bigger and bigger forest, we turned off the two lane blacktop and headed up a dirt road. Eventually we came to a modest, yet good-sized farmhouse. It was well back off the main road and there were several cars and trucks parked out front. As soon as we arrived, about twenty-five people and a couple of dogs came pouring out the front door and off the front porch, surrounding the SUV. They were all John's family and they were clearly glad to see him. The crowd parted as an old woman came out the front door, walking slowly toward the vehicle. Her walk was unsteady but two young girls attended her on either side. She worked her way through the crowd that had surrounded John as soon as he got out of the vehicle; they parted for her as she moved toward John. She was clearly far more than just the matriarch of this family. I could feel her presence, even though she made no intrusion into my mind. I was stunned by the power I felt in her presence. She was much more than her physical appearance let on. She slowly reached out with both hands and softly touched John's face. She was speaking in her native Salish dialect but she was also now reaching out to me in my head so that I understood every word she was saying. This was John's mother and she was clearly overjoyed to see her son about whom she'd been greatly concerned for some time. She shared a few private thoughts with him before she turned to me and put one of her hands to my face. She welcomed me. "You may call me grandmother," she said to me. "Everyone else does," She was still speaking out loud in Salish but her words were clear in my head. She turned to go back up the front steps of the house. "Now let's eat," she said as she disappeared back into the home attended by the two young girls. I could detect they were both aware of their connection yet novices in their skills.

Raymond took my arm and whispered as we walked to the house, "We were all really worried about Uncle John for a long time. We didn't think we would see him alive again once he went to the city the way he did. He had dropped off the radar. He thinks you are important, why I don't know but he thinks you are so important that he stopped trying to drink himself to death. For that alone we all think you are pretty important too. Uncle John was a very powerful medicine man before… well…before he was consumed by his own demons and went down that path with booze and all. He says he has seen something deep inside you that is what all the folks with the gift are talking about. Not just that you are connected but something more than that. I don't suppose you want to let me in on your secret power?"

"I wish I knew myself," I responded with a chuckle.

"Oh well, we are all glad you're here, if for no other reason than you brought him back to us." John had already been whisked inside the house. Raymond put his hand on my shoulder and we headed in the front door as well. Two more cars pulled in behind us and more people streamed toward the front door behind us.

For what seemed like hours, we sat around a big table that was piled high with food. Every time someone said goodbye more people would show up and more food would appear on the table. Everyone who arrived, brought food and other small gifts. They would work their way around to greet Grandma, then John, and then they would go out of their way to welcome me. It felt strange to be so welcome by so many people who did not even know me. There were a couple people that were also connected but not to the same level as John or his mother. I looked over at John feeling slightly embarrassed. I had been surprised to see someone at the ferry dock to pick us up. I had no idea that anyone was expecting us or for that matter that John had anyone that might want to see him. In the city I had first seen John as just another homeless guy, a person of no consequence and here he was a man with a big family and clearly the respect of the whole community.

"I can read people's minds and yet there is much that I still don't know about you," I said to John with my thoughts. "Clearly you are not what I thought you were at our first meeting; you are far more than most people I've ever met and I took you for far less."

John looked at me and smiled, "You will know everything about me soon enough. Come walk with me," he said, as he got up and motioned me to the back door. We excused ourselves to John's mother with our thoughts and everyone just carried on, eating, talking like a family reunion of sorts.

We stepped through the kitchen and out the back door. I stopped and took a deep breath of the clean fresh air and looked around. Several children were playing in the backyard that stretched across an open field all the way to the tree line of the forest. Only the grass near the house was cut short so the rest of the grass was tall enough to wave gently in the cool early evening breeze. It was late in the afternoon and the sky was silvery but not raining. We walked slowly across the cut grass and into the tall grass. The two German Shepherd mixed breed dogs that had been sitting by the back door watching the children play, got up and trailed us across the cut grass. Their minds were simple but I could feel their thoughts, I could feel that they considered themselves to be the appointed guardians of those human children they were watching. To them, Grandma was the Alpha of this pack and we were now a part of the pack. They each brushed against us as if to acknowledge us as welcome and then, when we left the cut grass area into the tall grass, they turned and went back to their spot by the back door, to their task of watching over the children at play.

Without a word John reached down and let his hand softly stroke the tops of the grass stalks as he walked along. It was almost as if the grass was reaching out to him. I could feel him reconnecting to the natural world after so long in the world of concrete and steel. "Try it," he said. "Listen to the grass and the trees," he added. It was the kind of cliché line one might hear from a Native American in a movie, but now I understood. We walked together into the forest and were enveloped in the moss covered quietness. The trees were old and tall and had seen the coming and going of centuries. The forest floor was covered in ferns and every tree, rock and stump was dripping with moss. Even without the rain the trees held the moisture close to the ground. The air was cool and still and the clouded sky was filtered even darker by the canopy of trees. John paused and closed his eyes. "Open your mind," he said. I leaned against a fallen log, closed my eyes and let myself relax. I slowed my breathing and took in the cool moist air. I could feel John's presence. He was calm and more relaxed than I had ever seen him. I could feel he was stronger, far more centered than he was only a few days earlier.

I could hear the thoughts of the kids in the yard behind the house, playing with the innocence of children. I could sense the dogs with them, silently observing their young wards at play, scanning the tree line, turning their ears to identify each sound. I could sense the people in the house and all the small animals hidden in the forest around us. I could feel the presence of Grandma, her physical appearance belied the magnitude of her power. She was connected to everyone and every living thing as far as I could sense. I sensed a few deer hidden in the forest not far from us and I could close my eyes and see through the eyes of a crow circling overhead. The air was moist and still and John was speaking in my head and Grandma, sitting back in the house, could also sense his thoughts.

"I want to train you, to help you learn how to use every aspect of the connection but this would take months if not years to do it correctly. I simply cannot take the time right now with my daughter looking to take on these scanners. I failed to be the father I should have been when Sparrow was younger and needed me most but I feel that she is getting into something now and I need to be there for her. I can sense the danger around her and I have to try to help her. Sparrow and Laura were holding something back from me. At the same time I can't leave you unprotected and unprepared for the challenges that are ahead of you. We cannot let them take someone with your capabilities. I'm going to ask Grandma to help us, to help me. Not just for my selfish reasons but because I sense something in you. There is something in your nature as well as your capabilities. There is a way that all that I have learned, all that I have been taught and every experience I have had, can be transferred to you, Alex. I can share all my knowledge with you in one moment. The problem, as I said before, is that I can't filter what I share. You will get it all. It is not something I do lightly but I just don't feel we have the time and you are unlike any other I have met. I believe you can absorb everything I have to give you and then build on that. This is deeply personal because you will receive all my knowledge along with all my other thoughts and experiences, my personal failures and shortcomings."

Grandma interrupted. "I will help you do this thing, John; I too am concerned for my granddaughter. The last time she was here she was evasive and would not share all her thoughts with me. I know she must be in some danger or why would she seek out training with Laura, the mind killer. She was being very cautious the last time I saw her and did not wish to explain to me why. I am worried she may, like you, go searching for her mother. I can help you to do this thing true enough but this is not without risk to you both. I see great strength in you, young man," she said to me, "I think you are capable of such a thing if you wish it. However, you will need to prepare yourself. There is much to discuss but for now, I am so pleased to see my son once again. Let's talk about this in the morning. Come back to the house now and meet those who have come to greet you." With that we walked back out of the forest and through the tall grass that was starting to collect the evening dew. The dogs stood up and waited at their post outside the back door. They sat back down as we passed them and entered the house. I felt so strangely relaxed and focused at the same time. The air was so clear, moist and refreshing. Each breath seemed to increase my connection. The forest was so quiet without the background noise that we have in the city. It was such a strange feeling, as we stepped back into the houseful of people that I had only just met, I felt genuinely welcomed.

THE FOUNTAIN OF KNOWLEDGE:

WE SPENT THE rest of the evening greeting visitors. In the city, John had been invisible, a nobody lost in a sea of humanity, but here they treated him like a long lost hero, like a man of great importance. I felt badly that I had so discounted him upon our first meeting.

As the evening wore on, Grandma moved to the living room. She pointed to the fire without a word and a young man next to the oversized fireplace put another log on the fire. People found seats everywhere and Grandma started telling stories. At first it was simple things about how things were when she was a girl. Then as everyone settled in around the living room and the light that had streamed in through the large picture windows turned to darkness, she started to speak about the time before the first white person came. The crowd of people, young and old, grew quiet as she spoke in her native Salish. Strangely, even the young people who did not have such a grasp on their own native language yet, were spellbound by her every word. Everyone settled in and became entranced as Grandma reached into every mind present to be sure nothing was lost from her story. The young and old alike were transfixed as Grandma, illuminated by the muted flickering of the fire burning in the fireplace, conjured images of the early people, their ancestors, living as they had in the old times when the people had a relationship with the land and sea.

A young girl, nestled in her mother's lap, turned and whispered to her mother as Grandma continued her conjuring, not just in words but imagery so clear in the minds of all who listened of times long ago, "Mama," the little girl said, "why can I understand Grandma when she speaks the Salish but not so much you?"

Her mother smiled at her and whispered back, "Because Grandma has great power that can see things we cannot see, hear things we cannot hear and understand things that can be confusing to the rest of us. She has great power. This is why we honor our elders, little isc (Salish word for squirrel). One day, young ones will look to you to tell the stories, so listen well," the mother told her child as they both immersed themselves once again into the imagery painted in their minds by grandma's words. This went on late into the evening. I closed my eyes and saw images of great potlatch feasts in the long houses where families gathered for the winter. I saw large cedar canoes plowing through the open waters of the Puget Sound.

Slowly, one by one, the guests started leaving. One of the ladies had made a bed for me on the living room sofa. As I lay down to sleep, it seemed like I had met everyone in John's tribe but not one word about Sparrow's mother? I wondered why. Although he made no comment, I realized that John likely heard my thought. I could sense the pain and a general sense of loss around any thought of her yet John, Grandma, even Sparrow shared nothing regarding her mother. I did not wish to ask about what I knew to be a painful topic. Just at that moment Grandma entered my thoughts. She spoke in her usual soft yet direct tone and said to me "All your questions will be answered tomorrow. Rest now," she told me. As I slipped off into slumber, the images that Grandma had conjured earlier crept back into my mind. They were so clear I could not tell if they were memories passed down from mind to mind or creations of her own mind that she simply was recalling. Then I saw more, I saw the face of John aging backward to his boyhood, I saw Grandma as a young mother and then as a young girl learning from her father, a gifted medicine man and healer. I saw her father age back to his youth and his teacher. I felt that as I experienced the images and thoughts of each of these souls, they somehow also could see me, traveling back in time as a watcher to the path of this gift through these people.

The next day after breakfast, John suggested we run a few errands. We would drive down to the local general store. As we rolled down the road in Grandma's pickup, John asked me, "So you traveled last night, didn't you?"

"Traveled?" I asked. "I had a weird dream if that's what you mean."

"You fucken traveled, son of a gun," John said, banging his hands on the steering wheel. "Your mind just tapped into the source, kid, all on your own. I knew you had the juice but, wow! Your mind went searching; you tapped into the shared consciousness that has traveled down to Grandma, to me and now you. Your mind just naturally was seeking out that connection that transcends time or our individuality. This is a big deal and for now that is something you may want to keep to yourself. It is extremely rare among those of us that have spent our lives developing our connection, let alone someone who has only been aware of his connection for five minutes. I know you're not exactly a spiritual person and to tell you the truth, lately, I have not been much of one either but this, this is a spiritual thing. Look I had my doubts before, I mean, I do sense something unique in your connection but I also wanted to shortcut your training partly out of selfishness, so I could focus on what is going on with Sparrow and get back to searching for my wife. Now I see that I have been given this opportunity, to get myself back on my path and to be a guide for you to find your path. Even now it is so hard for me to explain in a way you will understand what potential is locked up in your brain. Now I should explain, this shortcut in your training I want to try is like you said before: basically I will download everything I have in my head to you. I know this has got to sound strange to you but for me to do this alone, well, I didn't know for sure I could do it. To try to share a lifetime of experiences all in one load so to speak, but with Grandma's assistance, with her as the conduit, well, it's like the difference between dial up and high speed internet connections. Like she said, this is not without risk. If it is too much for you to process all at once like that, it's possible you could be injured."

"Injured?" I asked.

"It could fry your brain. If it works, you will have all my experiences in your brain. It will take a few days for you to settle it all in your mind but everything I know will be yours and you will be back to school in time for finals, slacker," he said with a half smile. "I don't want to put you on the spot but it's the only way I have to prepare you fully in the shortest amount of time possible and still have time to get back and see what is going on with Sparrow."

I looked at John. I could feel the weight of his words as well as his concern for Sparrow. There was something else he was not telling me, but I figured if what he said was true, I would know soon enough what it was. I had thought about all this for a few days now and as much as I liked all the new abilities I was starting to tap into, I did not like the feeling of vulnerability that I felt, knowing that there were others out there that could see into my head and manipulate me to their will. I remembered the thrashing Art gave me and he was not trying to kill me.

I looked out the window at the forest that lined either side of the country highway we were driving down. I thought about how different my world was today from just a short time ago. I thought about how alive I felt, as if I had just awoken from a long slumber. I could see things and do things that I had never dreamed of before and from what John said, this was just the tip of the iceberg. "What the hell, I'm in. So what do we need to do?" I asked.

"First we need to pick up a few things," John replied, pulling into the general store parking lot. It felt weird as we stepped out of the pickup truck, being the only white guy around. Everyone seemed to know John and they all treated me like they knew me too. I thought how strange that these people have every reason to be distrustful of some strange white guy in their midst, yet my experience was just the opposite. As we stepped into the store, I could tell right away the guy behind the counter was connected. I could sense his connection and he sensed me even with my guard up. He was talking to John normally. He gave John a bag of stuff that Grandma had called ahead for. "I will see you both tomorrow." He said as he shook John's hand and then turned to me and gave me a nod.

The rest of the day came and went before I knew it. Everything and everyone was so laid back and they made me feel at home in a way I could not explain. I did not know if it was the people or the rural atmosphere. There were fewer people around out here in the sticks. The few people that we did run into seemed much more at ease. They were not like city people anyway, always under pressure, always running late, always a bit defensive. I felt more relaxed than I could ever remember.

The next morning at breakfast I looked out the window. It was another cloudy day but not raining, at least not yet. "Today is the big day," John said as he slapped me on the back. He smiled but his trepidation was apparent. Grandma had been up for some time; in fact, I was not sure she ever slept. She wandered through the front room with her jacket on. She was on her way to the front door and she had the bag that John had brought from the general store and an overstuffed shoulder bag. "I'll see you two at noon, at the hot springs," she said in our heads without so much as a glance over her shoulder at either of us as she headed out the door.

Just as Grandma stepped out the front door, a big pickup truck with a lift kit and oversize tires pulled up outside.

She went out and got directly into the passenger side door of the huge truck. "So what is this hot spring?" I asked.

"Just think of it as a first nation's hot tub. Yeah, my people invented the day spa. Didn't I mention that? Seaweed wraps, hot springs, Sweat lodges," John said as he threw me a pair of baggy swim trunks. "You'll need these later," he said.

Just then Raymond pulled up outside in his SUV with music blasting. "How's my new paleface homeboy?" he asked with a grin, as he came in the front door. He paused and put a serious look on his face and said, "Just kidding. I don't want you to get into my head and make me crow like a rooster every time I try to talk to a pretty girl or something freaky like that." Raymond shuddered, and then made a sound like a rooster, "Cook-a-doddle- doooo." Oh man, that would put a serious wrinkle in this smooth rap of mine," he said with a worried look on his face. Then he smiled again.

"Ok, you two home-schooled; entertain yourselves for a few minutes. I need to get dressed for the day spa," John said as he left the room.

"Day spa?" Raymond asked. "By the way, it's homeboy, Uncle John, home boy!" he yelled after John as John walked down the hall.

"Yeah Yeah, home cooking, homemade, home run, whatever," John replied.

We got into Raymond's SUV and headed down the road. The tall trees on either side of the road rarely parted to offer a greater view of the forest around us. We sat there in the back of Raymond's SUV, John and I, not saying anything, just listening to the music which he had thankfully turned down. I looked at John and my thoughts went back to how much all these people respect him. Only a few days ago he was just another homeless wino living on the street in the big city. I see guys like him every day and never even imagined that these guys have lives, that any one of them could be important to someone. They were not always the lost souls we see on the street. Now I saw John as a father, a son and possibly the guy who saved my life by finding me just when I needed him.

"It's complicated, kid," John said to me as he picked up my thoughts. We pulled into a clearing where several other large trucks and SUVs were parked. I could see a few license plates from British Columbia, Canada. "Elders from the north," John said. We got out of the SUV. Raymond held up his fist and gave me the knuckle bump. No wise crack just a serious look as he said, "Later, homey." "His name is Alex not Homer or home run or whatever," John said without even looking at Raymond "Now can we go?"

John motioned toward a trail that led into the forest then started walking up the path. I nodded at Raymond then jogged a few steps to catch up to John. The tall evergreen trees blocked out the slate sky so that only shards of refracted misty light illuminated the moss and fern covered forest floor. We followed the path that led us up the hillside and around dark basalt rock outcroppings. Small streams periodically ran across the path as we walked along. All the background noise of the city was gone. There was no sound at all. The quite of the deep forest that surrounded us was punctuated only with the sounds of the streams trickling by and the various birds as they flittered from tree to tree. A squirrel would bark out every now and again. It was all so peaceful. As we walked, I could feel the presence of those waiting up the trail for us. Their presence was powerful and unrestrained. With several strong minds together it was like wading into the sea and feeling the waves of energy that emanated from their collective minds like the waves in the surf. I sensed Grandma, the guy from the general store and several others that I did not know. I could tell they were aware of us as well but they were linked in some sort of connection that seemed to synchronize their thoughts; it was as if they were all merging their thoughts. This was new to me. John paused and looked at me. "This is another part of what you linked into last night. You are still on the outside looking in but soon, soon..." he repeated as he turned and stared back up the trail.

I could smell the faint aroma of sulfur as we rounded a tall outcropping of dark rock. There in a clearing just ahead of us was Grandma and the others. The setting was primordial. The tall evergreen trees of the forest surrounded this clearing and in the middle of the clearing was a large pool of steaming hot spring water. It was on a mountainside so on the sloping landscape above, you could see the water seeping out of several cracks in the rocks just above the pool and trickling down and collecting in the pool built up on the downhill side with large rocks. On the other side of the pool there was a single small stream of runoff water that flowed through a rocky stream bed, down the hillside, disappearing into the trees and rocks of the forest below. The pool itself had rocks, carefully hand-placed all around it, forming a sort of flat patio in the middle of the forest.

Grandma stepped over to a particularly large rock placed at the edge of the hot spring. She was wearing a dark cloak with red design work and mother of pearl buttons This was the first time I had seen anyone in traditional Salish attire and all of first nations people present were adorned in traditional, similar black and red wraps with detailed patterns that represented various animals and spirits, all woven into a story and all adorned with the same buttons cut from mother of pearl, the iridescent inner side of the abalone shell. There were a few with lighter colored wraps, long fringes hanging down, and similar designs in black and yellow. Grandma also wore a hat intricately woven from very thin strands of cedar bark. There were a few guys over to one side gathered around a large drum. They were beating the drum and chanting, keeping a steady rhythm. None of them were connected. I could feel Grandma and the others using the drum beat to synchronize their thoughts. I could both hear and sense the steady peaceful rhythm they created.

Grandma was standing on the other side of a large, steaming pool of hot spring water. She smiled at us and motioned us to come closer. These hot springs are found along the west side of the Olympic Mountain Range deep in the forest. They are fed by the massive amounts of rainwater that fall, seeping into the earth only to boil up again from the heat of the volcanic action that percolates so close to the surface along this edge of the North-American continental shelf. That explained the sulfur smell. The other connected folks were standing on either side of Grandma. Some of them were chanting in rhythm with the drummers. John looked over at me. "I suppose I should have warned you that to us, this is a spiritual experience as much as it is a physical process. Just go with it."

Grandma motioned for us to get in the pool. Grandma then turned and picked up one of several abalone shells, filled with dried herbs, that she had sitting on a large rock next to the pool. John and I disrobed down to our trunks and set our clothing on a thick fallen tree on the side of the clearing. I could hear the chanting of the group and the rhythm of the drum as I slipped into the warm milk-colored water. As I submerged in the warm water I realized the rhythm was now in my head. I sat down and leaned back, resting my head on a rolled up towel on the edge of the pool. John did the same on the other side of the pool. The warm water lapped around my neck. Grandma poured out the contents of the shells one by one into the water. The rhythm of the chant flowed freely into my head now and I fell into that relaxed state of near-sleep. The warm water made me feel like I was weightless, floating with my eyes closed. I could smell the sulfur from the hot spring, and slowly other smells started to intermingle. I could smell a seaweed smell, then a sweet aroma like flowers, then lavender, ah yes lavender, and my thoughts drifted to Sparrow for just a moment.

Grandma bent down and touched her hands to the surface of the water; she rubbed them together, then stood up straight.

She closed her eyes and stretched out her hand toward John. They were now linked, her mind in his and his mind in hers. Then Grandma reached out her hand in my direction and we were linked as well, like a chain with her in the middle. I could feel the tremendous power of her mind now unfiltered and unrestrained. It was completely unexpected and overwhelming. We were now completely in each other's minds with Grandma in complete control. Then Grandma stepped back and brought her hands together.

    I felt John's thoughts start rushing into my mind. The chanting continued and I could feel all of John's life running into my head. I experienced his childhood as a truly gifted child growing up here on the reservation and his early training. I could feel his strength and mental powers as they developed. I felt like I was caught up in a raging river that was washing me quickly downstream. I felt his joy when he met and married his wife and I felt his pride of fatherhood at becoming a father. Then came his darkness--his wife disappeared and he was driven mad searching for her. No one knew where or why, she was simply gone. No note, no message, nothing. I felt like I was drowning now, as John's thoughts, memories and grief washed over me like I was caught in the white water rapids of a raging river. I may have cried out, feeling the depth of his pain all at once like that, as if it were my own. He went into the city looking for the scanners or anyone who might have seen her. He assumed that the scanners had taken her so he hunted these hunters without mercy, taking every thought he could get from their head, looking for some trace of his wife in the deepest parts of their subconscious. I felt his frustration as he discovered how empty their thoughts were. He had assumed that they had taken her and he declared war on them. He searched day and night, reaching out as far as he could with his mind for any person that was connected or not who had a thought or memory of her. The longer he searched without finding a single trace of her, the angrier he became. I was drowning now in John's thoughts, in his pain. He took out his rage on the scanners he found. His power was far beyond all that he came across. His power was so much greater that it took no effort at all for him to grip their mind and start to peel away the layers searching for any trace of his wife. The scanners would kill themselves if they could, stepping in front of a car, jumping off a roof or exploding a blood vessel in their own brain just to prevent him from getting too deep into their minds. He found the only way to quiet his rage and subdue his pain when he ran out of scanners to destroy, was with alcohol. His rage eventually consumed him. It was longer and longer between his encounters with scanners, so he started spending all his time drinking, waiting for the next scanner to cross his path, until the night that he felt my consciousness, that night on the bridge, in the rain. I felt something and I reached out with my mind. That was when John felt my consciousness, even in his drunken state.

"Alex...Alex..." Grandma was in my head trying to wake me up. I had floated off into unconsciousness. I awoke with a start. "Wow," I said aloud. My head was pounding. My heart was racing. I tried to stand up and lost my balance and fell back into the water. I felt like I had a massive hangover. John looked like he felt the same. "Sit still, you two, and relax in the spring for a few minutes," Grandma said in our heads. She was visibly exhausted as well. The others helped her walk over to a camp area they had set up, over behind where the drummers had been. My head was swimming with memories and thoughts of John's life. I leaned my head back against a flat rock as I sank down into the hot spring up to my neck again. I knew every moment of his life as if I was there. I also knew for the first time just how powerful John was. I lifted up my head and looked over at John but I was still a bit groggy and my head fell back onto the rolled up towel. I knew that he did not just have a vague feeling about his daughter, he had pulled something from Laura's thoughts, something that she was teaching Sparrow for a reason. Both Laura and Sparrow had done their best to hide it but Sparrow was in some kind of real danger.

"Ok kid," John said, "as soon as your mind settles and sorts all this out, you should know all the tricks of the trade that I know, as far as how to manage your connection and all the stuff you need to watch out for. You also know my sad story. I wish I had more time to spend with you right now because I think that you have a real gift. I really want to see what you can do. I was so lost and angry after my wife disappeared that I forgot I still had a daughter that needed me too. I still don't know what happened to my wife but if Sparrow is in some kind of danger now, I need to pull myself together. I need to focus." Finished with his little speech, John staggered slowly out of the hot spring.

I could tell he was mentally exhausted but also relieved. He was not so sure that this would work. In his lifetime he had never seen it done. An elder had shared this skill with him when he was quite young. "Look, John, You're right, I mean, I got all this stuff floating around in my head, I feel like I should have a handle on most of this stuff now. I got stuff swimming around in my head that you would not believe, OK, maybe you would, although some of it is still swirling around, sorting itself out. The important thing is I get what is going on now and the way I see it the choice is clear. We need to figure out who these scanners are. How many of them are there? Who is running them? All of us with this gift will either have to stand together or fall on our own one by one. You, John, need to get it into your head that you don't have to do this all on your own. I can help you now." I pulled myself from the warm waters of the hot spring and got dressed.

Then Grandma was in both our heads "He is right, you don't have to go it alone, you never did. The danger that threatens Sparrow, threatens us all. See past your anger and fear, my son. Protect my granddaughter and protect us all. Find the source of those who hunt us. Perhaps you will find the answer to all your questions with them."

We walked over to the small clearing where Grandma was sitting by a small campfire. She was drinking some tea that she had just poured from a pot simmering at the edge of the fire. We sat down next to her. The others gathered around and opened their minds to us; I now recognized them all. I was in their minds and they were in mine. There were no secrets between us. Several of them were shaman from various first nation tribes around the Puget Sound and up on Canada's Vancouver Island. There were also a few others with them that, although not first nation people, were clearly powerfully gifted.

One of them, a tall black man stepped up and shook my hand. "Welcome" he said with a smile. I could feel his gift was as powerful as any of them. He was an older man but with the physique of someone twenty years younger. He looked deep into my eyes as he shook my hand, then he turned. Placing one hand on John's shoulder, he looked just as deep into John's eyes and said in a soft yet firm voice, "Grandma's right. We are all in this together. It is time those of us who believe this gift should be used to do good, stood together."

John looked at him and nodded. Then John looked at me. "Ok, come on Tonto, we need to get you back to school."

"Tonto? Hey, shouldn't I be the Lone Ranger?" I asked.

John didn't answer as a few of the others chuckled. He turned away, got up and walked over to hug Grandma and I followed. I paused and leaned back away from her, looking at her now through the memories John had of her as his mother. It was confusing for a moment and I pulled her close again for another deeper hug. As I pulled back she smiled and took one of my hands. As she held my hand in her two hands, she was in my head and I felt the warmth of her soul, the sense of calmness and peace that enveloped me was like one feels as a child when your mother wraps you in a warm blanket and holds you close. I could not recall ever feeling so completely free of fear, anger or ambivalence. I felt weak for a moment and I sat down on a large rock, my hand slipping from hers. As I sat, absorbed in the moment, she turned to John, taking his hand as she had mine, sharing the same gift with him in the exact same way.

BACK TO THE CITY:

WE SAID GOODBYE to Raymond at the ferry dock and walked onto the big car ferry. "Later Uncle John and you too, home boy," he yelled after us with a smile.

"Yeah, Yeah, come on, home cooking," John said as we turned to walk on the ferry.

Lines of cars and truck loaded one after another as we made our way up the stairs to the passenger deck and out onto the open balcony overlooking the cars, trucks and motor homes slowly filling up the decks below us on the Cross Sound ferry. I took in the smell of the sea air and the sound of the seagulls circling overhead, calling out as if to announce our imminent departure. My mind was still swimming with all the thoughts and experiences I had absorbed from John. I was able to sense all the thoughts of the living things around me, even the same pod of Orcas we had come across on our trip over to the peninsula. They were several miles to the north of us yet I could sense them clearly and they me. I thought it curious that despite the clear connection, they did not seem to have much interest in communicating with me.

"Don't get your feelings hurt," said John. "They have good reasons to be suspicious of humans, even connected ones. To them we all look alike. I look forward to introducing you when we have more time."

I looked at him and I marveled how a man who I had seen as a nobody, just another meaningless part of the urban landscape only a short time ago was, in reality, not just a powerful being and a giant among men but he was also a son, a father, an uncle, a husband and all those things basic to all of us. These relationships gave him as much power and strength as the gifts brought to him by the rain. All these family relationships gave him strength and he brought the same to them. "You're a lucky man," I said to John.

John turned and looked me in the eye. As we stood there on the windy open deck he said, "Family can be a source of great strength for you as well. You have family too; just as imperfect as my own but they are your family just the same. Who else would welcome home a drunken Indian that had been MIA for a long time and treat him like he is welcome, he is home, where he is valued. When was the last time you saw your family?" he asked me. John then turned away without waiting for an answer that he knew I did not have. I stood there reflecting on my own family as if I were now seeing them through new eyes. They were imperfect but so was I. Could we provide that same kind of support for each other as I felt among John's family. I could only wonder?

The ferry horn sounded as its massive diesel engines rumbled into action, pushing us off from the dock and starting the Cross Sound journey back to Seattle. The blue sky was graying and cool and the clouds seemed content to just hover above us gathering the moisture from the water below and getting ready for another onslaught of rain. Off in the distance I could see a squall falling on the lower tip of Whidbey Island just to the north of us as we traversed the Puget Sound, traveling east. Slowly the skyline of the city took form in front of us as it emerged from the mist. I felt for the first time that I was in control now. Not just another cog in the machine. I could be whatever I wanted now. I was free. I could hear the thoughts of all those around John and me on the ferry. I could pick and choose who I wanted to hear and the same time I felt secure that my mind was guarded. I could feel the presence of John in my thoughts and at the same time, I was in his, as we both stood there in the cool wind scanning the mental horizon.

We searched through the multitude of minds before us as the mainland came into range, and the city drew closer.

I searched the few connected minds I reached to identify them. The few that we detected were all known to John and so I felt I knew them as well. I found Art at his antique warehouse. John laughed to himself. "Let him know you took the crash course," he said.

Art was in his office. He was sitting at his desk making a list of parts he needed on his next trip to the hardware store. I slipped quietly into his mind without detection. The next thing he knew, he was writing on his list "John and Alex are back in town." Art jumped up and stared at the note he had just written. He grabbed his own head with both hands and tried with all his might to shut me out. I was amazed that even at this distance I was able to wedge my way into his strong mind undetected. Even as he resisted me, I felt I was in control of him. I first reveled in my new power, then I felt immediately embarrassed and I pulled back out of his mind.

"Sorry about that," I told Art. As soon as I pulled out of his mind, I could feel Art's mind searching around like a blind man who is in unfamiliar territory. He could not yet even detect us. John reached out to him. "You're the one who wanted me to train him, old buddy," he told Art.

"Freaking A, where in the hell are you guys? How did the kid get so good so fast? I knew he was going to be good but damn, he snuck up on me like you, back in your prime, John. Damn, you guys scared the shit out of me."

"We'll check in with you in a day or two, old buddy," John told him--then he looked at me. "When we get to the city I need to do some checking. I need to find out what is going on with Sparrow. Remember as long as you're functioning like a regular person, keeping your thoughts in your head, you will be undetectable to any scanners. I have never come across one as strong as Art and you can see now where that puts you on the food chain. I will check in with you tomorrow. Just don't get cocky. Remember somehow they got my wife, at least, that is my best guess and she was stronger than Art. The truth is I don't know." John's face got serious. "Just remember to keep a low profile. You don't want to draw any attention to yourself. The truth is we don't know much about those who hunt us, where they come from or what they know but I think the time has come for us to find out."

I knew that, out of all the scanners he had come across, he had never found any memory or thought that would tell him they had even seen his wife. The truth is, they did not have much memory at all. Most scanners have had their minds wiped clean. He did find a few leftover fragments of memories in one but he did not get to explore that before the scanner self destructed. All of them had only a very short recent memory. It is as if they had just come into existence a week or two before John had encountered them and they had a bad habit of self destructing if they felt trapped.

John now chided me like a parent sending his kid off to his first day at school, "You will detect others out there but don't be in a hurry to meet and greet everyone that is connected. If the scanners catch someone that has your life story in their head, that could lead them right to you. So don't talk to strangers and look both ways before you cross the street. And don't forget, even those you do talk to, be careful what you share with them."

I just smiled at John and slowly his worried face gave way to a broad smile.

The ferry slowed as it eased into the docking gate area. It stopped, the gates were lifted and the cars started to roll of the main deck and off into the city. We walked, invisible, in the crowd of foot passengers off the boat and out onto the city streets. I thought to myself how different I felt to be disconnected from the earth again, separated by a layer of concrete. On the peninsula I felt connected to the moist earth under my feet and the living green all around me. Now, we walked up the hill, into the dark canyons formed by the tall buildings of the city. We walked together up the hill from the waterfront, yet we did not speak at all. Then again we didn't have too. John turned and went on his way, disappearing into a crowd of pedestrians migrating amidst the towering smoky sheets of glass like the herds of deer that browse the open meadows at dawn and at dusk but retreat to the security of the forest at night and during the fullest light of day. He was returning refreshed, restored and focused. He had closed his mind now to blend into the mass of humanity like a submarine slipping below the waves.

    I went my own way, to catch a bus back to the University District. I was back on my old familiar streets but everything felt new and different. I was alone now and I did not know when I would see John again. I was immersed in the thoughts of everyone around me. I felt alive, as if I had been born into a black and white world and only now learned to see a rainbow of color. I turned up my collar against the cold breeze as I made my way to the bus stop. Looked like rain. I smiled to myself.

SCHOOL DAYS:

BEEP, BEEP, BEEP...I awoke to the sound of my alarm. Oh, man. I had school today. I was about a week behind. I showered, dressed in a hurry and headed out the door. There was just a light rain falling, barely more than a mist. My head was swimming. I was careful to keep myself closed off until I could focus and slowly scan the area searching for any sign of someone who could detect me. I walked along the busy street full of students and commuters. One of my fellow tenants in the same apartment building spotted me leaving for school and decided to catch up and walk over to the campus with me. "Where you been, dude? I haven't seen you for a few days," he said.

"Sure you have," I replied as I reached into his mind and planted a few memories of me coming and going as usual. "Yeah, that's right I have seen you coming and going but I haven't really seen you, you know, like, I don't know what I mean." This guy was kind of a bubba so I usually tried to avoid him around the building but today seemed like a good day for my new friend to buy me breakfast. Especially after being in his head just long enough to plant memories of me coming and going only to find out he was the one who was stealing my laundry soap from the laundry room in the basement of the building. "Hey, how about we stop for a bit on the way?" he said.

"Great," I said. "I wasn't that hungry when I left the building but all of a sudden I feel a hunger coming on," I said with a smile.

After a good breakfast, courtesy of my buddy from the apartment building, I found my way to my first class. As I entered the hall I was scanning to see if there was anyone else connected in the area. I was surprised that as I scanned across this sprawling campus, with thousands of people, there were only a few low level connections. A few that might have felt some degree of intuition but no real connections until I detected one. She was closed off and very hard to detect at first. She was definitely not reading me, in fact she was not even aware that I had detected her. She was across the campus. I was well out of her range. I thought for a moment about what John had told me about not being in a hurry to contact every one of our kind I came across. I figured to play it safe, then I thought, a fellow student is not likely to be a scanner, not that I would know firsthand what a scanner felt like. I figured I would check her out later, real cool, just a quick look. After all, what could that hurt? She would never even know I spotted her.

I slipped into the lecture hall just as the teacher was preparing to get started. She looked down the roster to see who was current on assignments. As she scanned down the list, it was simple enough to get into her head and have her stop at my name and check off the two blank spots from last week's assignments. It was a breeze to take notes. I was listening to the teacher talk and think about the topic at the same time. I was able to absorb the teacher's thoughts directly. It was like my own, high intensity tutoring session. I could sense the thoughts of the students around me. I could relax now about school. Just as I started feeling a little cocky, the teacher spotted me just sitting with my eyes closed, not taking any notes, just taking it all in. She assumed I was sleeping. She was offended that someone would just sit there sleeping in her class so she decided she would make an example of me. She decided to call on me, figuring it would embarrass me. She was stunned that, not only did I have the answer to her question, but I was able to share some detail as to other views on the topic that she herself was working to define on a paper for publication. Her distain for what she thought of as a slacker student, turned to pleasure as she thought to herself, "This is a young man I should keep an eye on."

As I read her thoughts, I felt cocky for just a moment, and then I remembered what John had said about not standing out, even to the normal folks. The teacher smiled at me and made a note on her computer pad. I slinked out of the lecture hall as quickly as I could when she dismissed the class before she could catch me for an after class chat.

I strolled out among the multitude of students. I thought I would see if I could sneak a peek at the girl I detected earlier. She did not seem dangerous but I just had to see what she looked like. I strolled leisurely across campus, all the while being mindful to keep myself closed off. I would open up just enough to get a bead on her then close myself off again. Like swimming underwater and coming up just enough for a quick breath of air and look around before going back under. I had located her in the student union building at one of the coffee stands trying to decide what she would have.

As I entered the building I opened my mind just enough to get her ordering tea, Earl Gray. I was almost there now. I kept my head down as I came around the corner and stepped inside the building. I glanced up to see the coffee stand. There was a crowd gathered around it. She had just ordered so I figured I would just wait for them to call out her order. I kept myself closed off. I did not want her to detect me and I had no idea how skilled she might be.

"Tea, Earl Gray," the barista called out. There she was. A girl with black shoulder length hair approached the counter. She was Indian, A real Indian from India. At least I knew who she was now and she had not detected me at all.

I turned to walk away and I felt someone trying to get into my head. It was not her. Quickly I looked all around and I spotted him, across the hall. It an east-Indian guy and he had seen me too. Now he was fixed on me. He had apparently picked up on me as I was sneaking up on her. I had been really stupid, fixating on her to the exclusion of everything else. He was using all his focus to try to penetrate my head. I blocked him and I ran across the hall, I tried to lose him in the crowd, down a half a flight of stairs and back outside into the light rain that was now falling. He was on to me and I had no idea who he was other than a possible connection to her. I did not have time to figure this out right now. He had seen me. He did not get into my head but he knew I was connected and he knew what I looked like. I jogged around the corner of the building trying to move as quickly as possible without drawing more attention to myself. I cloaked myself to everyone in the area. I was now invisible. He was following me, still reaching out to try and get into my head. As soon as he rounded the corner I turned on him. He tried to keep me out of his head but he was not strong enough. I froze him immediately like Art had done with me. I walked over to him. He was panicking but before I could say anything to him, the girl was attacking my mind. I was so focused on him that I had forgotten about her.

She rounded the corner of the building at a full run. She was trying to place a vision of snakes everywhere into my head as she approached. I was trying to hold him frozen and block his mind at the same time I was keeping her out of my mind while simultaneously keeping all this invisible to the crowed of regular folks. Before I could get a hold on her she ran right up on me and punched me hard in the nose. I lost my focus and balance for just a moment and the guy was free now. She swung again and this time I sidestepped her. Now I was pissed. "Hey, that hurt," I yelled at her. They were both trying to penetrate my mind. The guy came hard at me with a lunging kick and I sidestepped that as well. He had overcommitted so when he missed he went past me. I turned and this time

I was able to focus and I grabbed them both with my mind. They were both frozen instantly.

There were a lot of people coming and going all around us and I did not like being in such a public place. I was still blocking everyone from seeing us while holding them. I could feel the panic and fear in both of them and I felt bad as I remembered what that had felt like when Art grabbed me. I held them both frozen a moment longer as I picked up my backpack with my books. I slowly walked over and looked into the eyes of each of my two captives. I did not say anything for a moment as I looked at them, trying to decide what to do now. People were just walking by us as if we were not even there now. I noticed the blood dripping from my nose as I bent over to pick up one last book and put it back into my backpack. I reached into the back pocket of my backpack and pulled out some paper napkins to hold on my nose. I walked over to the girl. "Nice shot," I said with a nod.

I then turned to the guy. I was speaking to them in their minds now. "If I let you two go, can we not do any more of this hitting and kicking stuff?" I asked.

The guy was less scared and now more full of questions, "Who are you? What do you want?" He thought I might be a scanner. Oh, he knew about them.

"Look, I said, if I was a bad guy now would be the time when I do bad stuff to you, right? So what about it? No more with the physical or mental violence OK? Can't we all just get along?"

"I suppose you're right," the guy acknowledged. He looked sideways at his still frozen sister. "Ah, your sister, now I get it. You got the overprotective big brother thing going on here," I said. She was still frozen and still a little scared but she immediately replied with just a touch of tone aimed at her brother, "I can take care of myself, thank you."

"She has a point," I said aloud as I released the two of them from their frozen state. I blocked my mind just in case. The guy walked over to me, looking me up and down. He was still just a bit angry. I took half a step back and dropped my backpack down. "I don't know about where you come from, but where I live, someone looks at you like you're looking at me that means they still want to do something to you. So what's it going to be? Can we talk?"

"Why were you stalking Sahira," he demanded. "Easy, guy, I'm not looking to swoop in on your sister. In case you didn't notice we are all a little unique. I was curious, there are not too many people like us so when I picked up on her vibe, I wanted to see who she was, that's all," I said.

He looked at her and scolded her. "I told you to keep your mind closed. This could have been much worse."

"Easy guy, no harm, no foul. Well, almost no harm," I said as I pulled the napkin away from my nose to see if the bleeding had stopped. "I'm Alex," I said as I offered my right hand, still holding the napkin to my nose with my left.

"I'm Jayanta, call me Jay and this is my sister, Sahira. I must admit, I am actually relieved to meet someone as powerful as you are who is not out to do any harm." He reached out and shook my hand.

"Well, I am obviously not all that good. I did not even feel you until you were right behind me," I replied.

"Yah, well, I had planned to meet my sister here and when I am just walking around, I try to keep myself closed down. It was just my luck that you did not scan around. You were pretty focused, but thank you," Jay said with half a smile. "I have been here two years as a student and I have only met two others of our kind. I have detected several others but we were warned about the ones called scanners so we try to pass undetected as much as possible. Wow, now that I think about it, you just froze us both, at the same time, wow. That could have been the end of us both, Sahira," Jay said as he gave his sister another cross look.

Sahira looked back at her brother for a moment then over at me with a curious expression. "Well, now that you have met us, now what? You could have killed us both if you'd wanted so you are clearly not out to do us harm. You are the most powerful person we have come across, even back home, but you don't seem to be at ease with your gifts."

I had to double check to be sure she was not in my head. "Look, I don't want to say too much but I am still getting used to all this. I did not plan to actually meet you. I just ... well, here we are so maybe we could grab a burger together or something?" I said.

Jay laughed. "How about the 'or something' we don't eat cows. Hello! Hindus! In our religion it is like asking one of your Green Peace activists to go to a sushi restaurant for a bite of a whale."

"Yeah, about those whales, well, never mind but OK let's just say I get your point," I responded.

We went back into the student union building, got some coffee and spent the afternoon hanging out, chatting about stuff just like three regular students. They told me about the part of India they were from, just to the north of Bangladesh but they were careful not to give me the specific name of the town. The climate is warmer but the rain is roughly the same as it is here. They told me that their parents had sent them here to study. Jay had been here two years and Sahira just one. They told me about their home and I told them about the Puget Sound and the many islands. Jay said that he had met an older woman that looked sort of like a librarian, shortly after he came here. From his description it sounded like Laura.

We really did not know each other well enough to allow each other into our thoughts yet so I could not see what she looked like in his head. He said she was not very friendly but she did warn him about the scanners. I started to tell them about the scanners—how basic most of their skills were and how little memory most of them seem to have. The danger is, they work as part of a team so when one becomes aware of you they will try to call for others right away. I wanted to tell them as much as I could without having to explain that the information I was giving them was actually from someone else's experiences. Sahira looked at me with a curious look again, "Sometimes you talk like you are as experienced as you are skilled but sometimes you sound like all this is very new to you?"

"Yeah, well, we will have to have that conversation another day," I responded. I nervously turned away and rubbed my temple with my right hand as I double-checked to be sure she was not in my head.

We swapped e-mail addresses and phone numbers. When I went on my way back home I was sure that I had said way too much but it was safer than letting anyone in my head. Still it was nice to have someone to talk to that was my age and that I could talk to about this crazy connection thing. I just hoped that nothing I had said would be one day pulled from their thoughts and used to track me down.

The rain had stopped and the clouds had lifted to a high ceiling by the time I headed home. With less moisture in the air I felt safer. The voices of those I passed on the street were quieter. As I tried to scan the area I found my range was much less than earlier in the light rain. It felt good. I was pondering what I was going to do for money. Having not shown for my last job for a few weeks now, it was safe to assume I would need a new source of income. As I walked home I tried to think of how I could use my new skills to make money without taking advantage of anyone or drawing attention to myself. I lay awake that night thinking about how I could help others and how I could help myself. I can always get a free meal and I guess I could go play cards with the frat brats up on Greek row and take some of their extra cash. I don't know--even that seemed kind of wrong. This was a strange thing, I could take what I want, manipulate most people any way I wanted--the only thing limiting me was my own morality.

The next day I came straight back to my apartment after class. It was actually a nice day with the clouds giving way to a little sunshine. My abilities were limited but it felt good to have the warmth of the sun again. I felt limited and yet at the same time safer. Just to be sure, before I went inside, I paused; I looked up and down the busy street. I dropped my pen in the street next to the curb. As I reached to pick it up, I touched my finger to the water running in the gutter. It was like plugging into a giant antenna. I made a quick scan to see who might be about. I made a quick inventory of those that I could detect. No scanners. I stood back up, put the pen back in my pocket and headed in the front door and up the stairs to my apartment. How sad that people like me have to avoid one another so as not to leave a mental trail in each other's minds that might one day be picked up by one of these scanners.

I unlocked the door and walked in; I meant to hang my coat in the hall but my hat fell to the floor and I was feeling just too lazy to go back and pick it up. I walked into the main room and was about to throw my backpack on the sofa when, to my surprise there was someone sitting there, on the sofa, sipping coffee. It was John.

"I would feel a lot more super powered if it was not so easy for you to sneak up on me," I said as I sat my backpack on the floor and pushed it to the side. Even as I spoke I could not read him or even feel his presence at all.

John laughed and said, "Closing yourself off is basic stuff. It's not too hard and it makes it easy for us to hide in a crowd. What is more challenging is creating a false level of consciousness so that one of these scanners can read you and think he is reading a regular person."

I knew from my link with John that he had done this many times. Scanners had walked right past him, scanning everyone in the area, passing right through his mind and never realizing that they had only passed through his fabrication of a conscious mind. They had no idea as to his true nature or thoughts, as they had only scanned a false outer layer of his consciousness. They had no way of knowing that John was now hunting them. John knew I understood what he was talking about. He gave me a nod and said, "This, boy wonder, is how we are going to catch one of these guys without them knowing they have been caught.

"Once these scanners know you are in their head they will find a way to self destruct. They will try to jump off a building or blow a blood vessel in their own brain rather than be caught and they will take you with them if they can. I have been thinking about this. We need to get into their heads without them knowing we are there. We need to catch them with their mind wide open, get into their head deeply before they can do anything. Then we are going to use one of them to trace back to their source. I've come to ask you for your help; I think that this is what Laura and Sparrow are planning or something like it and I would feel better if I, if we, were in on it. If I ask to join them they could say no and I wouldn't blame them, but if we ask them to help us, well, that's different," John said with a cunning smile.

I paused and looked at him. "So explain this to me again, we let them in our minds so we can sneak into their mind, only they are not really in our minds like they think they are and they will never notice we are in their minds until it's too late for them cause we are really getting into their mind when they think they are getting into ours?" I had an incredulous look on my face.

"It's about layers, grasshopper, like an onion," John said with a laugh.

"Ok, John, you know I'm going to back your play any way you want to roll but how about we get a real posse together on this? This sounds dangerous, not to mention confusing but this will affect us all so let's get as many folks in on this as we can. I know, you explained why everybody, as always, tried to hide from each other just as much as we are now trying to hide from these scanners but maybe it is time for us to stop hiding from each other and start working together. Remember what Grandma said, you are not alone?" I said as I stepped over closer to him.

John smiled a slow smile. He stood up, looked me in the eye and said, "Soon, but before we put too many people at risk let's find out what that risk really is. Let's find the source first, then we can decide what to do about it. At least then we will know better what we are all up against. Besides I detected a couple of scanners the other day which are working their way toward us. I think they will be in our area pretty soon. We should talk to Art and to Laura so she doesn't crush them before we get to them."

"Ok, fine, John, I'm in but I need to warn a couple of other folks like us that live in the area to stay clear as well," I said.

John looked at me for a moment. "So didn't we have a talk about laying low?

"Here just take a look in my head, it will be faster than explaining," I said.

John reached into my mind and saw my encounter with Sahira and her brother. "Ok, yeah, hey why don't you invite them to meet us tonight," he said. "We will see if Laura wants to meet them as well. I don't want to start outing everyone I know, just cause you want to be the ambassador for the, I-can-read-your-mind club."

I had started to fish around for my cell phone so I could send a quick text message. I paused to look back at John. "I'm pretty sure Laura already knows them but, yeah, ask her," I replied.

That evening John and I went out just as the sun was going down. It was a cool dry evening and all the streets were full of students from every corner of the globe, commuters transferring busses and what we call "Ave rats," the local runaway or throw away kids who live in or around the University District. They get by just pan handling, dumpster diving, or selling small amounts of drugs or other stolen items. When you mix in a few adult homeless and a few mentally ill folks then you have a good idea of the typical mix of people you might run into on any given day in the University District. We were headed for the same coffee shop where we had met Laura and Sparrow before. I had texted earlier to ask Sahira and Jay to meet me there about an hour or so after we were to meet Laura and Sparrow so we would have a chance to talk to them first. I had told them they would get a chance to meet my tutor but that was all I had said. I did not know if Laura would stick around to meet them again or not.

It was different without the rain as we walked the crowded, darkening streets. I could hear the thoughts of the people passing by on the street but not from that far away. I bent down to touch the little trickle of water in the street next to the curb again. As I did, I handed John a small tin of mints from my pocket with my other hand. He touched my hand to take the mints at the same time I touched the water with my finger and instantly we were both seeing farther and wider. I stood up and looked around; John gave me a nod and a smile as he said "Thanks" and tried to hand me back the mints.

I pushed them back to him and said, "How about you hold on to those."

"What?" John replied. "Look John, I'm not judging, I'm just saying we got the man off the street but we still haven't got the entire street off the man."

"I've been preoccupied," John said as he shrugged his shoulders. We walked on down the street, John sniffing his jacket and then holding his hand in front of his mouth and nose to try and smell his own breath. "Everyone is a critic," John muttered.

We arrived at the coffee shop and went in. It was dimly lit but the illumination from all the laptops gave the place a warm glow all around. The place was pretty full but we found a table by the wall. No sooner did we get ourselves situated than Laura and Sparrow strolled in, scanning the crowd both visually and consciously with a slow cool sweep. Laura looked as serious as always and Sparrow looked...I paused and looked at John just to be sure he was not reading me at all. He did not need to read me as he was looking right at me. I smiled at the stern look he was giving me.

"Hi Pop," Sparrow said as she dropped the cool demeanor and rushed over to give John a big hug. "You look different," she said to me in an offhand manner as she pulled off her coat and slid into a seat across from me.

She stared right at me with a deep, dispassionate yet penetrating gaze, then she gave me a warm and disarming smile. I was transfixed by the warm glow in her eyes from the reflection of all the laptop screens in the low light. Without realizing it, my guard was starting to slip. John looked over and saw the stupid look on my face. He gave a slow sigh of disappointment before he slowly reached behind me and gave me a slap on the back of the head. I realized she was trying to pry her way into my head. "Hey!" I said as I gave a cross look, first at John, then at Sparrow. I grabbed the back of my head where he had slapped me and rubbed it. John ignored me as he looked intently over at Laura, studying her as she hung her coat neatly and slid, ever so smoothly, in across the table from him and next to Sparrow. Only then did she meet his gaze. "You're teaching her well," John said to Laura. She responded with just the faintest momentary smile.

John turned to me with a serious look. "You see it is not just about how strong your mind is or the strength of your connection. It is also about combining your other natural skills and attributes with your mental capabilities to make you truly capable. She had you twisted before she even started to sneak into your head and you had no clue."

I looked over at Sparrow, still rubbing the back of my head and she gave me a smile with a cocky wink. John started explaining his plan to Laura but I was not paying much attention as I was not done with Sparrow. As childish as it seemed, I had to get her back. As she listened to John explain how he planned to trap a scanner and track them back to their source, I knew that I could not slip all the way into Sparrow's head unnoticed. She was very strong and John and Laura would feel it as well. Instead I just blocked everyone from feeling anything under the table. Then as casually as I could, I had her extend her leg as I reached over, under the table and pulled her boots and socks off her feet one by one, all the time I was pretending to listen intently. I was never really in her head, just blocking her from feeling her own feet.

After John had laid it out, Laura looked him in the eyes and said, "This will require some very delicate mental manipulation, John, not to mention a degree of teamwork and just a bit of luck."

John responded "Yes, but what if we are able to get into the head of one of these scanners? They may not lead us anywhere but until we catch one of them and are really able to get into their thoughts and trace them as far back as possible, we don't know. Look, in the past we just worried about stopping them. Between us we have the skills and capabilities to really find out who is behind them, maybe even stop them altogether."

Laura carefully leaned in and in a soft voice she said, "Someone will have to be the bait and we don't have the right to just sacrifice some unsuspecting person to who knows what and the hands of the scanners."

John held up his hand as if to stop her. "I would not let just anyone be the bait. I would be the bait."

Sparrow was stunned at her father's statement but before she could say a word. Laura sat up straight and then in a slightly angry voice said, "Out of the question. Ok, so we do not know where they would take you and what you might be subjected to and, should you be unable to escape, they could kill you or worse. They find a way into your head and then they would surely get us all, not to mention they might know you. You have certainly done everything that might attract their attention these past several months. No, I'm sorry, John. I can't let you put yourself or the rest of us at risk like that, absolutely not!"

John started to say something but I interrupted him. "I could be the bait."

Laura paused and looked over at me. "Commendable, you have the potential but you simply do not have the experience yet."

"You would be surprised how much I have learned already," I said.

"No, I will not put anyone else at risk. It has to be me," John interrupted.

Sparrow got up and walked around the table. She hugged John tightly then pulled back to look at him. "Pop, I lost my mom; do I have to risk losing you too?"

It was at that precise moment that Jay and Sahira walked in. Jay recognized Laura right away and I could feel his trepidation. I stood up and waved them over. John looked at them and then back at me. "Boy, that is a whole different kind of Indian," he said.

"I would like to introduce Jay and his sister, Sahira. Guys, this is John and his daughter Sparrow and I think you met Laura before. Jay looked around the table and then at Sparrow standing next to John.

"A little cold to go around barefoot, isn't it?" Jay asked with a smile as he looked down at Sparrow's feet. Sparrow looked down at her own feet in surprise, then over at me with a steely gaze. I looked at her with a smile and then over at Laura and John.

"See, I got mad skills now," I said as I sat back down. Jay and Sahira slid in at one end of the table, not quite sure what had just transpired regarding Sparrow's boots but they could not help but smile as she searched around under the other end of the table for her boots and socks. When she finally got her boots back on, she sat up and smiled at Jay and his sister before turning to give me an angry look across the table. I looked over at her and gave her the same smile with a cocky wink she had given me earlier.

"Mad skills," I repeated softly to Sparrow.

Laura looked over the top of her glasses at me but did not say anything. Then she looked at John and said, "We will continue this conversation later. He has clearly learned much from you already, including a bit of a swagger that he could best do without."

We sat around drinking coffee and exchanging small talk. I told how I had met Jay and Sahira. Sparrow interrupted after I got to the part where Sahira had smacked me square in the nose, by offering her a knuckle bump across the table and saying "Right on, girl."

She then gave me another quick sideways glance before going back to ignoring me. John explained to the two of them that we were expecting a couple of scanners in the area soon so they should be extra vigilant and not attract any attention.

"You two seem like a couple of nice kids," John said, "but I just can't tell you too much right now other than, we are going to have a little encounter with these scanners and we don't want anyone else to get caught up in the crossfire.

After an hour or so Jay and his sister left. Laura looked over at John. "Don't do anything on your own. I will talk to Art and we'll come up with something. You know too much for us to risk falling into the wrong hands and your apprentice here does not yet have the experience for such a plan."

"He has the benefit of all of my experience and knowledge now," John replied.

"Great, let me know when he has absorbed all that and we'll be all set," Laura snapped back.

John looked at her. "OK, he has absorbed all that," he said, somewhat sarcastically.

Laura glared at him for a moment then her eyes grew wide. She turned to me and looked at me for a moment with a curious look. "May I have a look?" she asked hesitantly as she reached slowly across the table to put her hand on top of mine.

"Fine, but just you," I said as I gave a quick, sideways glance back at Sparrow. She crossed her arms and looked away as if in a pout. I opened my mind to Laura, Sparrow tried to slip in with her but I was able to isolate her and block her out as Laura treaded softly around my thoughts. Laura lifted her hand off mine as soon as she had seen enough. She looked at John in amazement. Then she looked back at me.

"Amazing" she said under her breath. "How did you…, well, he may have the benefit of all of your experience and knowledge but his judgment is still questionable."

John chuckled to himself, "I think she's warming up to you, kid. She says the same thing about me." John gave me a quick elbow and a smile.

Laura looked back at him, "John, how did you…never mind, we still can't use him as bait, it's too risky."

"I told you, I'll be the bait," John said.

I looked over at John and then at Laura. "Sorry folks, let's review for just a moment, shall we? These guys may or may not have taken Sparrow's mom. If they have her, they may or may not know about all three of you so who does that leave that they will not recognize yet may have the skills to pull it off? Come on guys, you know this is the best way forward," I said as I raised my coffee cup as if to toast.

John shook his head. "We'll just have to risk that they don't identify me," he said.

I looked straight at John and said, "Look, John, this is part of the problem, this is not your problem alone, it's all *our* problem. Where would I be if you had not found me? This is not your private little war. We don't know how many of them there are or how powerful they are. We are eventually going to need to bring in everyone of our kind that we know because once we find the source, well, we may need to call in the cavalry. Like it or not, we are all in this together. We can fight this together or get hunted down one by one."

Sparrow sat back in her chair, crossed her arms and rolled her eyes. "Ok, John Wayne, so the plan is, we let them take you and we try to follow and see where you end up. When we find the place that they do what they do, we try to get in and get you out before they do it to you. Maybe we get to the source and find what happened to my mom in the process. Is that pretty much it?"

John cut me off. "I still say I should be the bait."

I looked at him with a smile and said, "So which one of us is the best tracker?"

I paused as John searched for a comeback. He knew he was the most skilled and experienced tracker even if I might now have his memories. "That's what I thought. I know you'll have my back. With you, Laura, and Sparrow tracking me, that's like the A team covering me," I said, as I looked around the table with a smirk.

John studied me for a moment without a word. Laura reached across the table and touched John's hand. He looked back at her and said, "Looks like you were right about his judgment. I could tell that what they were all most concerned about was, could I hold out long enough for this to work. I raised my coffee cup again and glanced over at Sparrow. I gave her a less convincing wink as I said "mad skills."

Later that night as John and I were walking back to my apartment, John reached into his shoulder bag, pulled out a bundle of cash and stuffed it into my pocket like it was nothing. "You're going to want to pay your bills ahead a bit and there are a few things we are going to need," he added. I stopped in my tracks.

"Wow! So, like do you always carry around that kind of cash," I asked as I peeked into my pocket and thumbed through the bundle of hundred dollar bills. "Getting money is never a problem for guys like us. I only take from those who deserve to lose it. This money was drug money," John said.

"Aren't there some kind of rules?" I asked. "We talked about this before, remember. What, rules? For guys like us? Who would write those rules? Who would enforce those rules?

Look, I have thought about this myself and the only thing I have to offer is this. The only one who can make any rules for you is you. Ok, for myself, I kind of have one rule. It's the only one I know but it seems to cover things pretty good," John replied.

"Ok," I said.

"It's simple: Do good whenever you can and when you screw up, try to fix it." John replied, Then he shook his head. "Boy, I got a lot of fixing to do."

The next day I got up and went to class like always. When I got back John was sitting at the kitchen table. He had some of my clothes on the chair next to him. He was busy threading a wire into the hem of one of my pant legs. Without looking up he motioned me over. "Left leg is a wire saw, right leg is piano wire, the belt buckle actually has a concealed blade in the belt and inside the collar on each side is a capsule of a drug called Nar can. They drug you up, you bite down on one of these and suck on it to cancel the effect. Over here you have your general handy stuff to have, like a can of Mace spray, a pocket size propane blow torch, a boot knife, a small set of pocket tools and a laser pointer. The handy stuff I will hold onto for you until we find out where they are going and catch up to you. Oh, put these on," John said as he handed me two metal rings. "These are the handles to your wire saw or they just hurt a lot if you punch someone with them."

"Wow, I did not expect to be turned into James, freaking, Bond," I said as I picked up the pocket torch and studied it, flicking the flame on and off. I started to say, I was not much of a fighter but then John *had* been. I flashed across his memories of serving in the military. He had trained extensively in Ju-Jitsu during his time in the service and continued his martial training after he got out. I had all of his skills and experiences flooding into my thoughts.

John looked sideways at me for a moment then reached out his hand, holding it open for me to return the torch to him.

"I just want to be sure that you have options, kid. Look, this could get really nasty. I do not want you to do this," John said.

"Yeah I know, John, but this is what jacked you up before, you want to protect everyone and handle it all yourself. You blame yourself for whatever happened to your wife and you definitely do not want to risk anyone else. I get it, but this is not your burden to carry alone. Like it or not, we are all in this. Besides, don't make me tell your mom, cause you know I will," I added as I turned and walked over to the sofa to sit down. John did not look up but he smiled to himself.

Well, we should probably get to work on your layers of consciousness, Mr. Bond," he said. The first lesson was to create an imaginary persona. John had me make up a fake identity and slowly we started building it with its own history, experiences and special moments. We sprinkled it with insignificant details to make it more believable and as similar to my own life so that if a stray thought slipped through, it would not seem out of place. I spent that night and the next several nights with John slamming around in my head like a burglar ransacking a room looking for any small thing of value. I had to compartmentalize any key thoughts or memory that might be dangerous for a scanner to find. I could not have any obvious holes but at the same time I had to secure every loose thought that could lead to anything that connected to the real me or that might tip them off that something was not right. It was mentally exhausting, but at the same time exhilarating. John looked around the false consciousness I had created for any defect that might give a reason to doubt they had total access, total control in my mind. He would exploit any weakness and I would try to redirect him back to the false consciousness.

Finally, late one evening, John said, "I think you're as ready as you are going to be."

"Great, because I've got finals tomorrow and the rest of this week and my brain is pretty fried right now," I said. The finals were no big concern for me now that I had the benefit of everyone else in my classes doing the studying for me. Still, I was going to need a degree of focus to finish my classes.

The next few days were pretty easy. I would get up, go to school, then come back to my apartment and go through a series of mental workouts with John. I would go up on the roof to practice some of the martial skills that I had assimilated and spend a little time just plugging in. I would close my eyes and see the world around me with my mind. I felt like I had known John all my life but the reality was that I really hadn't. In order for him to give me the benefit of all his years of training and experience in one afternoon, he had to surrender his privacy—even to a degree some of his dignity. He could offer no resistance, keep no secret. He had to open himself completely and let every experience, every thought flow freely. He had to expose himself completely to someone he did not know very well at all. Those thoughts that we all have, that we would be embarrassed to discuss, even with a close friend, he gave up without resistance. I know that the reason he did all this was only partly because he saw the potential in me. The main reason was because he knew that if I was at full power and possessed all his experience and training, between us we had a much better chance to find his wife and protect his daughter. I felt how deeply he loved his wife and she had loved him. I felt how lost he was when she disappeared. I looked at John and I knew, for him, everything was all about her and Sparrow. I was still humbled that he would trust me enough to share everything. I felt the love that he had shared with his wife, the mental bond that allowed their relationship to transcend what normal people experience. I wondered to myself if I would ever be fortunate enough to experience that kind of love? I understood now why it almost drove him mad to lose her.

My life was completely different now. I felt as if John had set me free from a destiny of compromises. I worried about the future but now I felt that I actually had the ability to do something about it. I had never felt so powerful, so in control of my own destiny and yet so vulnerable. Where there had once been a dull future with endless compromise, subject to the will of others, now I could see endless possibilities. Where once I saw a myriad challenges and threats, there was now only one thing that threatened me. I wanted to find where these scanners were coming from and stop them at the source for my own protection as much as anyone else. I had just been given this wonderful power over my own life and my future only to be told that I was at risk of losing everything. I did not want to just live day to day like I had been. I did not want to have to look over my shoulder, waiting for someone to come take it all away.

    I felt bad for these people, these scanners. They were just like me. They had discovered this rare gift, only to have it twisted, so they could be reduced to nothing but a tool, to be used as scanners and for what? Now that I had the tools to be in control of my own life for the first time, I was not prepared to surrender everything. I was not sure how far I would be able to go to keep my freedom. John had not been concerned so much with all that. He had lived day to day with just one goal. Perhaps he never contemplated the lives of those that had been enslaved as scanners. Perhaps he was focused more on those that mattered so much to him. I had never killed a person before; I was unsure if I could do it, even if I had to. One thing was clear to me, John had killed many. Through our connection I had seen yet another side to him; that was the side that was capable of efficient cold-blooded, murder. It certainly gave me pause. I wondered to myself if this was the price I would have to pay? John felt he had let both his wife and Sparrow down and now he was looking for redemption. He would do anything;--suffer anything to find his wife and to protect his daughter.

As I lay down to sleep that night, I pondered all that I had been through. I wondered where this adventure would take me and how it might change me? I had never actually seen a scanner but I had experienced all of John's encounters with them. What about my family, could any of them have the gift? Are any of them at risk? It was a long and restless night.

CYRUS:

THE NEXT MORNING I awoke to find that John had gone again. I rose, turned on some music and ran through some of the stretching exercises I had picked up from John. I got dressed and then went up onto the roof of my building. There was a heavy cloud cover and a very soft rain had just started to fall. I closed my eyes as I stood there alone on the roof. Slowly I lifted my arms straight out from my sides. I let my consciousness reach out, out of my body, into the moisture-filled air, through the heavy wet clouds above me. I reached as far as I could in every direction, listening, sorting the thoughts. It was like standing in the middle of a river, with the thoughts of every person flowing around me. I could hear the normal people's thoughts throughout the neighborhood. I could also sense Jay and his sister. Even closed off they could not hide from me now. I could feel the minds of those people with the gift some miles away. I could feel and be felt by those powerful minds at great distances. I searched as far as I could; perhaps I would find someone I did not recognize, even with all John's experiences. Perhaps his wife was out there. I reached farther. I focused my attention in one direction now; this gave me even more range. I slowly turned, scanning farther in one direction as I turned. Like a beam of light from a lighthouse, I probed farther and farther. I could feel the Orca whales in the Puget Sound. I could sense several tribal elders from various tribes on Vancouver Island stretching up into Canada. The island is much like the peninsula of Washington State, only bigger in sheer land mass. The forest is bigger, older, deeper and...there was something else there. I could sense a mind, a powerful mind, yet different. Before I could focus in on it, John was in my head.

"Enough of that for now," he said, "you still need to keep a low profile, for now anyway." I shut down and went back inside. There was so much out there; so many new facets to this gift. "How cool is that?" I thought to myself as I wiped the rainwater from my face. "How cool is that!"

The rain dissipated and the sun peeked out. I spent the afternoon in my apartment. I put on some streaming drum and bass music and sat down. I settled back and closed my eyes as I started going through the thoughts and experiences John had shared with me. I let them flow through my mind like a movie running on fast forward. As the stream of his life flowed past, something caught my attention. There, in the city, near the public market, there had once been a pub. A strange place off the main streets, it was open to the cobble stone alleyway adjacent to the public market and part of an old building of the same vintage as the market itself. It was once a place where people with the gift might congregate. I had felt drawn to it before but only vaguely. This pub had changed names and motifs over the years but I seem to recall some little trendy bar still there today. I remember I had sensed something down that alley but John had told me not to worry about it at the time. Maybe that is why John was hanging in that area? Ah, there was a memory that John had of a man, connected like us but not a friend. It seemed he did not want to associate with those who shared the gift but he ran this little establishment. Worth a look, I thought.

The clouds rolled in and then parted several times that day but as evening fell the clouds were back. There was moisture in the air but no rain, at least not yet. The sun was just going down as I stepped off the bus downtown and started walking toward the market. I could feel the thoughts of every person that passed me on the street, just ordinary people, living ordinary lives. I approached the market and then turned to enter the alley. I was on guard now, my mind closed and my eyes open. I could still sense a powerful presence there ahead of me but I could not tell specifically what or who it was without revealing myself. I approached the door of what appeared like any other English style pub. Were it not for the curious location, in the cobblestone alley adjacent to the old Public Market, there would be nothing strange about it at all.

As I entered the front door, I did not need any special power at all to feel the eyes on me. The man behind the bar approached me right away and asked to see my ID. This was not unusual. However, the rather large bald guy with tee shirt stretched tight across well-developed chest muscles, who was approaching me from the other side of the room, seemed like over kill in the bouncer department for such a quaint little pub. I could sense that the bartender was only mildly gifted so he was not the one I had picked up on earlier. I did not want to give myself away so did not resist as he looked into my mind. I let him into the false layers I had been developing with John. I wondered to myself if he was one of these scanners.

The bouncer was right up in front of me now with his hands on his hips. With his right hand he reached out and grabbed a hand full of my jacket just below my neck. Quickly, with my left hand, I reached across the back of his right hand that was gripping my jacket, sliding my fingers around the large muscle at the base of his massive thumb, and placing my left thumb between the two metacarpel bones, just below his two large knuckles adjacent to his thumb. It was a simple leverage grip that allowed me to pull back, releasing his grip on my jacket and then rotate his right hand back so his palm now faced himself. I then grabbed the other side of his right hand with my right hand. Now with two hands holding his hand which I had turned in an awkward position, as it now faced back at himself, applying pressure directly on his wrist, it was easy for me to step back with my left foot, twisting his hand backwards at the same time rotating it outward until he fell off balance, flat on his back. Still holding his right hand with both of my hands, I put my left foot on the side of his neck. I looked at the bartender, who had stepped back behind the bar was now reaching under the bar for something. I had no choice; I knew that there was someone else, someone strong enough to remain hidden from me. He was not reaching out to me so I could not pinpoint who or where he was. They must have sensed me or at least suspected me but I did not want to give myself up if I did not have to.

The regular people in the pub carried on as if they had no idea what was going on, like they could not see or hear us. They were being blocked but I could not tell who without opening my mind. I let go of muscle man and stepped backward out the door. The bartender had come around the end of the bar shotgun in hand. I put my hands up and took another step back. "We don't want your kind in here," he shouted.

"Hey, I don't know what your deal is, but give me three steps, mister, and you won't see me no more," I said with a cavalier tone. I realized I was now being scanned. I felt confident I could freeze these two when I wanted but not yet. I let whoever it was into my mind a little deeper, into the false construct that John and I had built. They were not trying to control me just to read me. I had to act like I did not know.

The bartender was still pointing the shotgun my way and the muscle man was standing behind him with a really pissed off look on his face, massaging his injured wrist. I was still backing away as I smiled my best disarming smile. "Sorry, dude, but hey, you put your hands on me so…"

I shrugged my shoulders as I took a few more steps back, then I turned and jogged away, waiting to feel the bartender decide to pull the trigger or the person in the pub try to grab my mind. As I turned the corner I did feel something. Someone was attempting to erase all that had just transpired from my memory. They were strong but had only penetrated my false persona. Still I acted like all was well.

I calmed myself and started walking, filling my thoughts with food. What was I going to eat? I remembered the tasty treats I had sampled from the local shops on prior days at the market. As I walked, I searched my memories from John to see what experience he may have regarding this place. Those people were certainly not the warm and welcoming type but they really did not want to do much more than run me off.

I walked along the city street, paging through John's memories that were piled up in my head. I found a coffee shop that I could step into. I ordered a pastry and coffee and took them to a small table in the back, still pondering what John knew about this place and its proprietor. As I sat down it started to come to me. This had been a popular spot for folks like us for years before John was born. There was a man that owned this establishment, no, the whole building…his name, I could not find his name. "Cyrus," came a deep voice from a robust-looking black man approaching me with a large coffee in his hand and a smile on his face. "My name is Cyrus. May I join you," he asked as he motioned with his free hand toward the empty chair across from me.

I had to check myself, to see that he had not somehow slipped into my head. As best I could tell, he was not even trying to read me. "Sure," I replied with a slight shudder. I did not know if that was the best idea, to invite him to join me, but he had caught me completely by surprise.

I played it cool as he removed his tailored, three quarter length, dark gray, wool outer coat and sat down across from me. He looked down at his coffee then up at me again with just a hint of a smile that he wore as a mask. "I do not think we have met," he said in a very measured tone.

I looked at him for a moment before I spoke. "Is there a reason we should?" I asked. I tried to give nothing away, even with an expression.

He just smiled a broad smile. "Perhaps we should start with my apology. My employees were quite rude to you," he said as he adjusted the lapel of his expensively tailored suit jacket. I pondered for a moment: do I admit that I remember that or not after he or someone tried to erase that memory?

Cyrus smiled, "I understand your dilemma," he said. "It was I that you perceived attempting to invade your thoughts and for that I also apologize. I mistakenly took you for, well, never mind, but I understand that there is more to you than the run of the mill, shall we say, gifted individual. I apologize for all that and I hope we can chalk that up to a simple misunderstanding."

I just looked at him with a blank look on my face as I was quite content to let him do all the talking. I took another sip of coffee. He paused for a moment, sipping his own coffee waiting for a response from me. "Well, you are quite right to keep your cards close to your chest. There is more to you than you are letting on I am sure; but I am a firm believer in the motto, Live and let live," he said.

I just grinned and took a bite of my pastry.

He continued, "Just the same, my establishment is not a place for people like us to congregate, not anymore."

He seemed a pleasant enough man, just clear in his desire to not interact with others of our kind. "I hope you understand," he said as he looked at me with an expressionless and penetrating gaze. With that he took another sip of his coffee and smiled another warm and genuine smile as he stood up. He carefully adjusted his fine silk tie, then turned away to put on his overcoat. He paused and turned to take one last look at me. He smiled again. "You intrigue me, young man. I am sure that…never mind, I wish you well and I ask that you simply give me my space and I shall give you yours. Do we understand each other?" I just raised my cup to him. "Please forget we have ever met," he said as he turned to walk away.

He had been careful not to make any attempt to read me. I had done the same so I did not really know just how strong he was but I could tell he was serious. John had met him before but their meeting was essentially the same. He had asked John to stay out of his business and John had accommodated him. Cyrus had been far more cautious about approaching John, as apparently Cyrus had witnessed John as he attempted to extract information from a scanner that had stumbled into John's field of perception one dark night some months earlier. He saw the scanner frozen in John's grip. He felt the blood vessel explode in the scanner's brain and he witnessed John's drunken rage at his failure to gain any information from the encounter. He had approached John much the same way as he approached me; and John, being embarrassed at his own conduct, was content to move on from someone who was neither friend nor foe. Cyrus was obviously not the friendly type but he did not come across as a threat either. I would have to talk to John about this guy but for now, I would keep my thoughts to myself and head home.

John was there at my apartment when I got home. As I closed the door behind me, I shared my encounter with Cyrus in my thoughts.

John winced, "Yeah, I was going to mention him, sorry. He is like so many of our kind. He just wants to be left alone. To be honest, I do not know that much about him. Anyway he appears to be harmless, although I could not tell for sure how strong he actually is."

I walked into the main room and sat down on the sofa. I looked over at John. "Any others like him I should know about?" I asked.

"Not around here," John replied. We talked a bit more about Cyrus and whether we should warn him about our upcoming plan to go after the scanners. What if he was somehow involved with them? We decided it was probably better to just work around him. We would do our best to keep our activities away from his corner of the world. John had been in communication with Laura and she was onboard with our plan. Now it was just a matter of when...

INTO THE JUNGLE:

A WEEK OR so went by and it had been pleasantly sunny, pretty dry. I continued to train and my skills continued to grow in leaps and bounds. Today, however, was going to be a cooler, wetter day. The clouds had parted from time to time over the past few days and given us glimpses of the sun but this was still the rain city. Today I would have the opportunity to really plug in and feel the rush. Today the clouds had rolled back in, I could feel the moisture silently collecting in the air and it looked like we would have rain by nightfall. I didn't know if that was good or bad.

The day went by and the shadows grew longer. John and I finally stepped out of my apartment building onto the urban landscape of concrete and glass. As I turned to lock the front door behind me, I could feel the weight of the moisture gathering in the air. I looked over at John and met his gaze. I watched him as he then took a long deep breath and looked around us real slow. He was scanning. I could feel his strength increasing moment by moment. I could also feel myself growing stronger and sharper with each breath I took of the moisture-laden air. Any second now, it was coming. Small goose bumps rose up on my skin in anticipation of the first contact. Then the first small drops started to fall. It was like a dose of adrenalin. John and I started walking down the street, on our way to meet up with Laura and Sparrow. I could smell the moisture that had collected in the air and it made me feel strong, the periodic little sprinkles gently fluttering in the light breeze. I could feel the real rain coming any moment now. John looked at me and smiled. Even as the first few real drops started to fall, we both could feel our perception spreading. We could sense the thoughts of those around us become clearer and clearer and at the same time our reach was expanding. With each drop of rain, I felt the rush come over me. We shielded ourselves now and the people on the street just moved around us. We were invisible to them yet they parted for us as we walked. We closed our thoughts off as we headed for the coffee shop. It was time and I was as ready as I was going to be.

Laura and Sparrow were already there when we arrived. Laura did not bother with any greeting. I could feel her studying me carefully as soon as John and I entered the coffee shop. We slowly found our way through the sea of students that filled the shop, some coming some going and some just glued to the iridescent glow of the screens on their electronic devices. As we sat down with them, Laura was actively attempting to penetrate my mind. She could not penetrate my thoughts at all but I could tell she was not yet convinced that I was ready. I gave her a wink and a smile. Laura just turned her steely gaze on John.

"I hope he's ready," she said to John with a rather curt tone, then she looked back at me and said, "Just remember that somewhere in the heads of these scanners is a booby trap that will make them self-destruct if you're not careful."

John interjected, "He ran into Cyrus the other day and from what I can tell, Cyrus could not get a read on him."

Laura looked at him and then back at me. "Cyrus, you say, that had to be an interesting encounter to say the least. You'll have to share that with me some other time," she quipped, "but now to the business at hand."

Sparrow leaned forward and looked straight at me with her penetrating yet disarming gaze. "Don't worry, we will try to get there before they turn your brain to mush," she said. Then she smiled and sat back in her chair.

"Just remember that you need to leave us a trail to follow," Laura added. "Let us know once you have enough info to deduce where they come from," John added, "or if it is getting too dangerous and we'll come bail you out."

Laura had picked up the trail on a pair of scanners that were in the downtown area about five miles to the southeast of us. She'd kept track of them for the last few weeks while training Sparrow in her stalking techniques. She shared with me their psychic description so I would recognize when I detected them and even before they started reaching out to me. "Whenever you're ready," Laura said with just a hint of trepidation in her voice.

I looked around the table, took another drink of the coffee and opened my mind just to start letting my idle thoughts about the coffee I was drinking, float out into the humidified atmosphere like bait in the water. Then I closed my mind again. We sat together for a moment sipping coffee and sharing uneasy glances with one another. I let my idle thoughts slip again and this time I could feel that I was being received by someone. "Here we go," I said as I got up, slid on my jacket and walked slowly to the door. I took one more look over my shoulder at the three of them, all watching me intently. As I turned and walked out of the coffee shop and into the rain they all got up and started putting on their coats as well. I don't think that they were ready for me to just jump up like that. I don't think I was ready either but I felt that the scanners were close now. I needed to separate myself from my friends.

I stood outside in the rain for a moment and looked up and down the busy University Avenue. I watched all the people hustling around in the rain. I thought about what I would do next; which direction I would go? Then I dodged the traffic and jogged across the street and into a magazine shop. The three of them just stood there. Not looking directly at me but looking at my reflection in the window of the coffee shop. They were closed off but they carefully watched the street full of people and the front of the shop across the street from the coffee shop that I entered. I felt their uneasiness, each one of them for different reasons but none of them were quite prepared for me to just put myself out there like this. They were all shut down so as to be undetected by the scanners but they studied the faces of everyone that passed on the street. They quickly settled into their role as the hunters now and I was the bait. They'd kept themselves from broadcasting but now they had completely closed off all their thoughts and disappeared from my perception altogether.

The rain was light but steady. I felt excited and a little scared. Every so often I would let slip another random thought about a magazine I was browsing or some personal observation about one of the other people in the shop. Eventually I walked out of the magazine shop and started strolling up the street. All the shops and stores were open on the avenue tonight and there were lots of people coming and going in the light rain. I stopped in at a little Mexican restaurant and picked up a burrito to go.

As I left the restaurant, dinner in hand, I let slip another random thought about the burrito I was eating. I walked slowly on in the rain, looking in the shop windows as I passed. I looked across the street lined with parked cars on both sides and I could see the reflections of my three shadows as they followed me up the street from a discrete distance, fading in and out of the pedestrian traffic. I had been in and out of a couple of music stores browsing the used CDs for about an hour when I first detected the scanners. They did not know where I was yet but they were headed my way, trying to get a lock on me. I knew exactly where they were as they closed in on me. I was excited as I felt them getting closer, eagerly searching for me. I ducked into another second hand music store and started browsing the used CDs.

They were in the area now so I let slip some thoughts about the music CDs I was looking at. Now they were closing in on my trail. I could sense their excitement. I had to control my emotions, calm my heart rate. I was not supposed to be aware of them yet. They had parked their car and were walking down the street only a few blocks north of me now. They had not pinpointed me yet but they were scanning hard. I stepped back out onto the rainy street. Even at night the lights from all the signs and store windows illuminated the street, reflecting off the parked cars and puddles of water collecting on the sidewalk and in the street. I started walking slowly south thinking about the two used CDs I had just bought. I let a few bits and pieces float out of my head like bread crumbs as much for the scanners as for John, Laura and Sparrow to follow. I could not sense them at all but they were in a shop just down a few doors from me and I wanted to be sure that they gotten a good look at the two scanners that were on my trail. I figured I would walk the scanners right past them.

As I walked down the street I felt the first one make his move. He had no tact at all. He just punched into my head trying to freeze me. He was not very strong so I pretended to panic and pushed him out of my head. I did not push him too hard, but at the same time, I did not want to be too easy. I broke into a run and I looked over my shoulder to see that two of them were after me. I needed to be sure they had seen me. I could not see or feel my three shadows but I knew they were not far. As I ran through the crowded street, pushing past the slower folks that just sort of meandered even in the rain, I caught a glimpse of John. He was inside a convenience store, looking out the window. I ran my two stalkers right past him. I knew he now had a good look at them. I tried not to think of John or any of them at all as I turned and ran through a parking lot and into an alley behind the business that lined the avenue. Both scanners were right on my heels. They were focused on me now, just yards behind me. Together they reached into my head. I could feel them both pressing hard into my thoughts so I let them into the first artificial layer that John and I had created just for them. Now we would see if they bought it.

They were trying to freeze me in my tracks so I played along. I froze as the two of them approached me slowly, their minds taxed to their limits. I stood frozen, obeying their repeated command to be still just as I had done when Art had frozen me. I mirrored my same emotions as well. My heart was racing and they mistook my excitement for panic. They stepped carefully from the shadows and I now I could see their faces.

They were two young men, just a few years older than I was. One was a rather average-looking guy. He had on a dark, full length raincoat and he stood a few inches shorter than I. His thin brown hair was pulled back into a short ponytail. The rain dripped from the ponytail in a steady stream as he stood there with his furrowed brow trying to press deeper into my mind. The other guy was a light-skinned black man, young and fit with short hair braided tight against his head in small rows. He used his left hand to hold the top of his short leather jacket closed at the neck; at the same time he reached out his right hand and placed it on the side of my head as he focused, reaching deeper into my mind. I slowly let them into my mind a little deeper and I could feel them start to relax. They were becoming confident now as they probed my thoughts that I had sprinkled around the artificial consciousness. They started walking me up the alley headed back to their car. They commanded and I obeyed, so they thought.

As we emerged from the alley and back onto the busy street I saw Sparrow out of the corner of my eye, standing at the bus stop among several other would be bus riders. Her mind was closed so, to these two scanners so preoccupied with me, she was invisible. As we walked past I gave her a wink. The same wink I had given Laura at the coffee shop. She smiled and turned away. They had me, I had them and they had no idea. We got to their car, a nondescript four door sedan and we got in. "Should I dose him, Mike?" my ponytailed captor asked his partner as he slipped into the back seat with me.

"No, you know he doesn't like to wait for the drug to wear off if we don't need it," he responded. Mike turned around and looked back at me from the driver's seat. I could see his uneasiness as he took one more, good long look at me to see what they had caught. He looked over at his partner, next to me and asked him, "You got him?"

The scanner next to me looked at me, then at Mike in the front seat. "Yeah, yeah I think so," he responded as he pressed harder into my mind. Mike turned back toward the front, adjusted his seat belt and we pulled out from the curb.

John and Laura were up the block waiting for the signal from Sparrow. John turned quickly, scanning the passing cars. He found a young university fraternity guy on his way to a party at one of the sororities, driving his dad's BMW with the stereo blasting. The next thing this young guy knew, John was in his head and he was pulling over to pick them up. "Where to, Dad?" the young driver asked.

"Pick up your sister down the block and get on the freeway heading downtown," John responded.

"Dad?" Laura said as she looked quizzically at John.

"Yes, sweetheart," he responded with a grin. Laura rolled her eyes and said nothing more.

As we found our way from the University District over to the freeway I could feel a mechanical repetition of instructions running over and over through the thoughts of these two scanners like a pair of religious zealots reciting scripture to pacify and reassure themselves. The ponytailed one next to me put the thought in my head that I needed to sleep as we entered the freeway on-ramp so I played along. He probed the part of my mind that I had let him into, then he smiled to himself, thinking how easily he'd controlled me. He settled back into reciting his mantra in his own head. I understood what John meant when he said there was a wide range of capabilities. These two were convinced that they were some kind of master ninjas when the reality was, their power was so much less than any of the four of us that they were like a couple of guys who had brought squirt guns to a tank battle and as yet, they still had no clue.

We went south only a short way before we changed lanes to the right, toward an exit lane in the downtown area, I, ever so gently, caused the driver of the car next to us to swerve slightly into our lane. As my two captors responded with surprise, they were distracted just long enough that they did not notice me slip the street and exit number into the subconscious of the driver of a large truck going the other way on the freeway. He would go past John, Laura and Sparrow broadcasting the exit number over and over like someone having an OCD attack. John and Laura would pick up on that for sure. These two were only looking and scanning what was in front of them now and their range was limited. This went off so easily unnoticed that now I was starting to feel a little cocky.

I continued to pretend I was asleep as we pulled up in the drive of one of the big high rise hotels downtown. "Wake," my pony-tailed captor commanded me as he looked gloatingly at his partner, self-impressed and self-assured with his apparent power over me. He then reasserted himself into my thoughts. He was so confident that he told his partner to park the car so he could walk me through the expansive lobby and present me, by himself, like a trophy to his puppet master waiting for us in a luxury suite upstairs. The one that awaited us was indeed far stronger than these two. I felt him as he scanned across the minds of his two minions as well as my own. At this distance he was only able to skim superficially through our minds, but I could tell this guy would not be quite so easily fooled as these two thick heads that led me to him.

I felt my confidence grow as we entered the lobby; the air was warm and dry. As we rode the elevator up, I could feel my captor become nervous as he felt his mental grip slipping. I made no attempt to escape but his abilities were so limited he was worried he might lose his grip on me anyway. If he dried out, this one would have almost no power at all. He grabbed my arm and rushed me to the room. There were two young women, with about the same capabilities as my pony-tailed captor awaiting us as we entered the room. They were repeating the same mantra of instructions, over and over in their heads, to the exclusion of most normal random thoughts. They took almost no notice of me at all other than to glance my way as they moved from the center of the room to stand along the wall. I was excited now to see what would happen next. I do not know if it was fear or excitement or a combination of both.

As I looked around the room I noticed that there were several humidifiers going, adding moisture to the air in the room. I did not know if I would have much time before the big boss who was in the next room detected the approach of John, Laura and Sparrow or something amiss with me. I distracted him by pretending to offer just a little resistance to my captor, just enough to make the boss man feel he needed to intervene.

He walked slowly into the room and I felt him take hold of my mind. He was far more powerful than the two scanners that had plucked me off the street but still nothing that approached the level of John or Laura, not even close. He made an impressive entrance nonetheless. He was a man of average height, in his early 30s, well dressed in a dark gray business suit and a bold red tie, he certainly had a flair for the theatric as he entered the room, throwing open both doors of the double door entrance to the bedroom before striking a pose, slowly reaching out toward me with one hand as he commanded me to sit and directed me to an oversized chair. I resisted just a bit. He then slowly walked across the room with his eyes fixed on me like a hypnotist and his hand still outstretched as if his power emanated from his fingertips. He stood, directing me with his outstretched hand, guiding me to the chair and then lowering his hand as I sat down. He pulled another chair just like mine over, directly in front of me. He sat down and leaned forward, staring directly into my eyes.

He placed both his hands on the arms of his chair and leaned slowly back, not blinking, staring deeper into my eyes as he settled into his chair.

His three attendants were all transfixed on him, reciting their mantra over and over in their own minds as they witnessed the spectacle he was putting on for them as much as for himself. He was clearly impressed with his own power. I pretended that I was resisting with all my might, then I slowly let him push into the first layer of my thoughts. I slowly gave ground until he felt he had all of me. I knew that he was totally absorbed with taking control of my mind to the exclusion of everything else around him. Everyone in the room was transfixed on his display of power and control. I offered enough resistance to occupy him but not so much as to make him suspect my true capabilities. He was fully engaged in probing my mind now and I was giving him just enough resistance to keep his full attention. He was not a brainwashed drone like the others. This one had free thoughts. This one would have answers. I was so excited but I was unsure if this was the time yet. How long could I draw this out? It was time to turn the tables but I did not know if the others were close enough yet. If I reached out to find them, the boss would know. I let him poke around a little more but I was too excited to contain myself much longer.

Suddenly the hotel suite door opened and Mike, the other of my two captors, stepped in. Behind him through the open door, I could see John, Laura and Sparrow stroll in, but Laura was preventing the rest of them from detecting them in any way. Now was the time. As I looked back into the eyes of my inquisitor and smiled, I saw a look of terror quickly overtake his face as he realized that the tables had just turned and I was in complete control. Just like that, he was frozen and as yet the other four scanners had no idea that anything had changed. They simply went on repeating their mantra in their own minds. Little did they know that Laura was already in their minds with them. I held their handler frozen as he struggled within his own consciousness. He tried to reach out to his minions only to find that he could neither speak nor project his thoughts. He was completely my prisoner, locked in his own mind like some alabaster statue. I could feel the terror overtake him but he made no attempt to harm himself. The four scanners had no idea that John, Laura and Sparrow were even in the room.

"Sleep," Laura commanded and all four scanners fell to the ground where they stood, fast asleep. "Monitor them, my dear," she said to Sparrow as she slowly approached our captive. He was frozen but for his eyes that darted back and forth in a panic. Now he focused his gaze only on Laura as she strolled slowly in his direction. Her gaze was fixed on him now and she approached him like a Jaguar approaching its wounded quarry for the kill. She smiled ever so slightly at him.

I stood up from the oversized chair, took a deep breath and shook myself off. I could see the focus on Laura's face, and I could sense her mind flooding into my captor's. She waved me away with one hand to let me know she had control of our friend now. I turned away and walked over to get a drink from the small hotel room refrigerator. Behind me, Laura softly slipped herself into my place in the overstuffed chair, with her eyes still fixed on her prey.

"Let me," John said in a terse tone as he stepped toward my former captor. I did not need to read his thoughts; I could see the look in John's eyes that reflected his intent. Laura simply raised one hand toward John without ever looking his way. John was still focused intently on our star captive but Laura closed her outstretched hand, but for one finger, giving pause to John's advance. Laura reached out with her other hand and gently stroked the side of her frozen captive's face. Her touch was soft and gentle as she stared deeper into his eyes and smiled again, ever so slightly. "Calm yourself, John. I find it curious that these scanners are all blank slates and programmed to take their own lives if they are caught but this one, this one, is fully intact and..." She hesitated for just a moment as she probed deeper into his mind, "I am detecting genuine fear."

Laura turned to look at the rest of us and smiled openly for just a moment, then turned quickly back to her frozen quarry. All the time her mind remained fixed on his, looking ever deeper into the mind of her captive. "I think that he has a great deal to share with us if we give him the opportunity, but John," Laura turned and looked directly at John now. "He has to live long enough to share all his secrets with us. This is what we have been looking for, after all. This is no programmed drone. Let's all get comfortable, shall we? I think we have a long and rewarding evening ahead of us."

Laura turned to the coffee table next to her and picked up the room service menu. She took her eyes off her captive for just a moment to scan the menu. I'll have the lobster and, ah, be a dear and order up some room service for everyone, will you, Alex?" she held out the menu in my direction as she fixed her gaze back on our host, frozen in the chair across from her. I think we will all be quite hungry soon enough and this is going to take a little time and a little finesse. Sparrow, please stay alert so that we are not interrupted without warning and, just a moment, yes," Laura said with a smile as she slowly reached over and ever so softly stroked the cheek of the former leader of this little cadre of scanners. "John, I believe I have found what we will need to unlock the minds of these soon-to-be former scanners," Laura said as she motioned for John to come closer and focus with her into her captive's mind.

No one, not even John had imagined that it might be possible to restore the blank minds of the scanners. Everyone had assumed that once erased, there was no restoring what had been lost. John looked at Laura and then at her captive. A look of horror came over John's face as he thought of all the scanners he had so readily dispatched. He put his hand on his face as he turned to walk away from Laura and her captive. We did not need to read his thoughts to know what he was thinking.

"There was no way for you to know, John," Laura said out loud. John just stood looking out the sliding glass doors that led to the balcony and the angry night sky beyond that was pouring out a wind-driven rain as far as could be seen. Laura turned back to her captive and focused on her task at hand.

Several hours transpired from the time I entered the hotel suite, as the newest capture for this little cadre of scanners. The scanners had been put to sleep and their leader was being interrogated in great detail. Laura had found many things, including the fact that all the scanners still had their identities. However, their individuality, all that makes a person who they are, had been compressed into a small corner of their mind and locked away. She explained that someone much more powerful than the leader of this small group had used a combination of hypnotic suggestion, perhaps drugs and the power to enter their minds, to lock away who they had been. This left them a blank slate and ready for reprogramming. Then to make them disposable, they had each been implanted with the drive to destroy themselves if caught. They all had been implanted with the idea that they faced a horrible and painful death beyond description if captured.

One by one, John reached into the mind of each scanner. They were mentally and physically restrained as we awakened them. Then slowly he reached into that deep corner of their mind and found the hidden trigger to release their true consciousness. Each one was different. This was a huge step. We now knew what to look for and how to unlock the true identity of those enslaved as scanners. We could now un-brainwash them.

I approached the scanner called Mike, one of the two that had picked me off the street. He was still laid out on the floor where Laura had dropped him into a deep sleep. I reached into his mind holding him frozen as I awakened him. As he opened his eyes I saw, first surprise, then panic in his eyes. I found the key and opened his suppressed consciousness before he could do himself any harm. He winced with pain as his true self came flooding back on top of his memories as a scanner. I released him and he grabbed his head with one hand as he propped himself up on the floor where he had been lying with the other.

"Damn," Mike said, as he looked up at me. I smiled and offered him a hand up off the floor. As Mike stood up he staggered a bit and I grabbed him to prevent him from falling. He then looked over at his former controller. I could see the anger wash over his face. I knew what he was thinking without even listening to his thoughts. Mike lunged toward our captive, who was still frozen in his chair, being examined by Laura. I did not do Mike the indignity of reaching into his mind to restrain him but instead I physically held him back from reaching his target.

"That bastard has been using us. We are all just disposable punks to him," Mike yelled.

"We know that," I replied. "I don't know why you didn't kill us outright or let us do ourselves in like we were supposed to, or maybe you still plan to; but all I am asking you guys for, is three minutes with that guy first, then I'll take whatever I got coming. Just three minutes."

Mike paused and looked around the room, looking for someone to give him the go ahead. I stepped directly in front of him. Mike's anger was escalating to a full rage. I put one hand on his shoulder and I looked in his eyes, "Look, up until tonight people like us were not safe and nobody knew who was hunting who or why. Tonight we plan to change all that. Things are going to change and with his help," I paused and looked over at the still frozen director of this group, "we are going to unravel this to the source. Anything you can tell us would be most helpful but for now we need to keep him alive, at least for now," I said as I motioned Mike toward the sofa.

Mike dropped himself onto the sofa and rubbed his hand over his face and then backwards over the small, tight braids of hair on his head. He then looked slowly around the room taking it all in. His former colleagues were all coming around as well, after being released by John and Sparrow.

"My head hurts," Mike said as he looked back at me. "I don't know what I can tell you. I had a life of my own before I met this young lady over here," he said as he pointed out one of the young ladies we had just released.

"Sorry about that," she replied as she forced a beguiling smile back at him. I looked around the room and addressed our four new companions. "Look guys, we know that none of you chose to be used the way you were. We are not holding you responsible for the stuff you may have done under the influence, so to speak. What we need to know is who did this to you? Who twisted you to do the things you did? Somehow your former boss here does not seem to be the one."

Mike looked back over at the former leader of his group and I could see the anger start to come over his face again. "His name is Andrew Rappaport," Mike said. "It looks like you folks already know that and a lot more about him but let me tell you about this weasel anyway." Mike paused and looked around at the four of us. "Say what are you going to do with us anyway? I'm getting the impression that you four really got the juice, I mean you are all way stronger than this schmuck. I mean, I don't think I ever came across anyone anywhere near any of you guys and now here are four of you heavyweights crashing our little party. No offense, I mean, I for one am really glad to see you. I don't get the vibe that you guys are going to do us any harm, but, yeah, I guess we would never have woken up if, ah…" Mike smiled at me as he started to calm down just a bit.

"I had only just discovered my ability to see other's thoughts when these guys took me. I don't know who you guys are or what you got planned but I want in. I mean I know I'm not in your league but, hell, even Tiger Woods needs a caddy, right? Besides, I'm not the forgiving type so I would like a little payback, if you don't mind?

I looked at Mike and asked, "Can I take a look again?" He looked confused at first, then responded, "Oh, in my head, yeah, why not. I guess you could anyway, even if I said no but thanks for asking," he said with a chuckle. I browsed easily through his mind and then, I told him, "I think you have more 'juice' than you know right now. The trouble is you never got a chance to develop it. Lucky for you, I know a guy who might be able get you on the right track." I glanced over in John's direction. "Hey, it's Art's turn," John stated right away, "and I will let you make the introductions."

We stayed in the hotel suite all night eating room service food and talking with our four new friends. Laura remained focused on exploring every nook and dark corner of Mr. Rappaport's consciousness and even his subconscious thoughts. We learned that Mike's full name was Michael Dechain. He was tall and well muscled, with the hands typical of a man who turned a wrench for a living. His light brown skin showed the nicks and scars of a physically active life. He had been a soldier in the Army, stationed at joint base Lewis-McCord. He was a heavy machinery mechanic and lived off the base in the city of Tacoma, just to the south of Seattle. One night he and some friends had gone out clubbing and he met Ms. Linnet Jones. Little did he know he was soon to be joining her team. She was one of our captured scanners, a woman of average height with straight brown hair that fell softly to her shoulders with just the slightest curl at the end. She had a very disarming smile and she dressed herself in a very unassuming yet feminine style. She was already in the service of Mr. Rappaport when Mike had the misfortune to cross her path. She invited Mike to her apartment and that was the last free memory he had until today. In our discussion, she remembered some others coming to collect Mr. Dechain and a few others, then bringing him back a little over a month later as one of several replacements for members they had lost.

As Linnet remembered the faces of those they had lost, I found them, one by one, in the memories I had been given from John. They all had the misfortune of crossing paths with John and I knew that none of them had survived the encounter. I did not say anything but I looked over at John as the gruesome memory of what he had done to them played in my mind. John's was clearly disturbed to see his own drunken rage played back before him, to relive the gruesome deeds for which he was responsible. I had only experienced his kindness and humility, but to relive with him his cold and deliberate attacks was disturbing to me as well. John looked over at me and I could see he wanted to say something but in his mind he allowed me to see, there were no words for the self-revulsion he was feeling.

Sparrow had been left out of the exchange but she had seen her father's reaction. "What, Dad?" she asked as she looked first at him, then over at me. She respected her father and would never just try to push into his mind without his permission but me, well, she just reached out to me and I had to hold her back from entering my mind. "What is it?" she asked me now.

"Go ahead," John said as he turned away from both of us and walked to the other side of the room to look back out the glass sliding doors that led to the balcony and the cityscape beyond. He just stood there for a moment staring off into the dark rainy night.

Laura had stopped her inquisition and was also now looking at me, intently waiting. "John, are you sure?" I asked.

"She has a right to know the truth about her dad," he responded. "Go ahead and share with them both," he said, without looking back my way.

I was hesitant but I shared those memories, as John had requested, in the raw and unedited way they had been in my mind. Sparrow looked on in horror at the image of her father as he led three scanners into an alley. They pursued him with the vigor and excitement my two captors had felt as they followed me into an alley. Laura and Sparrow both gasped as they witnessed John, first feign that he was frozen in their grasp and then turn, freezing all three, and riffling through their minds. He drew a knife from his sleeve as he turned, cutting the first one's throat as he stood there frozen. The next two he held in his mental grasp. He could see the pain on their faces and feel the horror and pain of their minds as John squeezed everything from their limited minds. I could feel them die in my own mind. I could feel the rage in John's mind at the time. Sparrow then started to cry as she quickly closed her mind and put her hands to her face. She had seen many bad things in her young life but the vision of her father as a cold and efficient killer even in a drunken stupor, momentarily overwhelmed her. Laura showed no outward expression but I could tell, even she was stunned. John did not look at either one of them. He just hung his head as he looked off into the night.

The four former scanners simply looked on in confusion as they had not been allowed to see the fate of those that they had known, however briefly, that had the misfortune of an encounter with John.

Of the four freed scanners, Paula Cruz, was the strongest of them mentally and possibly physically as well. She had jet black hair, straightened from its natural curl and pulled back into a tight thick braid. She wore tan Dockers and a pastel yellow polo shirt that contrasted against her amaretto skin. She had a serious face and the stocky physique of an athlete and seemed to be just taking it all and trying to sort it all out in her own head. She was actively blocking her own thoughts even though nobody was trying to read her. She started to move slowly for the door at first hoping not to be noticed. Sparrow turned quickly and looked right at her and she paused, seemingly surprised that no one tried to stop her. She looked over at me as she grabbed the door handle.

I waved my hand at her and said, "Look, we could use a little help here but I guess I can't blame you if want to bolt."

"You guys could stop me if you wanted," she replied as she stood there holding the door handle. "Yeah, but we're not those guys," I replied with a half smile. Laura looked over at her. " I understand, dear, just remember to keep a low profile, now that you have an idea what is going on, be careful."

With that Paula was gone.

The last of our four former scanners was still sitting on the floor leaning up against the wall finishing off a slice of pizza. "Like my former partner in crime," Mr. Dechain said, "I don't know what you all have planned but I'm in too, if you'll have me."

My former ponytailed captor stood up and said, "Richard Sullivan at your service," as he made a theatrical bow.

He was of slender build and average height. He looked to be close to thirty-five with a few tattoos visible on the pale skin of his arms, and clearly visible because of the cut off sleeves of his sweatshirt. His thin hair was pulled back into a pony tail and he had the gaunt and weathered face of a long time smoker.

"My friends call me Rick and you guys, having freed me from mental servitude, are now my new best friends," he said with a smile. He walked across the room stopping to shake John's hand, then Sparrow's. He approached Laura but she had only to glance away from Mr. Rappaport, momentarily in his direction, with a look that was disconcerting to say the least, yet enough for Rick to lose his smile and quickly withdraw the hand he was extending in her direction as if he had just touched something hot. He took a step backwards from her and turned to me. Putting a smile back on his face he then offered me his hand. As I shook his hand, I felt the guy had the look of a hustler. I stepped back from Rick and I looked around the room, "Look guys, we are not all that organized and we don't really have a master plan at this point. We will need to see what Mr. Rappaport here has to tell us before we can figure out what is going to happen next." I glanced over at Laura.

Laura was looking directly into the eyes of Mr. Rappaport. She slowly reached out with her right hand and gently stroked his cheek. She smiled and leaned forward, softly whispering the word "sleep" into one ear. He fell back into his chair fast asleep.

"Well," Laura began, as she stood up and took a few steps toward the center of the room, "It appears that, unlike the rest of you, Mr. Rappaport is a willing party to an organized effort to collect people like us. He can certainly take us to the next level but we should ask ourselves; what are we prepared to do and who among us is prepared to go however far this takes us? He does not contain all the information we need but I can tell you this is a far greater threat than we imagined. This small group that we had imagined to be the threat is, in fact, just one finger of a much larger organization. We will need more than a handful of us to face this challenge." Laura looked around the room at the rest of us; then she fixed her gaze on John. "We had assumed that if we all lived simple, quiet lives and avoided this threat as individuals we would be Ok, but what I have seen in the mind of Mr. Rappaport makes it obvious to me that this approach will be the downfall for all people like us."

I could hear a slight tremor in her voice as she continued. "They will simply send more and more scanner teams and one by one they will convert or destroy us all. Again, this threat is far bigger and much closer than any of us imagined. We can no longer hide and wait for them to find us. Alex, as you said earlier to John, it is time for us all to stand together or fall by the wayside one by one."

She looked over at John with the vision of him slaughtering those scanners still fresh in her mind and it was apparent on her face. "We will need to gather all the most gifted of our kind that we can while there is still time and come up with a plan. I will need to share what I have learned from our friend here..." She glanced back at Mr. Rappaport." Laura was silent for a moment, lost in her own deliberations. She looked over at John. "We need a gathering," she said.

Everyone was silent for a moment, then John said, "I guess I have always known this time would come one day." Turning back to the sliding glass door that opened onto the balcony, he opened the door and stepped out into the wind blown rain that swirled about in the darkness. He stood for a moment overlooking the beautiful panorama of the city lights against the dark night sky. The windblown rain pelted him and slowly the moisture started penetrating his clothing. I could feel him gathering his consciousness, focusing his thoughts. As the rain soaked him to the skin his consciousness now stretched out into the rainy darkness and across the moisture-laden clouds of the night sky. His reach was expanding now as he bowed his head and rubbed his hands together. He focused all his thoughts and gathered his energy as a weightlifter does before attempting a heavy lift. All at once he lifted his head, stepped to the railing at the edge of the balcony, stretched his arms out wide and let the rain drive itself into every inch of his skin. I could feel him reaching out with his mind, casting out through each rain drop and reverberating through the water laden clouds to minds far from us. He let loose a pulse of such energy that I could not have imagined. The others in the room were stunned by the blast he let loose from his mind. His compressed thoughts were sent traveling through the night sky and flowing through all of us like an earth trimmer. Then we felt the first returning pulse wave. It was Grandma. There were no words or specific thoughts, just a pulse of raw energy but I could tell just from the feel of it, that it was her. Then two more, then a steady stream of pulses could be felt bouncing back from powerful minds near and far like lightning traveling through the clouds.

 Michael had a stunned look on his face and so did the other former scanners. He and the others could feel the pulse but it was too intense for them to sort out any specific information from it. They had no idea what they had just experienced. Mike looked at me and said, "What the hell was that?" Before I could respond to him, more pulses continued returning from even farther away. I could feel each person's individual reflection in their returning pulses. I put my hand on Michael's shoulder again and told him, "John has sent up a flare and it has been answered. It has been sensed by all those that are now responding."

We all just stood there for a moment, absorbing the returning messages. I was amazed at how far away some appeared to come from. They had received John's signal and they understood what it meant.

John walked back into the room, soaking wet and with an emotionless look of resolve on his face. He walked directly over and took the wallet from the inside breast pocket of the sleeping, Mr. Rappaport. He pulled out the cash and handed it to Lynnette. "You three need to leave this place and lay low. When he does not check in, someone is going to come looking for him and maybe for you. You can't go back to your old life--at least not yet. We will contact you in a few days but stick together; it will be safer for now," John said as he looked the three of them over.

Lynnette started to ask, "How will you find...never mind." She smiled a nervous smile.

"We will find you," John said, as he gave her a wink. Michael, Richard and Lynnette left first, I could feel them close their minds as they disappeared into the night. Sparrow looked at John then over to Laura with a quizzical look on her face. "What if they are found? Can they find us through them," she asked.

"They may know what we look like but I think we are past the low profile approach now anyway, don't you?" she responded.

Laura looked at Mr. Rappaport and said, "Time to go, sweetheart."

He stood up from a dead sleep and said, "Is it time to go?"

"Get your coat, dear," she said.

"I'll just get my coat," he replied.

John said, "Sparrow, will you call Art? He has a few warehouses and we need a place for our friend here until we figure out what we are going to do with him." He put on his hat and took another bite of the sandwich that he had ordered earlier.

THE WAR BEGINS:

WE WALKED OUT through the lobby like we were doing a perp-walk with Mr. Rappaport in the middle. He was not restrained physically but Laura was in his head. Sparrow scanned everyone in the vicinity and I made us all invisible in the minds of anyone that may see us. John looked at the front desk and planted the command for the manager to erase any security camera tapes for the past several hours, thus covering our coming and going. Casually we walked out the front doors and into the rainy night. All the water in the world was not going to help our captive. As the water hit him and increased his power, so it did the same for the rest of us exponentially. Art pulled up out in front of the hotel lobby with one of his moving vans and we all calmly and quietly climbed in. Laura had been picking through the mind of Mr. Rappaport all the while, as we walked down to the lobby and out the front door. Once we were all seated, Art pulled away from the curb. It was a bit anticlimactic really. We sat quietly in the dark van as Art splashed down the wet city streets. The only sound was the windshield wiper slapping back and forth and the periodic deep sigh from one of us as we disappeared into the night.

The city never really sleeps. It was only an hour or two before dawn and the rain was nowhere near abating, yet there were street people moving from wherever they had found shelter for the night to start searching out their next meal. There were the early morning deliveries to the various downtown businesses. A delivery van like ours fit right in. We were all wide awake, Art at the wheel, Laura managing our prisoner, probing every corner of his mind, Sparrow and I scanning our surroundings and John lost in his own introspection. Art took a left and took us through the Chinatown area and over to the little Saigon part of town.

We pulled into a side street, then up an alley behind a Vietnamese grocery store. The back door opened and a Vietnamese man who was connected stepped out to greet us. Art pulled in behind the store and stopped. He then turned and said, "No worries, folks. This is my friend, Hung. He's cool." Everyone stepped out of the van. Hung had a look of trepidation on his face as he scanned the group. We were all closed down but no one was hiding their abilities from him. Hung took a step back as soon as he realized the nature of this group assembled before him. He looked quickly over at Art, then back at the bunch of us.

"Holy shit, Art," Hung said. He put one hand to the side of his own head as if to check to see if it was still there. "Who are these guys?" he asked.

Hung was more connected than our captive, Mr. Rappaport, but not by a lot. Until that moment Art was the strongest mind he had come across and his concern was written across his face. "You freak-in, Dink-a-dow, crazy man, bringing these high rollers to my little grocery," Hung said, as he looked us over one by one. "So this is the big boss of the scanners," Hung stepped over in front of Mr. Rappaport. He looked Mr. Rappaport up and down and made an indignant face at him.

"Not the big boss, I'm afraid. I'm going to need you and your crew to hold onto him for a bit, OK?" Art asked.

"My crew? Hey, I'm just a grocery guy, Art," Hung replied as he looked nervously around at the rest of us.

Art paused and looked Hung in the face. "Really, you don't think that these guys are going to know about your gambling operation? They all got more juice than me, buddy, but relax, nobody's judging. I just knew that you'd be the right guy for the job, am I right?"

"Yah, no sweat, Art, of course," Hung replied. "Anything I can do to help you guys get rid of these scanners, man. You know I am in." Hung smiled a nervous smile and invited us to a different building across the alleyway. We started moving in that direction as Hung ran ahead of us and banged on the door. A couple of Vietnamese men opened the door and looked us over with a cynical eye. Hung directed them in Vietnamese to make the room ready and they disappeared back into the building.

Laura asked, "Will you be able to restrain him?"

Just then Hung's wife stepped out of the building. It was apparent that she was also gifted as she had managed to shield herself from our passive scans of the area. She simply smiled and nodded at Laura. She gestured toward Mr. Rappaport and he walked obligingly toward her. Laura smiled and released him to her custody. "Ok, buddy, we gotta go. Keep him on ice and I will be in touch," Art said as he shook Hung's hand.

With that we got back into the van and pulled backwards out of the alley onto the side street. I could see Hung's wife disappear into the warehouse with Mr. Rappaport walking obediently next to her. Hung looked carefully up and down the alley before closing the door behind himself, leaving the passageway as if this little transaction had never transpired. We headed back to Art's place just as the night sky was giving way to a lighter shade of gray. The rain washed over everything in a slow steady rhythm. The windshield wipers slapped out a rhythm of their own as the van bounced down the street, splashing through the puddles. We all sort of sat back and processed the events that had just transpired. Things had been set in motion now and there was no going back.

We pulled into the parking lot on the side of Art's Antique furniture warehouse. Art put the van into park, shut off the engine and we all stepped out of the van in silence. We looked around cautiously and scanned the area as we moved toward the non-descript door on the side of the building that leads directly into Art's back office.

Everyone entered the office and dropped themselves into a seat except Art, who went directly about making a fresh pot of coffee. John was deeply disappointed and embarrassed. Rather than getting to the heart of the problem, we had discovered a far greater problem and he was no closer to finding any sign of his wife. His brutality had been laid bare for all of us to see and he could not bring himself to look anyone in the face right now. Sparrow and I were both tired and Art was just focused on the coffee for the moment. Laura, on the other hand, was already analyzing that which she had gleaned from the mind of Mr. Rappaport.

Art put out the coffee additives and handed each of us a cup of hot coffee before clearing some papers off the chair at his old rolltop desk and sitting down himself. Art took a sip, then looking over at Laura he said, "Let's have it, sister. What are we up against here?"

"Please make yourself comfortable and I will show you, as best as I can, those thoughts and memories I have gleaned from Mr. Rappaport, she replied." With that we all settled back, closed our eyes and opened our minds to receive what she would share with us.

Slowly, Laura's thoughts materialized in our minds. We saw images of Mr. Rappaport as he managed his small group of scanners. Every day he would get into the mind of each of his people and recite with them their mantra, 'Living to serve, serving to live. Capture means death. I will choose my own death.' His job was to reinforce the programming and contact his superiors when they had a loss or a capture. Then Laura shared a visit from someone who appeared to be his superior, which had occurred only a few weeks earlier. Mr. Rappaport was accustomed to the periodic visits of those, like himself, slightly more powerful than the typical scanner but they were also programmed. They would deliver new scanners to him and take new captures to be programmed. Today was a visit of a different type that had him nervous to say the least.

A new black Suburban with dark tinted windows pulled up in the expansive drive of the hotel. A large man in the front passenger seat then promptly jumped out and quickly surveyed the area before opening the door just behind his. Up in his hotel suite, Mr. Rappaport sensed the arrival and paused to dab the perspiration from his brow with a handkerchief he had pulled from the inside breast pocket of his suit. He summoned his scanners to the main room and he looked them over nervously. Down in the lobby, a middle-aged woman, elegantly attired from her Prada shoes to her full length, fur collared coat, strode directly to the elevator. She was accompanied by two very large, dark suit and sunglasses type attendants. Mr. Rappaport paced nervously to the door, then back to his group of automatons where he fussed over their appearance, then back to the door. He paused for a moment then opened the door just as his boss arrived outside.

With a wave of his hand, he invited her inside. She smiled a beguiling yet confident smile as she caught his eye for just a moment before he quickly looked away.

"Let me take your coat," he said with just a hint of a stutter as he reached to take her coat from her shoulders. She stepped away from him before he could get a hold of her coat as if she had not heard him at all. Smoothly, yet with purpose, she glided over toward the scanners that were standing in a nice line, repeating their mantra to themselves. "I don't plan to stay that long," she said casually over her shoulder, as she walked. He quickly retracted his hands and stuffed them nervously into his pockets as one of her attendants pushed past him. The other stood by the door which he had closed behind them but only after quickly surveying the hallway up and down. She walked slowly in front of the scanners, reaching into each one's mind, inspecting their conditioning. "Good, It appears that you are maintaining their conditioning," she said as she turned to look Mr. Rappaport directly in his eyes again. This time her gaze was not momentary. It was a deep and penetrating stare.

"The question I have come all this way to ask you, Mr. Rappaport, is what is happening to your scanners? Are they having problems with the conditioning? Are they escaping or are you just irresponsible with the resources we are giving you?" There was a cynical tone in her voice. She had stopped and was standing directly in front of Mr. Rappaport, looking unblinkingly at him now. He was looking at the ground, afraid to meet her gaze. Finally he summoned the courage to look her in the face. "There is someone out there," he managed. "Someone is killing my people," he said.

"Well then, who is it?" she replied.

"I don't know." He started to offer some explanation but she shut him down with a wave of her hand as she turned away and walked over to the window as if to take in the view.

"Mr. Rappaport, how is it that you have evaded this person? Could it be that you have sequestered yourself away up here with this beautiful view and wonderful room service and left these poor drones to fend for themselves?" she asked. She did not wait for an answer; she simply turned and walked back over to where he was still standing in the middle of the room. She stood directly in front of him, looking him directly in the eyes. She continued, "If this problem is beyond you, I can send someone else and we can find something less challenging for you." He looked nervously down at his feet then over at his scanners. There was an awkward moment of silence before he stuttered, "I can, I can handle, I want to handle this."

"Good," she replied as a slow smile spread across her face and she turned and walked to the door before turning to look back at him. "I look forward to your next report," she said.

With that, one of her attendants opened the door and she followed him out. The other pushed past Mr. Rappaport as if he were not of any consequence, as he took the door handle to shut it behind them. He paused momentarily just before he closed the door and gave Mr. Rappaport a grin. As soon as the door closed, poor Mr. Rappaport fell down on one of the sofas with his hands on his head.

Laura paused after sharing that with us. She looked around the room. "I think that this woman or someone else will return to check on Mr. Rappaport. I think that we need only wait to see who shows up and allow them to lead us to the next level." Laura then looked around the silent room. John took a sip of his coffee, then added "I agree, there is no point in sitting back to see what they do next. This is right up my alley so…"

Laura cut him off, "No, John, Sparrow and I will do this; you have a more important task. Besides it could be weeks before they show up. You may be back in time to relieve us. I am quite sure Alex will be keeping tabs on us as well," she said with just a quick sideways glance in my direction and a hint of a smirk as she looked back at John.

He knew she was right but he didn't like it. "Ok, just be careful," said John. "If they come looking for Mr. Rappaport they will be expecting some trouble, so just hang back, get a few clues and let them go. We don't know what we are getting into yet and we still need to get everyone together on this."

"Who exactly is everyone?" Sparrow asked her dad.

John paused and looked back at her. He gave her just a momentary smile. "You will see," he replied as he stepped forward to put his arms around her. John hugged her tight the way a father does when he knows he is really letting her go, letting her be the strong person she is, letting the little girl become a memory and the young woman step forward.

Sparrow stepped back and took her father's hand as she looked at his worry-worn face. "I can do this, Pop," she said. She let his hand fall as she turned toward the door. Laura stood up and gathered her coat as she moved toward the door behind Sparrow.

As Sparrow opened the door, Laura looked back over her shoulder at John. "We will go back to keep an eye on the hotel right after we contact a few singular individuals I know, who have the prerequisite skill set to be capable and have a vested interest in the outcome of our endeavors, and yes, John, You have my word." She said no more, she simply turned and followed Sparrow out the door.

Art stood up and motioned John and I toward the door behind them. Art looked over at John and said, "Not to worry, guys. Me and my friends will keep Mr. Rappaport high and dry in a quiet corner."

I mentioned Mr. Dechain to Art and suggested that he has some skills yet to be developed and that John had mentioned it was his turn. Art just looked back at me over the top of his glasses. "Yah, we'll see about taking on a former scanner," he replied.

John and I stepped out the side door from Art's office. It was cool outside with just a light mist floating in the morning air that drifted off the water and into the city. I stood next to John and squeezed his arm. "I know how you feel, John, as weird as it is, I mean she is my age but, I feel, I guess, your feelings. Damn," I paused for a moment.

John looked at me with a quizzical look on his face. "What?" he said.

"I will keep tabs on them both," I responded, "but what is this thing you have to do that Laura mentioned."

"I am going to have to face the people, my people. I am going to ask for their help but first I must be judged by them for what I have done," John replied.

"I should go with you," I said.

"No, I don't know for sure that they will want to see me and if they do, there may be some that are not pleased with some of the decisions I have made--one of them being sharing everything with you," John said as we walked along in the cool morning air.

I looked at John but I did not say anything as we walked. I reflected on how much my life had changed, how much this man had given me. I thought about how many of his personal thoughts and feelings he had shared--the thoughts one normally does not share but John had sacrificed his dignity for me. I thought about Sparrow.

"I will watch her for you, John," I said aloud.

"I know," John replied as he slapped me on the back and smiled at me. "Keep an eye on them both, Tonto," he said as he turned and started south along the waterfront. "Hi ho silver and away," he said without looking back.

"Hey, hey, I'm supposed to be the lone ranger," I yelled back at him as he disappeared down the street. I knew he was headed back to the rain forest of the Olympic Peninsula first and then north, across the straits—across to Vancouver Island, Canada, the main shipping lane where the Pacific Ocean pours into the Puget Sound and the inside straits between the Canadian mainland and the deep ancient forests that cover the 460-kilometer-long, Vancouver Island. He had shared his thought with me. This is where he would go before the other powerful minds among the first Nations people.

This was the turning point. This was the first time anyone had tried to bring together those who had learned the secret of the rain to organize for a single purpose. I was headed back to the University District to try to get my head around this new dimension to my life. A few months ago I was just another cog in the machine that is our human society, just another grain of sand on the beach of humanity. Now I'd discovered this rare gift that both expands my existence to yet unknown dimensions and threatens my existence at the same time. For the first time I felt I was truly alive. I had been rather cavalier about going out to trap the person running these scanners without a great deal of thought as to where this could take me. I had no idea that this would be just the tip of the proverbial iceberg. I had never really stopped to consider if this was a fight I was prepared for. Everything had happened so fast. How deep was I prepared to go? I suppose I was better off to have discovered this part of myself, to have been found by these people that would help me understand and develop my abilities early enough to be able to fight for myself, as opposed to simply being discovered by a scanner and turned into another drone, just another cog in the machine. We would see soon enough. John was somewhat vague about this gathering. I had the benefit of all John's memories so I knew without him saying, where all the elders would gather. All those powerful enough to receive and understand the thought pulse John sent out, would collect their associates and apprentices to come together in just a few nights. This would be an unprecedented gathering. Not everyone may agree that this is the way forward, not everyone may come. Even John had never actually attended such a thing. He had a memory of a gathering like this that had been passed down to him and he had, in turn, shared with me. A meeting called by a chief of the Duwamish Tribe years ago, that included elders even from tribes he had conflict with. This was 150 years ago, and from that time forward no such gathering had occurred. This would be greater; it would involve more people--diverse people from different backgrounds with many differing points of view. John may find himself on trial. He had taken lives; he had shared everything with a non-first nation's person. He had walked away from his family and people that he was responsible for. How would he be judged?

I turned and started heading the other way. I closed myself off and walked on in the mist that had turned into a light rain, toward the stairway that ascends the hillside under the Public Market. I enveloped myself in a cloud of invisibility that I was able to cast into the minds of the few street people that might be about. As I got closer to the market, I could sense all the venders and shop owners hustling about to get ready for the day--scattered people coming and going on the street around me. The steady patter of the rain was now a comfort. I felt for the first time in my life that I was the master of my own destiny and I resolved not to allow anyone to take that from me. I moved undetected and unseen through the city. I was no longer just a cog in the machine.

Sometime in the late hours of the morning, just as the streets were filling with all the people on their way to school or work, I got to the front door of my building. As I placed my key in the lock I could sense every one of my fellow apartment dwellers. I could hear their thoughts and feel their emotions along with those of everyone else on the street and passing by in the cars and trucks on the road. I could sense all that and keep myself hidden from even those right in front of me on the street. As I stepped into the small lobby of my building and put my key back in my pocket and closed the front door behind me. I suddenly became aware that I was sensing something strange. To be more precise, what I was sensing was nothing. It was as if there was a big hole with no thoughts or emotions passing through or around it. It was strange that what I felt was simply a hole that should not be there. Then it came to me, I realized what I was sensing. For those of us with the gift, thoughts flow through space in a linear way and there was something or someone blocking that flow. My sensitivity was so acute now that I was detecting someone that believed they were blocking themselves from detection. Although I could not sense them directly, I sensed the void of conscious thought that they were creating. Someone was waiting for me up in my apartment. For just a moment I was apprehensive and I thought about running. Then I realized that whoever it was, I had the advantage. They had not detected me yet.

    I went up the stairs quietly until I stood in front of my apartment door. I started to project the vision of the front door into my room so that as I opened my front door to walk in and confront my visitor, they would look and only see an empty hall and a closed door. I slowly slid my key into the door and quietly turned the lock. Whoever was waiting in my room did not appear to have noticed. I opened the door as quietly as I could and stepped into the apartment. It was dark with only the glow from the streets signs outside filtered through the half closed blinds. I could not see the person yet so I stepped slowly and quietly just a few steps into my apartment. My visitor must have heard a squeak from my wet shoe on the wood floor. I froze as he turned and looked directly at the door. He only saw the empty hall and closed door that I was projecting but he must have felt something was not right. I was starting to see his outline in the darkness. I still could not sense him. He stepped back. Reaching around to his back, under his three quarter length black leather jacket; he pulled a large-bladed weapon. As he stepped to the middle of the room, the dim filtered light crossed his face. It was Jay and he still had not detected me. All he could see was the image of the closed door and empty hallway that I was projecting. As I reached over and switched on the light, I dropped the image and then opened my consciousness so he could both see and sense me. For Jay it was as if the lights went on and I appeared out of thin air at the same time.

"Boo," I said with a smile. Jay exploded backwards, falling across a small table and onto the sofa by the front window. "What the hell? Damn, I nearly pissed myself. How the hell did you do that?" he asked as he fumbled and almost dropped his rather large knife.

"Is that a really big knife or are you just glad to see me?" I replied as I stepped back and pulled off my wet jacket. "You don't think you are overcompensating for something with that thing?" I said with a smirk.

Jay stammered, "That was wicked. How did you know I was here? How did you"... I cut him off. "Mad skills, bro, mad skills," I said.

"I'll say," he replied.

"So what brings you here?" I asked. "My crazy sister was just sure you were in some kind of big trouble. I told her you could handle yourself but she would not let it go until I promised her I would come by and check up on you. I can see that you are quite alright though," Jay said as he gathered himself together, stood up and replaced the long blade behind his back, under his coat.

"Yeah, well, I am glad you dropped by actually," I said as I stepped into the kitchenette. I put some water on to boil and pulled out my French press coffee maker and set it on the counter. I held out the package of ground coffee toward Jay and he nodded approvingly. I turned back to fixing the coffee and Jay sat down on the sofa. "Your sister was not wrong. Better sit down and I will share with you what I've been up too."

As we sat down for a cup of coffee, I looked over at Jay who was expecting me to launch into a long story. "Look, Jay, I would like to share with you what I have been up to with greater detail than just words can convey."

Jay gave me a blank look.

"I would like to give you my thoughts for the last couple days," I continued.

"You can do that?" Jay asked.

"Yeah, but only if you're cool with it," I replied.

Jay understood I was asking him to trust me in his head. I set my coffee cup down and I placed my right hand on the side of my head to help me focus on just the last few days. I reached out my left hand and touched Jay's forehead with one finger. I had John's memory of how to do this but I had never done it myself. I must have seemed a bit unsure because Jay looked at me for a moment, "You sure you know what you're doing," he asked?

"Yeah, no sweat," I replied.

Jay closed his eyes and all the events of the last two days flowed instantly into his mind. Jay twitched as he absorbed my thoughts, then he leaned back in his chair. He looked and me and smiled. "Wow, what a rush," he said.

"I would understand if you and your sister did not want to get involved but the truth is this will affect you guys and everyone else like us and, I hesitated, we could use your help. You have seen what we discovered about the small groups these guys work in but we do not know how many of these groups are out there or how big their organization is, let alone who is behind it. We don't know if this threat is local or worldwide. We are going to try to do something about it. Laura is watching the hotel now but once we find out where the next level is we are planning to step into them. I would like to ask you and your sister to help. My teacher, John, has gone to get the support of as many powerful minds as he can."

Jay just smiled. "Is that Sparrow girl going to be involved?"

I looked at him for a moment dumbfounded. "You know I'm talking about a large scale gathering of people like us, right? Some of the most powerful minds on the planet coming together to see if we can work together and free ourselves of those who want to hunt us down and enslave us and you're thinking it might be worth going if there is a chance to hook up with a hot chick?" I asked.

Jay just smiled, then he said, "So that's a yes, she'll be there, right?"

I shook my head and gave half a laugh. "Did you feel that pulse last night?" I asked.

"Oh yeah, I was going to ask you about that. What was that?" Jay responded.

"That was her dad," I said with a grin.

"Whose dad?" Jay asked.

"John, he is Sparrow's dad--remember you met him in the coffee shop with Sparrow and Laura. He is the one that sent out the pulse. He's the one who has been training me," I told him. "Dang, I have only met this beautiful young woman once, she does not yet know any of my finer qualities and now you tell me her dad could kill me if he ever gets into my head," Jay said.

"Still want to see her again?" I asked.

"What's life without a little adventure? Of course I do," Jay responded with a big smile.

"It's your life, but I need to crash now. How about we hook up later after I sleep?" I asked. With that, Jay got up and headed out the door. I checked the locks and jumped into bed, just as the rain was subsiding and the sun was about to come up on a new day.

It was almost noon when I woke up. The sun had somehow burst through and dried up most of the rain-soaked streets. This was great. I could be more relaxed, less moisture in the air, less chance of any scanners being close enough to pick up on anything. I showered, got dressed and was out the door. Walking down the busy street with the sun peeking out at me between broken clouds gave me a warm feeling. I could still hear the thoughts of the people passing by me on the street but their thoughts were softer and faded out of range quicker. I pulled out my cell phone and sent a text message to Jay. "Lunch?" I got a response from Sahira, his sister, inviting me to their apartment for lunch.

Their apartment building was one of the nicer ones in the University District. I was about to press the buzzer but they had both sensed my arrival and the door to the spacious lobby opened before I could reach out for the button. Sahira greeted me at the door to their apartment with a somewhat flirtatious smile. I stepped back and put my hands up, as if to guard my face.

"You're not going hit me in the nose again, are you?" I asked.

She looked at me with a sideways glance before she smiled again and said, "That depends on how you like my cooking. Now please take off your shoes and come in," she said as she turned and walked back into the apartment and Jay came to the door.

"Come on in, man," he said as I stepped in and kicked off my shoes. I looked around the apartment. I could see that the décor was modern but clearly east-Indian. A nice living room with a pass through counter to the kitchen allowed the aroma of the curry that Sahira had simmering on the stove, to float throughout the apartment. On the other side of the small living room was a set of sliding glass doors that opened onto a balcony just wide enough for a couple of chairs and a very small table. Jay grabbed a couple of cold sodas off the counter and passed me one as we walked through the living room toward the balcony. As we passed the open door to Jay's bedroom, I noticed several large knives hanging on the wall. Jay saw me stop and stare for a moment. "My uncle is a Sikh. Most of them have a family tradition of being warriors. I learned from him, how to use them," he said.

"That could be a useful skill to have," I told him as we went out onto the balcony for a moment to admire the view. "Pretty swank," I said as I looked across at the apartment buildings that lined the street like canyon walls.

"Our parents sent us here to go to the university but also to find ourselves," Jay said as we stepped back inside.

I sat down on the large designer sofa. Jay sat down in a large matching chair across a glass topped coffee table from me. Looking over Jay's shoulder I could see Sahira through the pass through to the kitchen. "Look guys, there is a good bit of trouble coming our way and to be honest, I don't know if you want to get mixed up in all this."

Before I could go on, Jay cut me off. "Hey, how long do you think these guys will take before they show up in our hometown if they are successful here?"

"So I see that you have been thinking about this already. Fair enough, but if you're in, you're in all the way. Like I told you last night, John has gone to a get together of sorts in a few days to convince as many of our kind as possible to help us." Jay looked at me and smiled. "Our kind," he repeated.

Over a leisurely lunch, we shared stories about our upbringing. Jay and Sahira were from an upper middle class family that could well afford to send them halfway across the world to go to school here and the University of Washington. Jay told me how they had always known that they had the gift and they were taught from the time they were very young by an uncle that also had the gift. He had helped them to develop their skills until they were of high school age. Then they were introduced to a new teacher that was older and even more skilled than their uncle. He had been their teacher until they came here to go to school.

Jay told me that there were others like them where they came from and they would see a few other young people coming and going at their teacher's house. He told me a story about getting in trouble for misusing his skills at his middle school as a young boy. Jay was a skinny kid growing up, and one day a bully in his school decided to take the lunch that Jay's mother had so lovingly packed for him. When he resisted the bully knocked him down. "I made him pee his pants standing right there in front of everyone. I felt quite clever until I got home and my uncle was waiting for me. He told me that it was time for me to start learning how to fight."

"That sounds pretty cool," I interrupted.

"Yeah, well my uncle was a great teacher but he made his point about not using our abilities wherever we wanted. He told me how important it was to not let others know about our gift.

Sahira joined Jay and me in the living room. She dropped herself into the other end of the sofa that I was sitting on. I looked at both of them and said, "I am jealous of you two. It seems like you have grown up with the ability and it is a natural part of your lives. I did not even know that I could do such things until only a short time ago."

Jay looked at me with a confused expression. "How is that even possible after that trick you did on me last night when I was waiting for you or the way you transferred all that information to me in just a moment?"

"I'll just say I have a really good teacher for now," I told him.

I had noticed that Sahira had just been listening and observing me. She was not attempting to read my mind but she was reading me. "Our teacher back home was a venerable man but I doubt his skills were on your level," Sahira said. She had a most sincere look on her face as she looked at me. Her eyes stared with such intensity, as if she might simply look right into my head and see my thoughts. "It is true, you do not even know the extent of your own abilities yet," she stated with a certainty in her voice as unwavering as her stare.

"How did you do that?" I asked. "You were not in my head; I have been paying close attention."

"The same way she knew you were in some kind of trouble the other night," Jay added. "As best I can describe it, it is like seeing the ripples on a pond after something disturbs the surface."

"I do not always see what disturbed the surface, but I can sense the ripples," Sahira added.

"Now that is something new to me, I will have to watch my ripples from now on," I said with a smirk.

I did not say much about John to them other than he was my teacher. I figured it was up to John to decide what he wanted to share about himself. I was genuinely curious about Sahira's strange perception that seemed to function in a way that was outside my understanding as of yet. After a wonderful meal and an afternoon of mostly the normal conversations young people have about the latest cell phone or tablet, I told them I would get back to them as to the where and when. As I put my shoes on to leave I paused to remind them. This lady we saw that had intimidated Mr. Rappaport would likely be coming back around, and she looked quite dangerous. I shared her image with them both. "Be careful," I warned them as I headed out the door. "I will see you in a couple days."

Later that day at home, I took some time to sit back and review some of the thoughts and experiences John had shared with me. I wondered how John was doing? From the memories he had shared, I knew some of the people he was seeking. Most of them were Native Americans from many of the First Nations tribes spread along the coast of Washington, British Columbia and up into southern Alaska. In the old days, even after the first white settlers started showing up, some tribes made war with each other and the new European settlers. The Snohomish Tribe raided the Duwamish. Most all the Puget Sound Tribes feared the war-like Haida, who still today occupy two large islands and a number of smaller islands off the northern coast of British Columbia. There was also the Southern Kwakiutl from the eastern center of Vancouver Island and across the channel, covering many small islands and some mainland villages. Both of these two tribes had raided the local Salish-speaking tribes for many, many years to take slaves and other loot even up into the 19th century. Although those days were long over, they were still in the collective memories of tribal elders. Then there was also the Tlingits from southern Alaska that had taken the head of a prominent white settler on Whidbey Island in Washington back in the late 1850s.

These were the people that John went to convince that this was their problem and not just something going on in the white man's world. Where John was going was very rural, very remote and extremely wary of outsiders. Small towns and villages nestled into the massive temperate rain forest that covers the Olympic peninsula in Washington, Vancouver Island, the coast of British Columbia north of the City of Vancouver Canada and all the way up to southern Alaska.

JOHN'S TRAVELS:

JOHN AWOKE EARLY from the comfortable deep sleep he had not felt for a long time. The smell of breakfast cooking gently beckoned to him from down the hall. Being at home in his mother's house surrounded by family and friends who looked on him with the respect one gives a gifted and devout man, he was wrapped in their collective warm feelings and thoughts and he wore them like a garment. It was a far cry from the life he had been living on the city streets, numbing himself with alcohol, invisible to the throngs of people that passed him daily. Deep in the moist, cool forest of the Olympic peninsula on the Quinault Reservation, he was safely sequestered from the outside world that had almost consumed him. His mental and physical strength grew with each breath he took as if he was connected to the land and the people in a way that allowed him to draw his strength from them both.

John walked down the hall into the living room following the smell of his mother's cooking. He peeked into the kitchen and there she was, directing two young teenage girls that looked like they were cooking enough to feed an army. One of the young girls had the gift and had sensed him coming. She turned with a cup of hot coffee ready just as John appeared. She smiled at John as she handed him his coffee, then she quickly went back to the dough she was hand rolling on the large prep table with Grandma giving a steady stream of directions and commentary to her two young apprentices in their native language. As John walked into the living room, slowly sipping his coffee, the smell of breakfast filled the house. John dropped softly into an oversized lazy boy chair. He set his coffee on a small side table with one hand and reached out with his other hand to grab Raymond's foot that stuck out from under the blanket on the sofa. He gave it a little shake. John knew that Raymond had every intention of going with him. He also knew that Raymond had no idea where they would be going.

John started putting his boots on. "Come on, home school," John said.

Raymond woke with a start and looked around before he realized where he was and what was going on. He started to pull himself together and find his shoes. Hopping on one foot as he tried to walk and put on a shoe he blurted out, "It's homeboy, uncle, Homeboy."

"Ya, Ya," John said as he walked toward the door. Raymond had smelled the food cooking in the kitchen behind him, but at the same time he heard the rumble of a big turbo diesel engine out in front of the house. A big truck pulled up just as John opened the front door. The deer that had been quietly grazing on the open grass next to the tree line were just disappearing into the forest. The first rays of the sun were starting to dissipate the morning fog as John stepped out onto the front porch. Two large men stepped out of the truck. Without a word they stepped up on the porch and picked up the two backpacks sitting there packed and ready, prepared overnight as John rested. Raymond stumbled out onto the porch still putting himself together, followed by Grandma and her two young apprentices. Grandma handed a basket full of fresh cooked food to Raymond. She looked him in the eyes and told him in her Salish dialect, "You stay with him, wherever he goes you stay with him and bring him back."

"Yes, Grandma," Raymond responded in English. The two girls handed the other two large baskets of food to the driver and his partner. Raymond looked at the other two baskets and then back at Grandma with a look of confusion on his face. In her Salish dialect she said, "I need you to make a couple stops on the way. Some of our family is hungry today." With that, she turned to John and put her hand to his face.

He closed his eyes for a moment, then he smiled at her. "I will tell them, Mother," he said in a soft voice. The driver and his partner set the food baskets in the bed of the truck. One of the girls ran back into the house and brought out paper towel wrapped around some fresh baked biscuits with meat inside them. They were hot right out of the oven. She handed them to Raymond with a smile then turned quickly and ducked behind grandma. John and Raymond turned and looked at Grandma. The driver stood stroking his long black ponytail with one hand as if waiting for something. She nodded to them and everyone turned and got up into the big truck. Grandma stood on the porch and raised her hands, sending a prayer behind them as the engine roared to life again.

The big truck turned around and headed down the dirt drive that led back to the two lane highway. They got to the highway and paused to look, not a vehicle in sight from either direction. They turned north and headed up the west coast of the Olympic peninsula, along the winding two lane highway, shrouded by massive evergreen trees on either side, which only offered small glimpses of the cool wispy sky. Occasionally the trees would part, offering a view of the Pacific Ocean, its turquoise horizon melting into the blue-gray sky. They made two stops as they traveled north, winding up a dirt road to a small home nestled back in the forest each time. Each time John exited the truck and took a basket to the house. Each time he was greeted with hugs and handshakes, each time the people receiving grandma's basket would not let John leave without giving him some small trinket of thanks. After half a day traveling through the rain forest and the few small towns that dot the remote rural highway, they came to Neah Bay, on the Makah Reservation. At the far tip of the Olympic peninsula, it is a very isolated place. Everyone they passed stopped to look at the truck as it rolled into their small town. This is the kind of place where everyone knows everyone; you are either a local or a tourist but this big truck did not look like either.

They pulled in and parked in front of a small grocery and gas store under the watchful eyes of the few people going about their business in this remote corner of the state. The peninsula protrudes out into the vastness of the Pacific Ocean and marks the entryway to the inland sea of the Puget Sound. The straits between the top of the Olympic Peninsula in the state of Washington and the bottom of Vancouver Island in Canada are 95 miles long and 12 miles across to Vancouver Island. This passageway is referred to as the Salish Sea. It is the very far northwest corner of the continental United States.

Raymond had fallen asleep in the back seat of the truck, so John and the other two left him sleeping there as they went inside the small store. As John walked through the open door, he was greeted by a small boy who stood blocking his path. They smiled at each other and the boy held up his hands for John to pick him up. John lifted the boy who hugged him as if he had been waiting for John for some time. They were quickly guided to the back room by a smiling young lady with raven black hair. She stroked the boy's head as John walked by, carrying the boy on one arm. In her Salish dialect she told the boy softly, "Listen and learn."

The boy had the gift and had felt John as he approached. They had been communicating for half an hour before his arrival. To someone who did not understand, it might have appeared that the boy had been sitting alone on the floor of the store talking out loud to imaginary friends. The boy's mother understood what was happening; she knew that a powerful medicine man was approaching. John's two guides waited in the store as John went through to the backroom. Several elders were sitting around a small table talking and drinking coffee in what looked like a storage room. Only one of them had the gift but John greeted each of them with the respect due an elder. One of them motioned for John to join them at the table. As John sat down, the boy hugged John one more time and then went over and stood by the connected elder who was his teacher. The teacher looked over at the boy and stroked his head. He then looked back at John and said, "He will soon surpass my abilities. I hope to send him to visit with your mother soon." John replied, "The boy and his mother will be welcomed into my family when he is ready."

Outside, Raymond was still lost in sleep and did not notice the three children peering in the truck window at him. The children stepped back from the truck when John and his two guides emerged from the store. The little boy from the store was holding John's hand as they walked together to the door. The children that had been watching Raymond sleep, looked at the boy, then at John. Their expressions all changed. They knew the boy was special, and they knew the man before them holding his hand must be special as well. They greeted him with a respectful greeting in their Salish dialect. John smiled at the kids and knelt down to look them in their smiling faces.

"Know who you are," he said and he passed a vision that had been passed down for a few generations, a memory from an elder of their tribe. He and a small group paddled the open ocean, harpooning a gray whale and towing it back to share with the tribe. The children stood motionless with a blank expression on their faces as they absorbed this vision, then when it was done, they all came alive again with a startled look on their bright young faces. John stood up and smiled at the children again. "Know who you are," he repeated.

John turned and slapped the side of the truck and Raymond awoke with a start. Raymond opened the door and stepped out, yawning and stretching as he looked around to see where he was. "Come on, homemade," John said, as he turned and grabbed their two backpacks out of the back of the truck.

"It's home boy, "Raymond replied with a somewhat exasperated tone. He then reached to take his pack from John.

John just smiled at Raymond before he turned and thanked the two men that had brought them this far. He threw his pack over one shoulder and grabbed a couple sandwiches from the last food basket. He then turned back to Raymond and handed him a sandwich. He looked Raymond up and down and smiled. "Come on, we are going for a little boat ride," John said as he turned and started walking down the street toward the marina. Raymond jogged a couple steps to catch up with John and then he asked, "What about those two grizzly bears? John looked back at Raymond as they walked. He smiled and said, "I told them you had me covered from here on, home cooking."

"It's homeboy, Uncle John, homeboy," Raymond said with even more exasperation as he and John walked down the small-town street, the three children from the store trailing them at a distance.

John and Raymond walked through the town and down to the Marina. As they walked out one of the piers, the seagulls scattered in front of them. They stopped at a fishing boat tied up at one of the slips. The three men onboard stopped the outfitting of their vessel long enough to greet John and Raymond as they came onboard. The captain invited the two into the pilot house as the two crewmen without a word went to cast off all lines. The boat pulled away from the dock. The captain smiled and looked John up and down; in his Salish dialect he told him it was good to see him again.

As the big, twin diesel engines churned the water, nudging the boat slowly forward, away from the dock, the captain explained, "All the big tankers have to pass through here so keep an eye out. They can sneak up on you when it is gray like this." The boat's bow lifted as the captain pushed the throttles forward. The big diesel engines churned the water and the small marina slowly started to fade into the gray-green of the land behind them. It was a 12-mile crossing to the twelve thousand square miles of mostly ancient forests that make up Vancouver Island. With the fog, the island was not yet visible. Once they crossed they were headed some distance up the outside of the island so they would be at sea the better part of the day. John looked at the captain and smiled. "Don't worry," he said to the captain as he closed his eyes and extended his hand out the window to feel the sea mist. "I have asked for safe passage and our cousins have come to guide us."

The captain knew John was a powerful medicine man. He had heard the legends so he was only mildly surprised to see a number of large blips on his sonar coming quickly on an intersecting course with them. Still he looked at the screen, then over at John with just a bit of concern on his face. John stood, one hand in the moist sea breeze, speaking quietly under his breath. The captain smiled to himself as he looked back forward. One of his young deck hands was standing on the foredeck, scanning the soupy fog for boats, floating logs or the supertankers that transit these straits. John walked out to join him.

The young man looked at him. Politely, struggling with the little Salish he could speak, he found the words and the courage to ask. "They say that you are a medicine man?" the young man asked.

John looked at him and smiled. Just then the pod of Killer whales that had come to guide them surfaced all around the boat, matching their speed and direction. A very large male took up a position in front of them. John pointed to the big male and looked back at the captain. The captain nodded to show he understood; he was to follow the big Orca. He waved back to John. The young man stood with his mouth open, staring at John.

John looked back at the young man, still smiling. "Is that what they say?" John said. With that John went to join Raymond and the other deck hand below decks. The young man paused and looked around the boat, now surrounded by the black and white of their escorts appearing for a breath and then disappearing in a beautiful rhythm all around their boat. Then he stumbled as quickly as he could to the wheelhouse.

He burst in, trying to use as much of his Salish dialect as he could muster but slipping back into English as the words flooded out. The captain smiled, his eyes fixed on the large whale now leading them. The captain reached out his hand and put it on the young man's shoulder as he turned to look at him. "Perhaps the bait fish would be a good offering for our cousins when we reach our destination," he said to the young man.

"Yah, for our cousins," he replied, first in English then in the best Salish he could muster. "I'll get them out of the freezer," he said, first in English then in Salish, as he turned to leave the cabin.

The boat cruised on into the mist accompanied by their escort. The drone of the engines and the sporadic breaching of the whales faded into the vastness of the open sea.

LAURA'S WATCH:

BACK IN THE city, Laura and Sparrow had decided to spend the afternoon visiting with Mr. Rappaport. They found their way down to the little Saigon area of town and into the Vietnamese grocery. As they entered the store, Laura scanned for the consciousness of Mr. Rappaport's hosts. Both Hung and his wife were keeping their minds and that of Mr. Rappaports well concealed. Sparrow asked one of the workers to speak to the manager. As Hung came out of the back he had a look of apprehension on his face. He had detected Laura's scan because she had made no attempt to conceal herself. He looked relieved when he saw the two of them. He waved them to the back of the store and into the receiving area. They walked through the back of the store and out the back, across the alley to the storage building where they kept Mr. Rappaport. As they entered the building they could feel the dry heat which would certainly limit Mr. Rappaport's abilities. Hung's wife sat at a desk outside the room that was confining Mr. Rappaport. She was diligently going over their receipts and keeping her mind also on her guest.

Ms. Nguyen turned and smiled as Laura and Sparrow approached. "Good timing," she said, "I am ready for lunch. Can I bring you something?" she asked them as she shared images in her mind of some of the food they offered at their hot food bar at the back of the grocery. Laura approached her and took her hand as she got up from her desk. "Just some of your delightful sandwiches would be wonderful," Laura replied.

"One of the benefits of our gift, is that when you share a thought or two with someone, you know right away what kind of person they are. You and I are going to be good friends, I can tell. My name is Thuan," Hung's wife replied. Hung waved at two of his employees that had been sitting to one side, just outside the door to Mr. Rappaport's room. They got up, one folded the newspaper he had been reading and let it drop on his chair before they wandered off. "Well, I will leave you ladies to it. Let me know if there is anything you need," and with that Hung went back to his work.

Laura shared the plan in her thoughts with Sparrow. Sparrow sat down at the small table where the two workers had been sitting. Laura set her purse on the table next to Sparrow, adjusted her hair and blouse, then opened the door and stepped into the room with Mr. Rappaport. He was lying on a bed with his back to the door. He turned over somewhat lazily until he saw who it was. He did not see Laura but the image of the woman from his organization that had visited him to inquire as to why he was losing his scanners. He leaped to his feet and started to explain how what had happened to him was not his fault until he realized that something was not right. He stopped talking. He took a deep breath and sat back down on the bed. "Ok, what now?" he asked.

Laura dropped the image and showed her true form to him. "Yeah, I remember you," he said with a tone of resignation in his voice. "Are you my executioner?" he asked.

"I could be, but I do not have to be," she responded. Laura sat down at a small table and then waved her hand for him to join her at the table. He studied her for a moment before he slowly got up and trudged over, pulled out the other chair and plopped himself down. He looked down at the top of the small table top, afraid to make eye contact. "I hope we can do this the easy way, Mr. Rappaport, what do you say?" she asked him. The full time he was focused on Laura, he had not noticed that Sparrow was slipping ever so gently into his head, just in case he decided to do the unexpected or self-destruct in some way. "These people will kill me, you know," he said with a slight hesitation in his voice.

"Not today they won't," Laura replied in a calm voice. He looked up and met her piercing gaze. His demeanor was that of resignation. He was offering no resistance and he did not even attempt to shield his thoughts. "Ok, say I go along with you and give you everything I have, what guarantee do I have you won't just melt my brain later?" he asked.

Laura just smiled, "None whatsoever, Mr. Rappaport, none," she replied. "To be quite honest, we are in somewhat of a quandary as to what we will do with you. What you have here is the opportunity to influence our decision-making process, nothing more." She leaned back in her chair, her gaze still fixed on him as if her eyes alone could penetrate his thoughts.

Mr. Rappaport leaned back and looked down at the table again, rubbing the back of his head with one hand and nervously tapping the table top with the other. Finally he started with, "Ok, ok, well, I don't know that much, you see. I just ran this bunch that you rounded me up with…."

Laura cut him off. "I will be the judge of that."

"Say, by the way, what happened to those guys anyway, or do I want to know?" Mr. Rappaport asked.

"Let us just say they are no longer your concern, shall we?" Laura replied with a cold and calculating demeanor that would surely lead him to think the worst.

Laura sat calmly with her hands folded on the table top in front of her. Her gaze never left him. He twisted and turned as he agonized over what to do, all the while careful not to meet her gaze. "Ok, but you have to promise me," he started and she cut him off again. "No, no promises, no deals," she said firmly but without raising her voice.

"You don't give a guy much choice," Mr. Rappaport groaned.

"Not really," she replied.

"Is this going to hurt?" he said.

"That also is up to you," she replied. "I will need your full cooperation. Perhaps you would like to lay down and just relax."

Mr. Rappaport got up and turned away from her, careful so as not to meet her gaze. As he stepped over to the small bed that was against the wall, he weighed his options. He quickly realized that there were none. He lay down on the bed and closed his eyes. Laura did not move. She sat frozen at the table. Slowly she projected her mind to his. She made no attempt to conceal and he offered no resistance. First, her thoughts surrounded him and entered his conscious thoughts in her usual soft and reassuring manner. As he relaxed even further, his breathing became softer, like a person in a very deep sleep. Sparrow was there, waiting at the edge of his consciousness, waiting for Laura to take the lead and now, together, they entered the deepest part of his subconscious thoughts. "Take me to the beginning," Laura whispered in his mind, and her command reverberated in every corner of his neurotransmitters, quietly disappearing into the far reaches of his brain. An image of Mr. Rappaport started to take form. He was a few years younger and had discovered that sometimes he had the power of suggestion over some people sometimes. He was just a street hustler. He would take advantage where he could but he was not clear on why it worked sometimes but not at others or with some people it was easy or others it did not work at all.

Mr. Rappaport was sitting back at his desk, front and center of a large car dealership. His fellow salesmen loved and hated him at the same time. He had been the top salesmen month after month from the day he had started there. He was staring at the front door, waiting for his next big sale to walk in and there she was. It was as if she was moving in slow motion. As she approached the front door he observed her long auburn hair lightly fluttering in the soft breeze. Her full length, form fitting designer wool jacket, was neatly gathered at the waist, so as to flatter her stunning figure. As she stepped gracefully toward the front doors, her power over men was obvious as three different men rushed to open the large glass doors for her.

Mr. Rappaport did not move from his desk as he confidently stared at her, reaching out with his mind, beckoning her to him. As she stepped through the doorway, she met his steely gaze. She paused and removed her sunglasses. Mr. Rappaport stood up and walked around to the other side of his desk but never completely turned his back on her. His confidence was exploding as she walked past other salesmen who attempted to engage her, only to be dismissed as if they did not exist. When she approached, he pulled the chair out for her, inviting her with his twinkling eyes and confident grin to be seated. As she did so, he slowly returned to his seat of power. They looked at each other across his desk, each one smiling a beguiling smile, their eyes interlocked with one another. Without looking away, he called out to one of his underlings to bring them a couple lattes and then nodded to her for approval. She nodded in return. Now was his opportunity. He reached across his oversized desk and touched her hand. She slowly looked down at his hand touching her then back up at his face. She set her sunglasses down on his desk with her other hand and then met his gaze once again. As she did so, her smile widened. He could barely contain himself now; he reached out with his mind, attempting to plant the idea that he was the most handsome man she had ever laid eyes on.

Suddenly the woman was in his head. "You have got to be kidding," she said to him. Her words were clear yet her lips did not move. He was stunned. He tried to stand up but she had him. He was frozen. His cocky gaze quickly turned to a look of sheer panic. She calmly leaned back in her chair and shrugged off her coat to reveal her designer blouse and a display of jewelry that was worth thousands of dollars. "Not to worry," she said with a smile. "I am going to release you in just a moment but I want it to be clear who is in charge here, Ok?"

He was panicked now. He mustered all his strength to try to assert himself, to push her out of his head, but to no avail. She just sat there smiling. In his head he could hear her voice.

"By all means, get it out of your system," she said. She leaned back in her chair. He struggled for a moment longer before the futility of it all set in.

"Are you done now?" she inquired, in his mind. He lowered his eyes to his desk. She released her grip on him. Slowly he leaned back in his chair, unsure of what was to come next.

As he looked back up at the woman, she smiled again, speaking to him normally now so as not to attract attention with their outward silence. "Relax, sweetheart, you are about to embark on a wonderful new adventure. Now be a dear and go give them your notice, tell them you have just been recruited for a much better-paying job, which is true by the way, and meet me outside at my car."

With that she stood and picked up her coat. Mr. Rappaport ran around his desk to help her put it on. He was still ambivalent to say the least but the notion of more money and the allure of getting a better understanding of the gift he had, hooked him. Besides, this woman had an allure that had nothing to do with her psychic abilities.

They went to a swank hotel suite which was already occupied by several preprogrammed scanners. She trained him as to how the gift worked and how he could maximize his skills. She explained that his role was simple. He would manage the scanners with whom he was entrusted and if he were to encounter anyone with a higher level of skill than they could manage he need only report them to her. She explained that his skills were more than the typical. She smiled and leaned in close. Which would you rather be, one of them, as she gestured toward the scanners standing in a row, or their boss?"

From that day on he was running a group of scanners. They would move around from city to city. He would send them out searching. They would bring in those that they could capture. She would come or she would send her two oversized bodyguards to take the captured away for programming. Sometimes one that they had captured would come back to them, ready to use, sometimes not. He did not know what happened to the others and he was too afraid to ask. He had referred a few to her that were beyond the abilities of his scanners; none of them were known to Laura.

Laura and Sparrow exited Mr. Rappaport's mind and he slowly regained consciousness and sat up on the edge of his bed. He did not look over at Laura at all. He simply looked at the floor waiting for whatever might come next. Laura stood up from the table where she had been sitting and walked to the door, she then paused and turned toward Mr. Rappaport. "Stay on your best behavior, Mr. Rappaport. Your future is as yet undecided." With that she opened the door and stepped outside to meet Sparrow and Thuan, who were eating some Vietnamese sandwiches. "I am afraid I will need to leave him in your capable hands a bit longer. I will have to take one of these delightful sandwiches to go," Laura said, as she picked one from the table as she walked by. "Come, Sparrow, we have a very adept quarry to seek out." She headed for the door with Sparrow right behind her.

THE COUNCIL:

NIGHT WAS STARTING to fall and the fishing boat carrying John and Raymond had been paralleling the outside coast of Vancouver Island for several hours. The captain had turned on the running lights and the pod of Orcas that had been accompanying them were keeping a steady rhythm rising to the surface for a breath and submerging again, just below the surface. The boat slowed and turned inland as a narrow entry to a large cove opened up to them. The captain slowed even further and turned to John, "Is now a good time?" he asked.

"Sure," John replied. John stepped to the back of the boat as the two crewmen brought up some tubs full of bait fish. John closed his eyes, held up his hands and thanked their escorts for a safe journey. The leader of the pod spy hopped next to the boat so as to see all those on board. Raymond came out of the cabin just in time to look the large Orca directly in the eye. He stood there paralyzed with amazement for a moment. Then he stepped carefully over to one of the tubs to pull a big handful of fish. He stepped carefully back to the side where the pod leader had been. He looked around and then leaned out to look into the dark water just in time to meet the pod leader coming up again just feet away from him. He reached out and let the fish slip into the water and the whale sucked them in. John was still standing there with his eyes closed and his hands up, communicating with the pod. He smiled and said, "Looks like you got a friend, Raymond."

They stayed there bobbing up and down with the waves, sliding fish into the water as each Orca took its turn approaching the back of the boat. When they finally finished putting the last of the fish in the water, the whales turned and departed, their tall dorsal fins slipping beneath the surface of the dark waters.

The captain throttled up the engines and they moved slowly into the cove. Darkness had enveloped the land and the sea but across on the other side, perched on a rocky outcropping overlooking the water and framed by the mammoth old growth trees that stood just behind them were several buildings. It was a first nations fishing village. The lights from the buildings reflected across the surface of the water and danced with the waves. The outdoor lights among the cluster of buildings stretched down to the water and out the floating dock. It gave a warm and inviting appeal to what was otherwise as lonely an outpost of humankind in the wilderness as one could imagine. There were no roads to bring a person here, surrounded by nature and only accessible from the sea.

As they pulled into the dock they were greeted by some from the local tribe at whose village they were now guests. They greeted John and his party with the respect of a visiting medicine man. One of those greeting John was a local medicine man who had known John from the time they were children together, he was called Tall Elk, a big and robust man who stood a full head taller than everyone there. They took each other by the shoulders and touched their heads together to share a day's worth of conversation in just a moment. They then laughed and started walking arm in arm up the walkway to the meeting house where others from the village and around the island waited to meet John. The rest of them had secured the boat and were about to start walking up, when John spoke in Raymond's head. "Bring my backpack, home cooking," he said. Raymond jumped back onto the boat, grabbed the backpack and tried to hurry to catch up with the rest of them, thinking to himself, "Uncle, why can't your great mind digest the words: home boy?"

The local tribe had a slightly different dialect from the Salish dialect Raymond sort of spoke, so it made it all the harder to communicate. Most of the younger people would have preferred to resort to English but none of them wanted to disappoint their elders so they kept at it, using only the occasional English word. As they entered the hall, the elders were all seated at the far end. John stepped forward and greeted them, Raymond came up behind him and handed him his backpack. John stepped forward, offering small gifts to the elders, everything from special packages of medicinal herbs to expensive watches. He then introduced the captain and his crew and Raymond.

John's friend, Tall Elk, then stood up and introduced all of those seated among the elders. Then he said to John, "We have another guest with us tonight that has been hidden from you until this moment. With that they pointed to one side and John recognized someone he had not seen in many years, a shaman powerful enough to keep his consciousness hidden even from John. They had been friends and rivals in their youth but they had not seen each other from the time they had been rivals for the woman who became John's wife.

"Frank?" John said. This had truly caught him by surprise.

"Call me Storm Cloud," he replied as he pushed through the crowded room to hug John. John did not share his thoughts with him as he had with Tall Elk, but they hugged and laughed. "We have much to catch up on," Storm Cloud said to John, "but not now, not here. Now is a time for eating and rejoicing in the company of our people." He pulled back and waved his hand to expose the room full of happy faces. "Come, let's join the elders and pay our respects first," he added. With that he put his hand on John's shoulder and they moved to join the elders as the party kicked off.

Some of the tribe dragged a big communal drum out and started a beat. They invited their guests to give them a song, so the captain that had brought John to this remote place started them out. He called out a tune as he found a spot around the big drum. As a child Raymond had been forced to go to the traditional dance class at their rec center every weekend. As a child he had hated it but today, as a young man with several attractive young ladies looking on, he was glad for every lesson as he stepped into the middle of the floor to show them how they do it in his village.

John looked on and smiled, sitting with the elders, Frank Storm Cloud and Tall Elk on either side of him, both friends from his youth. He told them about his wife's disappearance, much of which had already reached their ears. He told them about his fall from grace and how he had slipped into alcohol. He did not tell them about Alex, not yet, although several of the elders that were present had been there when Grandma had performed the transfer. He was not sure what was already known but he did not want to start the conversation tonight. Tomorrow he would face the council to explain why he had come, and why he was asking for a gathering. They would extract everything from him, he would be judged for his actions, but for tonight, he did not think it was the time to put it all out there, not yet. He turned to Tall Elk and said, "I will also ask for permission to go to the sacred place to see if the old man will speak with me, if the elders will permit it."

"You will have my support tomorrow," Tall Elk said as he slapped John on the back of his shoulder. "For now you must tell me one thing, is that your younger sister's boy," Tall Elk said, as he pointed at Raymond dancing solo to the drum. "He looks like he has his uncle's moves," Frank added with a chuckle.

"Don't tell me you two are still jealous because I had the best moves, back in the day," John said. With that, Tall Elk and Frank both got up and started to the center of the floor. They were halfway there when they both paused and looked back at John. John stood and removed his coat before joining them. Raymond turned and saw the three coming. He then danced backward into the crowd and found a seat, leaving the floor for them. As he sat down, three of the young ladies encircled him, offering him refreshments and questions, all in the Salish dialect. The night went on and John and his friends danced their traditional dance, singing the words together and sharing the images in the minds of everyone present of ancient times, when the people lived and hunted, sharing the waters with the Orca and the land with the wolves, and so it went long into the night.

The next morning John and Raymond awoke in their cots in one of the smaller out buildings, The captain and his crew had gone down to sleep on their boat and there was no sign of Frank Storm Cloud.

"Ouch, muscle cramp," John cried out.

Raymond, just half awake, laughed to himself.

"What are you laughing at?" John said with a cross tone.

"You and your buddies were really busting a move or two out there, Uncle John," Raymond replied.

"Yep, still got it," John said with a confident tone, to which Raymond just burst into uncontrolled laughter.

There was a knock on the door, "Come," replied John, as he tried to sit up without straining his sore muscles too much. The door opened and Tall Elk entered. John was surprised, as normally he would have sensed his presence long before he knocked on the door. He was concealing his location which suggested he was hiding himself from someone else, someone powerful.

"Come in, buddy. What's going on?" John asked.

Tall Elk stepped into the room and glanced over at Raymond.

John turned to Raymond "Hey, Mr. Dancing with the stars, why don't you go get some breakfast? I will be right behind you," John said, as he started to get up before being forced to sit back down with another muscle cramp. "Ouch, come on over and give me some of that muscle cream I can smell on you," John said in Tall Elk's direction.

Tall Elk walked over toward John but said nothing as he waited for Raymond to leave. Raymond took the hint, grabbed his sweatshirt and closed the door behind him as he headed for the big communal building.

Tall Elk made a sign, passing his hand over his head so John would know to also conceal his thoughts. Normally in a remote place like this, they could let their guard down so John was concerned but he did as requested. "Listen, buddy," Tall Elk began. "You were right to hold back with Frank last night. I just don't want you to get blindsided with the elders' council today. You remember how he was about none First Nations people and allowing them to develop the gift? He hasn't changed. You remember, my father was there when you gave your lifetime of skill and training to an outsider. Your mother had asked him and the others not to share this with anyone for a short time. She said the reasons would become clear soon. He is going to try to shut you down today, buddy. He thinks this is a white man's problem and we need to stay out of it."

"How do you know all this?" John asked.

Tall Elk made a face of disbelief. "You know your mom is my aunty. Of course she asked me to keep you out of trouble. Anyway, how many times did you do the same for me?"

John patted him on the shoulder and the two of them headed slowly up to join the tribe for a communal breakfast, groaning about their sore muscles.

As John and Tall Elk walked into the hall, Raymond looked up and smiled. He started to mimic the chant from the drum circle last night, he then pointed with both hands at his two elders who had just entered. The young people around him laughed.

John and Tall Elk found a spot at the far end with the other elders. They started exchanging pleasantries with them. John noted there were several others present that had arrived in the night or early this morning. John stood up and started to say, "Hey, there are a lot more boats here this morning," when

Frank slipped in next to them. He smiled. John looked at him quickly and forced a smile before going on with a greeting for each of the late arrivals.

John was now starting to feel the pressure. Many from the First Nations people with the gift had come to this remote little fishing village to hear him, for John to account for his behavior and to hear his request. He was widely known as the most powerful medicine man but that was before, before his life had collapsed.

John sat down and started eating as Frank put his hand on John's shoulder. He then leaned in and whispered in his ear, "I am so glad that you found your way back from the white man's world, my brother. I was afraid that it might have destroyed you but here you are, back amongst your people."

John did not say anything; he just nodded and smiled as he took another bite. One of the host tribe elders stood up and made a short announcement. "Ok," she started, "we are gonna have an old people's meeting this afternoon but everyone be sure that you're here for dinner because afterward, we have a great story from one of our visiting elders so come and learn your history."

With that everyone broke up. The children went out to play. The young people cleaned the hall and helped with the dishes and that included Raymond. John and Tall Elk left together, along with Frank.

"I will need a quiet place to prepare," John said.

"Let me know when you are ready, I have a spot I use that should do," Tall Elk replied.

John started to head back to where he had slept to change and Frank was in his head, "We have not always agreed, my brother, but you are and always will be my brother," he said.

"I know," John replied.

John was changing when Raymond entered the room. "Why so serious this morning?" Raymond asked.

"Well, I have to convince the other folks with the gift to help me get to the bottom of all this stuff with the scanners," John replied.

"Why wouldn't they, uncle?" Raymond said with a tone of confusion in his voice.

John thought for a moment, "Why not indeed?" he said. "Before I go before the elders, I am going to go and clear my mind but I would like you to come with me."

"Sure, uncle, I got your back," Raymond replied.

Just at that moment Tall Elk knocked. He stuck his head in the doorway and looked the two of them over. "Ready to go?" he asked.

The three of them walked up past the communal building and then they took a small dirt path that led directly into the deep old growth forest. They walked until they came out of the forest again at a small clearing. The primordial rough and broken basalt rocks that make up all of these Pacific coast islands become smooth as they meet the never-ending pounding from the surf and the tides. It was a beautiful vista that looked exactly as it might have to their ancestors hundreds of years ago. The small village was only accessible from the water. Behind the village, as far as you could see was wilderness. The shoreline was very rough, cutting into and out of the forest, lined with large craggy basalt outcroppings and just the small patch of beach every now and again. Across the inlet you could see the sea birds settled in the sparse branches of the trees that lined the edge of the forest on the other side. In the forest behind him he could hear the chirping of the squirrels declaring their territory and the cawing of the crows doing the same. Tall Elk smiled and slapped John on the shoulder as he turned to go. Raymond just stood and watched John as he gazed out across this raw natural vista. Slowly Raymond stepped back and sat down on a fallen log at the edge of the forest. He watched his uncle roll out a mat and kneel down. He observed as John asked for the council of his ancestors.

Time seemed to stand still as John sat there, slowly chanting to himself. Raymond tried to still his mind and just take it all in. He thought to himself, he did not know what help he could be as an ordinary person among all these elders, many of them with great power, but he was resolute. His grandmother had asked him to accompany his uncle and she had asked one thing of him, "Bring him home to me."

She could have sent many older or gifted people but she asked him. He observed as John meditated, and Raymond found himself at peace observing everything around him, listening to the tapping of a woodpecker, watching a deer mouse rustle through the ferns and moss that covered the forest floor.

Some time had gone by when Tall Elk reached out with his mind to both John and Raymond. "The council is ready, please come."

John got up and rolled up his mat. He turned to Raymond and smiled. As he walked past Raymond, who was still sitting on the log, he handed him his rolled up mat and said, "Come on boy wonder, this looks like a job for a caped crusader." John laughed to himself as he walked up the trail with Raymond right behind him.

The council had gathered outside in a clearing surrounded by huge old growth trees--trees so large their branches reached across the clearing toward each other as if to create a roof. Sections of trees had been laid on their side for seating in a semi-circle and John approached this gathering place from the open end. Raymond had to stand back as his uncle entered the center.

John raised his hands and offered his thanks and his respects to all for coming to hear him. He was speaking now in his Salish dialect. Raymond knew that, by rights, he should not stay but he thought of his grandmother's words. Just then, in his head the medicine man from the host tribe spoke to him. "You may stay; we ask only that you be mindful of yourself in this council." Raymond nodded and took one more step back, looking left and right to be sure he was not out of place.

John began to speak; "First, I wish to humble myself before you, my brothers and sisters. I have shamed myself and I have shamed all of you. Before I speak on the reason I have requested this meeting, I must share with you my conduct that may give you concern as to how you will measure my words and actions going forward." John stopped and looked around. Everyone nodded in agreement. John closed his eyes and bowed his head. He let his consciousness flow starting at the moment he realized that his wife was missing to the moment he met with Laura and Sparrow to see if Laura would be Alex's teacher. He did not show them her answer. The faces of the council members went from sharing his sorrow and pain as he searched, to expressions of horror as they watched him encounter the scanners and descend into a spiral of murder and alcohol searching for his wife. John stopped and although it would have been rude for him to scan their minds, he could read their faces.

Raymond, who had been standing by the entrance, had experienced the complete stream of consciousness that his uncle had shared. Although he knew much of this, he struggled to remain calm and still. Raymond stood there, with his hands folded in front of him as a single tear ran down his cheek. He saw his uncle standing alone as many of the council's faces clearly showed their shock and displeasure. Raymond had not imagined all that his uncle had been through and all he had done.

Now the chief from the host tribe spoke. His gift was very small in comparison with that of John, perhaps like many of the scanners. "Many of us had heard many things. Opening yourself in this way leaves no room for misunderstanding. You honor us with your honesty and openness. However, perhaps now is a good time for us to drink some tea and consider all of this before we hear the rest?"

John nodded and stood quietly as several young people with trays carrying a pot of tea and mugs entered the council area. Raymond stopped one young man circulating with the tea and poured a cup, then he brought it to his uncle who stood alone in the center. He held the cup in two hands as a sign of respect as he offered it to John. John looked up at him as he accepted the tea. Their eyes connected for just an instant. There were no words.

After some time, the chief stood up and spoke again, "We have seen the past, perhaps we can now go forward now."

All the young people disappeared and Raymond stepped back. Everyone settled again. An elder, powerful with the gift stood to speak, "What you have shared with us is disturbing on many levels, John, deeply disturbing. We all understand your conduct is not why you requested this council, it is to discuss these scanners. However, before we go forward, I must caution you that although we are not here to discuss your conduct today, neither can we ignore it. You have taken lives. You have allowed yourself, a respected and truly gifted leader amongst our people, to diminish yourself to just another drunken Indian. You have shamed yourself and all of us along with you, this you know. What now gives you the authority to demand our council?"

John stood silent. He could feel the mixed emotions of those around him. Raymond was back by the entryway standing quietly, as he knew he had no right to even be there. Although they were all speaking in the Salish dialect that Raymond struggled with, their thoughts were also in his head. He saw his uncle speechless before them. He waited for a moment and still, the elder stood, staring at John and waiting for an answer that John did not have. Raymond knew that it was not his place but he took a deep breath and stepped forward to his uncle's side.

The elder turned and glared at Raymond; she could silence Raymond with the bat of her eyelash yet she did not. John waved him to step back.

"My uncle does not demand," Raymond started. The chief of the host tribe cast a withering glare at Raymond and said, "Is it your place now to address your elders?"

"No, elder, it is not," Raymond replied, "but I speak for my uncle where he has no words."

John reached out and pushed his nephew back as he whispered to him, "No, step back."

Raymond pushed past his uncle. "Please, he could have hid himself from you. He did not need to share with you his mind."

The elder, who was still standing, froze Raymond with the wave of her hand.

"John, what have you to say?" she inquired. John now lifted his head and waved his hand. Raymond was released and the elder swayed just a bit as she felt the power that now protected the young man. "I am responsible for all that I have done and I will accept whatever consequences you, my people, will extract from me. However, as my nephew said, I do not demand, I request."

John now stepped up and pushed his nephew behind him. "I wish only to inform you of a threat that threatens all of us with the gift. I do not ask for forgiveness as I will not forgive myself. I ask only that you protect yourselves and our people. I am here today, as is my duty to all of you, my people, to bring you this warning. I suggest that the best way to protect one another is to work together to track this threat to its source and then decide what we will do."

Now Storm Cloud stood to speak. "It is true, this is a threat to some with the gift. We have all seen it through your eyes. I must ask you, my brother, and we have differed on this issue before, is this really an issue for us? Have you found any of us among the scanners or have we, any of the tribes gathered here today, lost one of ours to these scanners?" He paused and looked around the council. "In truth my brother this is just another problem in the white man's world. As my father and grandfather before have all said, we should have never helped any of them to develop the gift. We should have kept it from them. I say let them do what they will with one another. The fewer of them with the gift, the better, I say." Storm Cloud paused and looked around, smiling a small smile before sitting back down. Storm Cloud paused momentarily as he sat, now looking down at the ground. "I know, my brother," he continued. "I know it is your wife that you have searched for; you believe that they have taken her. It is this madness that drove you to the city and to alcohol and to do the terrible things you have done. In truth, you do not know where she is or if she just left on her own."

Storm Cloud, was sitting now and he had lowered his head so as not to even look at John but he was keenly aware of the impact of these last words. "I thank you for the warning and I will be happy to help you look for your wife but I say, let us look to our own." As Storm Cloud finished, there was much talking among those assembled.

Tall Elk now stood to speak. He was a large and imposing man and his gift was strong. His strength could be heard in his voice and felt as his thoughts reverberated in everyone's consciousness. "John has given his life to the service of his people. Does anyone here refute this?" He paused and looked around the council. Everyone was silent. "John's power is great, so if he believes that these scanners have taken his wife, I do believe this. If John believes that this is the time for us to search them out, then I will stand with John and together we will do what must be done. As it happens, I too have been blessed with the gift to some degree, and I will remind all of you here that there is that which we see with our eyes and hear with our ears. For those of us with the gift, there is also that which we can sense in other ways. But beyond that there is also that which flows through the spirit world, that can touch any of us, gifted or not by the rain. I will tell all of you present that this does involve us. We are a part of this. I do not know how or why yet but I have spent some time reaching out, searching the conscious thoughts of people far and wide and listening to the spirit world. There will be a time when John shall stand before us to answer for his actions but that is not today. Surely we must all know more before we can judge him. Today, I stand with John. We must find the source of this poison today and not wait for it to grow stronger." With that, Tall Elk stepped out of the council, walked over and stood by John. The council members spoke among themselves. Then, one by one, others stepped down to stand with John in the center. Raymond slowly stepped back as the center of the council became crowded with his elders. Storm Cloud sat with his head down, not speaking, not saying a word. The chief of the host tribe looked around as still more stepped into the center. "Ok, now," he said as he raised his hands in front of his chest. Everyone can return to their seats."

Raymond had moved all the way back to the entrance now, just to make room for all the members of the council that had stepped into the center to support John. He kept his head down but he could not help but smile just a little.

As everyone took their seats again, the chief spoke. "I understand that some may still not wish to be part of this but it appears that the majority are prepared to confront this menace. Those who choose not to be a part of this may speak before leaving the council now. Storm Cloud stood again. "Although I do not agree that we should interfere with the white man's issues and I choose not to participate, I hope you all know that I am still your brother, and you can always call on me if you are in need or any danger whatsoever. At this time the only danger I see is not to me or you, my people, it is to the white man doing what they always do." Storm Cloud walked to the entryway. As he passed John, he patted John on the shoulder but never looked up or made eye contact with him. The elder medicine woman also stood and looked at John without speaking for a moment. Slowly she started to walk down to the center where John stood. She stood in front of him and waited for their eyes to meet.

"Do not bring this trouble upon us," she said.

"It is already upon us," John replied softly.

The elder medicine woman walked out of the council meeting. A few more left, but the majority stayed. The chief said, "Ok, John, now tell us the rest."

John did not open his mind but he did explain. "We have now found a way to release these scanners, we no longer have to worry about them killing themselves and more importantly, we do not have to kill them," John said with a lump in his throat. He paused for a moment, then continued. We discovered all this at great risk to my friend, Laura, who many of you know, my daughter, Sparrow, and my young apprentice. We have captured a leader of a small group of scanners and he, unlike the others, is not brainwashed as the ones you saw. As we speak Laura is searching his mind to find out who he answers to and anything else that may help us track this to the source.

Another elder stood to speak. He was perhaps the oldest among them so when he stood, all the side conversations of the council stopped. He spoke softly in his native language but he projected himself for all to hear in their mind clearly. "We must divide into groups to spread the word and find these scanner groups. We will disassemble their groups as John and his people did. We will free those we can. We will find the source." This elder was there when John transferred his knowledge to Alex yet he made no mention of this to the group. He continued. "A member of each group will meet with you and we will also examine this leader of the scanner group that you have captured."

The remaining council group stamped their feet or hit their walking sticks on the logs they sat upon in agreement. We must reach out to all those gifted by the rain, be they first nations or any other people." With that he banged his walking stick on the ground.

John replied, "Thank you, elder." The elder looked sternly at John, then nodded. As the elder sat, the host chief stood again. Ok, folks, it is about dinner time and I am looking forward to see who has the best story for us tonight. One last bit of business. John has requested to seek the council of the old man of the forest. He will go into the forest tomorrow if there are no objections?"

As the chief looked around the council each member nodded in agreement. "Ok, folks we are adjourned," the chief said as he stepped down toward the center and joined everyone else as they moved slowly toward the entryway and down the path to the communal building.

Raymond joined his uncle on the path to the main building. "Uncle, who is the old man of the forest? Was he here today?" Raymond asked.

"He might have been but I did not see him," John replied as he slapped Raymond on the back and they continued down the path.

The dinner was just a bit more subdued than the previous night. Storm Cloud and a few other elders had left and many more visitors had arrived. Tonight was simply a coming together celebration. After much food and much talk the chief of the host tribe stood up and said, "It is good that we should come together like this with our cousins, that we should share and renew our culture. Tonight a great and powerful shaman from the north has come to take us all on a trip to visit our ancestors as they were in the time before." The chief waved his hand over toward the massive stone fireplace.

Some of the young people helped to shift all the tables into a semi-circle around the towering fireplace. The lights were turned down and a big cast iron pot full of water was set on a hook and swung in close to the fire. A woman stepped forward in her traditional dark robe with red design. The mother of pearl buttons would shine as she moved and they caught the glow of the fire. She started her tale speaking in her Salish dialect. As one powerful with the gift of the rain, she let her words and images flow out to the crowd and permeate their minds. As she turned and moved waving her hands to describe the details of her story, she would undulate her hand fan made from eagle feathers across the steam that was creeping out of the cast iron pot. As she did so, it would swirl and take the form of the great bear or their ancestors paddling their big seagoing canoes. The audience remained spellbound as she conjured the words and images into the minds of young and old, gifted or not, long into the night.

The next morning at breakfast Raymond asked, "So, uncle, you going to see that old guy you were talking about yesterday?"

"I will see if he will speak with me today, yes," John replied.

"Can I come with?" Raymond asked.

John looked across the table at Tall Elk and asked, "What do you think?"

Tall Elk looked across at John, then over at Raymond. "He is much revered and if he does come to see your uncle, you will need to be respectful, more so than yesterday. No matter what, remain still and silent. Can you do that?" Tall Elk asked

"Yes I will," Raymond replied.

After breakfast Tall Elk met the two at the trailhead. John had his satchel and Tall Elk handed Raymond a huge salmon on a carved cedar tray. Raymond looked at him quizzically but said nothing. Tall Elk smiled and patted Raymond on the shoulder as he put one finger up in front of his lips to remind Raymond to be silent. They walked up the trail about a mile until they approached a grove deep in this ancient forest. The sky had been a medium gray but the trees obscured most of that now. John pointed at a moss-covered rock for Raymond to set the tray with the offering, then he stepped back and so did Raymond. No words were spoken. John then pointed to a fallen log even farther back for Raymond to sit upon. "Remember, no matter what you see, do not speak and do not move," John said in his mind.

Raymond took note of the serious look on John's face. John stepped forward, knelt down and began his meditation.

Some time had gone by and Raymond was doing his best to remain still. Suddenly Raymond noticed that the noises of the forest and gone quiet. The squirrels chirping to claim their territory, the occasional woodpecker or crow, nothing was making a sound. Raymond was on alert now, but he dare not move or look around. He kept himself still but he listened carefully. He did not move his head but his eyes darted left and right. Suddenly there was movement. directly in front of them, on the other side of the rock where they had placed the offering, a part of a giant tree seemed to move. Raymond dared not move but he fixed his eyes now on the side of the tree. A large form separated itself from the tree. What had seemed to be a part of the tree covered with moss and lichens now stood erect like a large bear standing on its hind legs but it was shaped more like a man. It looked at John and John stood. Raymond could see they were communicating but he could not hear them and Raymond was without the gift. He watched as John knelt again and so did the creature. John gestured toward the fish and the creature picked it up with ease. The creature then stood and looked directly at Raymond. Raymond put his head down. As he slowly peeked up again the creature was gone. John looked at him and smiled.

Raymond's eyes were huge. John grabbed the tray and walked toward Raymond who was now standing, looking all around. "Uncle, was that a…?"

Raymond was interrupted by John putting his finger in front of his lips. "Yes," John said, "we call them many things, tree people, Sasquatch and so on. You must not speak of this. They are ancient creatures more connected to the natural world and more gifted by the rain than any human. They walk with one foot in our world and one in the spirit world. I had to share with them what is going on in the human world among those of us with the gift but, of course, they have already sensed some of these things. They are wise and they are childlike all at the same time. We must protect them from the human world." With that John patted Raymond on the shoulder again and they headed back to the village. It was time to head home and then back to the city.

As John and Raymond headed back down the dock to the boat that had brought them, they were accompanied by several powerfully gifted individuals as well as a number of young girls smiling and making commentary on their dancing cousin from the south. The elders would travel with John to the city. They would see this Mr. Rappaport. Then they would return to their people and search out any scanners in their area. The crewmen on the boat were just loading a couple coolers full of bait fish as the party boarded. Just then the Orca pod that had accompanied them to this little fishing village arrived at the mouth of the inlet. One of the larger Orcas breached, lunging high out of the water then crashing back into the sea with a huge splash. The captain smiled as he saw them out there waiting. Tall Elk stood on the dock and looked out at the Orcas, then he smiled at John. "You have always been lucky with your friend," Tall Elk said as he looked out at the Orcas.

The twin diesel engines rumbled into action and the boat headed out toward their waiting escort, out toward the vastness of the open ocean. Tall Elk raised his hands and closed his eyes, sending his prayer after them.

THE BIG BATTLE:

LAURA AND SPARROW had been keeping a low profile in the city. They had taken coffee at the local coffee shops and eaten at several of the local restaurants all in the area of the hotel where they had abducted Mr. Rappaport. They were awaiting the return of the woman with the long brown hair that had left such an impression on Mr. Rappaport. The weather had been somewhat overcast with brief periods of sun but the forecast was calling for rain soon. I was back in the University District. Jay and I had been working out on the roof of my apartment building regularly. Sahira would join us from time to time and today was one of those days.

Jay and I were going through a few routine sparring drills and Sahira was meditating. She was sitting peacefully and then without warning she opened her eyes and blurted out, "We need to check in on Laura and Sparrow. It feels like something is going to happen soon." There was more than a little concern in her voice. Jay and I paused and I opened my consciousness. The moisture was starting to collect in the air, as it does before a rain. I closed my eyes and stretched out with my mind until I found them. Laura and Sparrow were closed off but I could search every mind in the area one by one until I detected them. They seemed fine but I grabbed my cell phone so as not to blow their cover should someone else be searching. I texted Sparrow, "Anything going on with you ladies?"

"Not right now," she replied.

"Sahira seems to think something is getting ready to kick off so stay sharp, I'll check in later," I said to Sparrow. "I remember you made your brother come check on me and you were right so I figure better safe than sorry, I said to Sahira. "We can check in again later too."

Evening was coming and the sky was now getting darker. A gentle shower started to fall. Laura went to the sliding glass doors that led to the balcony of their hotel room, just across the street from the one that Mr. Rappaport and his crew had occupied. She opened the door wide and let the moisture-rich air roll in. Laura went back to a table where she occupied herself with a chess game against herself. Sparrow watched a reality show on the TV...

Suddenly Laura felt something. It was a scan. She waved at Sparrow who had also felt it. It was powerful. Laura went to the balcony, looked around and saw nothing. Both she and Sparrow were on high alert now. Their minds were shut down tight. Laura looked across at the hotel room that had been Mr. Rappaport's. The lights were out. She looked down at the drive in front of the hotel. There was nothing. She looked over at Sparrow and said, "You'd better let Alex and Art know."

Sparrow sent out the text messages, "Someone is in the area and they are looking. We are going to get out on the street and hopefully spot whoever it is."

Laura looked at Sparrow. "They've probably figured out that there is nobody in the hotel so they are going to be on guard. Let's proceed with all due caution, shall we?" Laura said, as she grabbed her jacket.

Laura and Sparrow headed down to the lobby of their hotel. Keeping their minds closed and themselves invisible to all those around them, they strolled with purpose through the lobby and out the front door, unseen. Out on the street, the moist air filled their lungs and the smallest of droplets started to fall. They hurried across the street and into the lobby of the hotel. They split apart but stayed in visual range of one another. Sparrow slipped in behind the counter into the back office, invisible to those brushing past her in the hallway. She took up a spot at one of the desks where she could see through the one way mirror. Laura sat down and took up reading one of the magazines in the lobby.

It came again, a longer, slower scan, more localized this time. This person, whoever they were, certainly knew what they were doing. They moved their focus slowly down the street, scanning each person in their cars, on the sidewalks, and close to the windows where they could be readily detected from the street. The scan passed through the lobby of the hotel without a trace of detection. The two kept their composure and their focus, hiding in plain sight. Ten minutes had passed before they felt yet another scan; this time they could feel that the person doing the scan was just outside the lobby in the hotel drive. They were close now.

Laura examined her defenses. What if this person was too powerful for her to handle? Had she been arrogant to assume that she and Sparrow would be able to handle whoever showed up? Oh, well, too late now for second thoughts.

Laura watched as the hotel lobby doors opened and the auburn-haired woman she had seen in Mr. Rappaport's thoughts stepped in, flanked by two large attendants. They were moving through the lobby, trying to do a cursory scan through the minds of every person they passed. They were moving casually but headed for the elevator. The woman passed within feet of Laura and yet, it appeared Laura was undetected. Laura calmly flipped the page of the magazine she was reading as the woman scanned the lobby, looking directly at Laura before moving on to the elevators. As the elevator door closed and started its ascent, another black Suburban pulled up out front in the drive. It parked over to the side next to the one that had brought the auburn-haired woman and her companions. Laura had just stood up to follow the woman when she caught the other Suburban out of the corner of her eye. Laura stood looking out the window as Sparrow came out from behind the counter to join her. They both stared at the Suburban for a moment but no one got out. They did not dare try to scan for fear of detection. Sparrow looked at her phone and saw the earlier response from me. It read "on my way." Sparrow sent a second text. "Our friend is here. Second load of goons parked out front. Be careful."

Myself, Jay and Sahira were indeed on our way swerving through traffic on the interstate in Jay's BMW, Sahira trying to direct her brother as he cut left and right through traffic and I was trying to conceal us from any scans or police.

Laura and Sparrow looked at the second parked vehicle with the dark shaded glass for a moment longer before deciding what to do next. Finally the two turned and started walking toward the elevator. Perhaps they were just more low level scanners, Laura mused. She did not want to engage with them and let the bigger fish escape, so away they went. They both looked at the black Suburban one last time as the elevator doors closed and they started to ascend.

When the elevator doors opened they could see a maid cart and a couple tourists in the hallway and down at the other end, one of the two associates of the auburn-haired woman standing outside the door looking up and down the hallway. Laura whispered to Sparrow as she approached. "I am counting on you to address the two book ends so that I may focus on our friend."

Sparrow nodded. They came to a stop just a few steps from the door. Sparrow raised her hands and dropped her guard, becoming visible to the man in the hallway. Then she instantly reached deep into the minds of both the man in the hallway and the one inside the apartment. The auburn-haired woman felt this intrusion and turned, immediately putting up her guard. Laura tried to open the door but it was locked. She reached out to take hold of the mind of the auburn-haired woman but she was strong. Sparrow, still holding the two goons frozen, saw Laura struggling with the door so she motioned Laura back from the door. Sparrow took a step back and then launched herself forward kicking the door open. Laura ran into the room and smacked right into the wave of energy coming from her quarry. Laura's mind was now fully engaged. She moved toward the woman, who continued to press back against her. Sparrow was focused on her two targets. Outside in the hallway they had been unable to hide their entry from the tourists and the maid who were startled by what they had just seen. Sparrow instructed the man outside to reach in and pull the broken door closed again, then turn and smile at them. Laura slowly approached her adversary as each of them threw wave upon wave of energy at one another. The auburn-haired woman stood her ground. She reached out her hands toward Laura as Laura approached her. She squinted her eyes as if looking into a blinding light. Laura continued to advance. Now the woman took a half a step back. She was not able to hold her focus so she turned slightly away from the intense energy emanating from Laura. Sparrow was focused on holding both of the two attendants but she turned her head to see how Laura was doing. Sparrow could feel the pulsations in every water molecule in the air as their two wills collided.

Laura stepped forward, her demeanor calm, as she stretched out one hand toward the auburn-haired woman who appeared to be withering where she stood. Laura's hand gently touched the cheek of the woman who was now half doubled over. She raised both her hands in front of her face as if she could block Laura's will from being imposed upon her with them but to no avail. Laura spoke to her in a soft and soothing voice. Her words penetrated her mind and echoed into the far reaches of her consciousness. "Relax dear," Laura said softly.

The words seemed to affect the auburn-haired woman right away. She stood up straighter and looked directly at Laura now. She was indeed more powerful than Laura had anticipated but fortunately not more powerful than Laura. They stood there facing one another, Laura's hand on the woman's check. The woman relaxed further as Laura spoke again. "Everything is going to be Ok," Laura said as she watched the woman's face relax even more. She smiled at Laura and repeated, "Everything is going to be Ok."

Laura smiled back at her with her beguiling smile and told her, "We are going to be good friends dear."

The woman appeared quite calm now as she smiled back at Laura and said, "Yes, yes, we are going to be good friends."

Laura patted her on the cheek and smiled back at her; she was completely in the woman's mind. "Sparrow, invite our other friend in the hallway in now and have these two make us some coffee," she said, without taking her eyes off the woman. Laura smiled and waved one hand toward the sofa as she told her, "Let's do sit down and have a chat, shall we? Things have been so very hard on you, haven't they?"

Sparrow had been traveling with Laura for several months and had seen her do many things but watching her take this powerful woman, and feeling the waves of energy radiating from their struggle was impressive.

The other man entered the hotel suite and smiled. Sparrow had them both under control. "Can you two make us some coffee please," she said with a smile. As the two men headed into the kitchen area Sparrow walked over and sat down next to Laura. Laura was now sitting next to the woman, holding her hand in a comforting manner. The woman looked over and smiled at Sparrow.

It was at that moment that they felt another scan. It was very powerful and it was close. Sparrow quickly turned to Laura and said, "The other SUV," as she stood up quickly. She waited a moment as she did her best to screen them all. Laura was focused on controlling the auburn-haired woman. The two men were well under Sparrow's influence for the moment. Another scan came, even more powerful. Sparrow could tell that they had been detected by someone very powerful. She could feel a voice attempting to penetrate their consciousness even as Sparrow closed her eyes and pushed every bit of energy she could muster back at the voice.

The voice spoke. "I see you," it said. The voice pressed in on Sparrow's shield and Sparrow dropped to her knees, using everything she could muster to push back. Laura looked over at Sparrow and then back to the woman. "I'm sorry, dear," she said as the woman looked back at her with a quizzical expression on her face. Then Laura stood up abruptly and hit the woman in the head with a lamp that had been sitting on a small end table next to the sofa. The woman fell off the sofa to the ground unconscious as Laura turned all her attention to supporting Sparrow's shield.

Sparrow stood and looked at Laura as Laura now moved to her side. Just then the two assistants who had awakened from their trance-like state rushed at the two of them. Laura held the shield and Sparrow turned and stepped forward, placing her foot directly in the abdomen of the first, onrushing assailant. He fell backwards against the second man. As the second man stumbled to get around the first, Sparrow reached into the mind of the first and made him grab his partner from behind. As the man turned to see who was grabbing him, his partner punched him squarely in the jaw knocking him across the room. As the man stood up after punching his partner, he smiled at Sparrow. She then punched him in just the same manner, and he fell to the ground. Sparrow recoiled from the punch with the sharp realization as to just how much that hurt her hand, she looked over at Laura. Laura was collapsing under the pressure so Sparrow quickly moved to bolster her shield.

Laura and Sparrow moved out into the hallway and looked down the hallway at the elevator doors. They could see that someone was on the way up. They ran the other way, down the hall to the staircase. As they entered the stairwell they could hear a large number of people exit the elevator and run down the hallway toward them. Sparrow grabbed Laura by the hand and together they started running down the stairs. They looked over the railing and several floors down they could see and hear several people running up toward them. Laura and Sparrow were focused on keeping themselves protected from whoever it was that was pressing to enter their consciousness. They could not afford to split their energy for use on any of those closing in on them. They entered one of the lower floors and started walking quickly down the hall toward the elevator.

It was at that very moment that Jay's BMW rounded the corner, at the end of the block that the hotel was on. I could sense everything that was going on but at the moment I was devoting my energy to shielding our approach from everyone. I could feel the presence of someone very powerful who was focused on Laura and Sparrow.

"Pull over here," I said to Jay, just as we turned the corner. Jay pulled over and we all jumped out of the car. The rain was falling gently but steadily. "You two go help Laura and Sparrow," I said, as the rain started to saturate my hair and drip down my face. I was searching for the source of this powerful consciousness. I searched left, then right and I realized it was directly in front of me. I started walking quickly toward the front of the hotel as I reached out with one hand, surrounding the black SUV with my consciousness and focusing all my thoughts on containing the reach of the one in the vehicle. Whoever they were, they were clearly surprised by me. Immediately this powerful person turned all their focus on me as I was approaching the vehicle at a brisk walk. Inside Laura and Sparrow instantly felt my presence and that of Jay and Sahira. They also felt the one who had been pressing in on them disengage to focus on me outside.

Laura and Sparrow stopped running and looked at each other. Laura smiled the faintest of smiles just as the stairway door opened behind them and they both turned to face their pursuers as they emerged from the stair well. Outside I suddenly felt the full force of the person concealed in the Black SUV. I was bombarded by a powerful stream of raw energy hitting me like a high pressure hose of blinding power. I stumbled back a few steps and struggled to refocus myself, then directed every bit of energy I could muster forward, pressing back against the stream emanating from the SUV. Slowly I started walking toward the vehicle again, my arms up as if to shield myself from the stream of energy that was blasting me. So much energy was passing through the air and the moisture contained within that air that you could actually see the ripple as the energy passed through each rain drop.

Inside the hotel three men had entered the hallway from the staircase and ran toward Laura and Sparrow. Laura turned toward them, blocking their feeble attempt to penetrate her mind with the wave of a hand, as one might shoo away a fly. Then she pressed forward with her other hand, delivering a wave of energy that rolled down the hallway and knocked them all backwards off their feet. The elevator door opened behind them and out rushed several more. "My turn," Sparrow said as she turned and raised her hand, blocking the surge of energy as these new assailants attempted to reach her mind with a co-ordinated effort. Then Sparrow took a single step toward the oncoming group and pushed both hands toward them, sending a large rolling wave of her mental energy, taking them all off their feet. As the group attempted to get to their feet, Sparrow approached them. Laura followed Sparrow, walking calmly as she gathered herself and dispassionately observed Sparrow's skills. Sparrow approached the first man, still attempting to lift himself from the floor, slamming her foot down on the back of his neck driving his head hard against the floor. The next one was halfway up when she quick-stepped over to where she could give him a solid right cross before he could raise his hands to defend himself. As he stumbled back, she turned to the next one that had just gotten himself to his feet. As Sparrow approached, ready to engage him in physical combat, Laura cleared her throat and Sparrow hesitated and looked back at her. Laura shook her head disapprovingly. Laura was focused on Sparrow as she raised her hand in the direction of the one Sparrow was about to engage and froze him. "Really Sparrow, is all that really necessary," she said.

A second man ran toward them and Laura, without looking his way at all, froze him as well. She turned momentarily away from Sparrow, to observe the two frozen men, then she motioned with her hands as if she might clap, causing the two to run hard into one another and fall to the floor. Then she looked back at Sparrow. "See, no need to exhaust oneself unnecessarily," she said, raising an eyebrow.

Jay and Sahira entered the lobby of the hotel shielding their consciousness. They sensed what was going on a few floors up with Sparrow and Laura, than they sensed several scanners loitering by the elevators. They casually crossed the lobby approaching the elevators. As they approached, a couple of the scanners turned and attempted to scan Jay and his sister. Jay turned to his sister and smiled, "I got these guys," he said. Jay and Sahira walked right in among them. Jay reached out and pushed the button to summon the elevator, smiling at one of the two scanners that were attempting to scan them both, but were clearly bewildered by the lack of any reading whatsoever.

Sahira turned her back on the pack of scanners and cast a curtain across the minds of all the other people in the lobby, preventing them from seeing or hearing anything in the area in front of the elevators. All the scanners immediately turned toward her but before any one of them could move, Jay opened up a can of Whoop-ass that nobody saw coming. The two closest to his sister were first. Catching the two by the back of their collars he yanked them both backwards, turning to face them as they moved backwards past him on either side, he raised his hands and with a mental blast, drove them further back, hard against the wall. As the two scanners' heads slammed hard against the finished marble wall, two more lunged at him. Jay turned to his left, raising his left hand, sweeping it across in front of his own face, blocking the punch that was aimed squarely at his face. Jay let his left blocking hand slide down to the assailant's wrist. He then closed his left hand around the wrist of the right hand he had just blocked. Jay hooked with his right hand, catching this assailant squarely on the side of his jaw. He then continued his turning motion, pulling on the right arm of his now-collapsing assailant and sending him tumbling backward, toward the other attacker that had been approaching Jay from the other side. As the second man lowered his hand to catch the first that was collapsing backward toward him, Jay took a step toward them and stretched out a high roundhouse kick, reaching over the collapsing first scanner and catching the second directly alongside his head as both his hands were occupied holding the first already-unconscious scanner. Jay took a half skip backward and watched the last one fall, then did a quick shuffle with his feet as he winked at his sister.

"Stop showing off," Sahira said as she pointed at the last scanner, who appeared to be undecided as to what to do. Sahira let fly a pulse, sending that scanner stumbling backward until she let fly with another that took him off his feet. The second pulse hit him like a bolt of lightning. Just as he hit the floor, the elevator door opened in front of them with a ding. The two of them stepped into the empty elevator, turned to face the front and stood patiently; listening to the homogenized music as the doors closed and the elevator proceeded upward.

Outside, I had my hands full. Energy pulsated toward me on a massive scale. As I pushed back against it, it would change form, first attempting to pierce then trying to smother. I knew he had to press forward but with each step I felt the pressure increase as if I were walking against a hurricane force wind. Suddenly, the vehicle that concealed this unknown assailant lunged backward from its parked position, directly toward me. I quickly reached into the mind of a valet who was about to pull out of the hotel drive to go park a guest's SUV. That SUV lunged backward, striking the black SUV, preventing it from hitting me where I stood in the middle of the drive. The Black SUV now spun its tires to go forward, peeling out of the hotel drive and into the downtown traffic. I ran down to the sidewalk where I could see the Black SUV as it wove wildly through the traffic. I quickly reached into the mind of a delivery truck driver and just as the black SUV pulled alongside the truck, the truck swerved over, slamming into the Black SUV, driving it up onto the sidewalk where it ran directly into a street lamp pole. I ran up the street toward the Black SUV as did many other people on the street at the sight of such a crash.

Back inside the hotel, the auburn-haired woman had recovered herself and made her way down the stairs to the floor that Sparrow and Laura were on. Sparrow had just pushed the button for the elevator when she and Laura both felt the presence of that woman. Laura turned and raised one hand but before she could focus her shield, the auburn-haired woman sent a focused beam of penetrating energy, slamming into their consciousness like a punch in the face. Laura took the brunt of it as she had just time to step in front of Sparrow before it hit them. Laura collapsed to the ground woozy from the blast and Sparrow stumbled back but was able to regain her focus, firing back with a rolling wave of energy. The two large attendants that Sparrow had left lying on the floor upstairs entered the hallway behind their boss. Sparrow's attack had only slowed the advance of the woman but it knocked both men to the floor clutching their heads, attempting to regain their balance.

The auburn-haired woman smiled at Sparrow and focused now all her energy pressing to penetrate both Sparrow and Laura's conscious mind. Sparrow focused all her thoughts on shielding both herself and Laura. Sparrow reached down with one arm to help Laura off the floor. Laura was still trying to regain her full consciousness. The auburn-haired woman's two attendants had picked themselves up and walked past their boss now, heading down the hall toward Laura and Sparrow. Sparrow did not dare split her focus to deal with the other two or the woman would be in her head. Sparrow and Laura were backed up to the elevators when the door opened behind them. It was Jay and Sahira that stepped out of the elevator. Sahira reached out and took hold of Laura's arm with one hand as she reached with her other, helping Sparrow to scatter the focused beam of the woman. Jay lunged past the ladies, driving his foot squarely into the midsection of the first of the two attendants, sending him tumbling backwards down the hall. The woman slowly reached forward with both hands pressing back against the combined efforts of Sparrow and Sahira. The woman was able to let fly a psychic blast toward Jay, causing him to lose his footing momentarily before he stepped back and recovered, joining his energy to that of his sister and Sparrow. The woman stepped back a half step against the combined waves of energy. The second attendant was standing just over the shoulder of the auburn-haired woman. She turned and yelled at him, "Do something, you idiot." He put his best, albeit limited, effort in shielding his mind as he started down the hallway toward them.

As the back and forth with the auburn-haired woman had been going on, Laura had pulled herself together and just as several of the scanners entered the hallway behind the woman in her support, Laura stepped forward. Pressing her will like the first light of dawn, against that of the other woman, slowly now Laura's consciousness advanced, pressing back that of the woman. Jay stepped forward as if to crash into the oncoming enraged attendant but just as the big man launched a powerful right hand, Jay side-stepped him to the outside, catching the man's right wrist with his right hand. Jay then lunged in, driving his left forearm against the big man's straight right arm at the elbow, at the same time pulling back on the man's right wrist. The elbow shattered with a sickening crunch. Jay quickly let go of the man and as he collapsed to the ground, Jay followed with a straight left to the back of the head to render him unconscious.

Sparrow and Sahira were occupied engaging and freezing the scanners so they could unlock and free them from the psychic bondage that they were under. All the time this was going on Laura and the auburn-haired woman had been approaching each other slowly. They were locked in an unseen combat. Laura had folded her hands in front of her chest as if she were engaged in prayer. The woman had her hands outstretched; her painted and manicured fingernails like claws all pointed at Laura. As the physical combat raged around them, the scanners dropping one after another, they approached one another until they stood only inches apart. Laura's face was calm, focused. The woman was starting to show pain. Laura looked deep into the eyes of her adversary. The woman reached both hands toward Laura's face but Laura caught her by the wrists and bent her arms, pulling her closer. The woman opened her mouth as if to scream but no sound would come out. Laura furrowed her brow and whispered to the woman, "Relent."

The woman shouted back at her, "Never."

As the woman screamed, the last of the scanners hit the floor and Sparrow, Jay and Sahira all turned to see what was transpiring with Laura. A small trickle of blood started to run from the woman's nose. She screamed again as she pushed with her last bit of energy, trying to force Laura out of her head, then the woman collapsed.

Laura was still holding her by the wrists. Laura slowly let the woman's body fall backward onto the floor, dead. The woman's eyes were still open and her mouth, as if she was still trying to let go of one last scream. Laura took a deep breath and shook her head, looking down upon her adversary's twisted body. She stood up straight, realigning her clothes and brushing back her hair before turning to face Sparrow, Jay and Sahira. She could see the shock in their young faces. None of them had ever witnessed such a thing, and what they had witnessed was a horrifying death. They were all stunned.

Laura searched for something to say but before she could find the words her mind quickly was drawn to the battle going on up the street. "Alex," she said softly.

At that moment the rest of them quickly remembered and could feel that I was engaged with an incredibly powerful person just up the block.

"We have to help him," Jay yelled.

"No," responded Laura, "I will go to help Alex, you three need to clean up. Wipe the minds of everyone that has seen any of this. Get the scanners that we have released out of here. Laura had moved back to the elevator and pushed the button. Sparrow looked at the dead woman on the floor and started to ask, but Laura cut her off, "Leave her; people have heart attacks every day." Laura got on the elevator and the doors started to close. "I will try to clear the minds in the lobby as I go through but you might want to check as well," she said just as the doors closed.

The doors opened in the hotel lobby and there were people helping the injured left by Jay and his sister. Laura paused, raised her hands and put everyone into a frozen state. It was at that precise moment she then released the scanners from their mental prisons and awakened them. Several of them immediately got up and ran for the nearest exit. Laura then walked briskly toward the front door of the hotel lobby, clearing the memories of what they had witnessed from each person she passed.

As Laura stepped out the front door, she turned her head quickly at the rumble of an accelerating motorcycle engine coming at her. It was Art, flying up the drive on a full size Harley Davidson, "Jump on," he yelled over the rumble of the engine. Art had to brake hard to stop right next to her. Laura looked at Art with a look of disbelief. Before she could offer any protest Art said, "Come on."

Laura hesitated for a moment, looking apprehensively at Art on his big motorcycle before she finally threw a leg over and grabbed him around the middle. Art looked over his shoulder and grinned just before putting the gas to it and launching them down the drive and into the traffic.

Up the block, they could actually see the vehicles crashed up onto the sidewalk and feel the waves of energy flowing outward in every direction from the collision of my conscious energy and that of this other powerful person. Laura was trying to shield herself and Art as they approached but the way that Art was cutting between cars and then up on the sidewalk full of people it seemed almost pointless. They could hear police sirens in the background growing louder. As they approached they could see the visible energy waves rippling through the raindrops as they fell and so could every person passing on the street.

I was stuck standing in the rain, attempting to approach the crashed SUV but I could barely take each single step. Just as Art and Laura approached, the driver of the SUV jumped out of the driver door and started firing a hand gun at me. He was not the powerful one that I was locked in combat with so it was a simple matter for me to deflect his aim upward. At the moment that I was distracted by the driver, the passenger from the SUV got out the other side and started running away. It was at that moment that Art with Laura on the back of his bike, came roaring up the sidewalk and slammed into the shooter, sending him flying over the hood of a parked car. Art turned back to Laura as they came to an abrupt stop, "You got all this?" he asked. Laura could not wait to get off that bike.

"Yes, I do," she exclaimed as she practically leaped off the back of Art's bike.

"Let's go," Art yelled at me. I immediately ran over and jumped on the back of Art's bike. Art put the gas to it and the two of us roared up the sidewalk and back out into traffic, dodging pedestrians and other vehicles. In the rear view, Art could see Laura reaching into the minds of those around the scene of the accident, altering their memories. Just as they approached the intersection, a police car with sirens and lights came skidding around the corner. The person we were chasing had just reached into the minds of the two officers, leading them to believe that they were responding to a mass shooter who was escaping on the back of a motorcycle. The police attempted to cut us off but Art swerved over into the oncoming traffic and gunned it, going south between two lanes of oncoming traffic. I could not get a look at my foe as he ran up the street and ducked into the lobby of a building. Art rode his bike onto the sidewalk, up to the front of the building just as he reached into the minds of two pedestrians and had them hold the doors open. Art and I roared into the lobby of this building just as four security guards under the control of our adversary came running toward us, weapons drawn. Art spun the back tire of his big bike, turning the bike around and he gunned the engine, leaving a big black spin mark on the polished floor. We went back out the way they had come in, with the guards firing at us as we cut left and right through the crowd. The guards were quickly released by my fleeing foe as they ran out the door after Art and myself. They seemed to awaken from their momentary trance. Art waved his hand and the guards paused in a state of confusion and looked at each other. The two of them rode up to the end of the block and turned, circling the block, with me scanning, searching for the one that had just eluded us. I searched from mind to mind, flying from the consciousness of one person to the next but found nothing. "It's no good, Art, he's gone," I said.

Art turned his bike around and we rolled back toward where we had left Laura. She was still scanning and adjusting the memories of the people in the area. Laura knew as soon as she saw us that the big fish had got away. We paused and scanned the minds of all the people coming and going around us in the rain. So many people, they were not going to find him this way. Sparrow, Jay and Sahira came walking up the street with several of the newly freed scanners following them, perhaps out of gratitude, perhaps because they had no place else to go.

I reached out with both hands and grabbed all three of them, hugging them, then quickly released them. "Sorry, guys, I'm just glad to see you all in one piece, so ah, nice work anyway." I shoved my hands into my pockets. "Anyone got any ideas as to who that guy was," I asked, as I looked around at everyone present. There was no response. The cadre of former scanners all appeared fairly stunned. I looked over at Laura and Art and asked, "So what are the chances that someone this powerful is someone nobody knows? We need to figure this out. I need to reach out to John and see what he can tell us." With that I turned, facing the waterfront, and started reaching out with my mind over land, over water to the deep forest of the peninsula. First, it was Grandma that answered me. "We will summon all those known to us with this level of power. We will see who this person is that would so misuse the gift of the rain. You may not have seen him but you have all felt him and that may be enough, we will see," Grandma said.

John responded as well but he was much closer than I expected. He was on board a ferry boat that had just docked and he was headed up the hill toward us. "I will be there soon," was all he said.

Just then a big moving van pulled up alongside them on the street. It was Mike Dechain driving one of Art's Antique Furniture warehouse vans. He jumped out and ran around to the street side, giving Art a fist bump as he smiled and nodded at the rest of us. Mike addressed the new former scanners,

"Alright people, I know you're dazed and confused. Anyone who is interested, we are offering you the opportunity at the very least, to get the low down on what is going down. Step this way and let's get the hell out of here. Of course, this activity is purely optional, folks," he said as he held the door open. Art looked at the rest of us and we studied him. He had not mentioned that he'd actually taken Mike on as a trainee.

"What?" Art said. "I got tired of moving all that heavy stuff around so I hired a guy." He turned away, climbed back on his Harley and slowly disappeared into the rain city traffic. Mike smiled at me as he closed the door to the van. "Art made me hang back this time but just so you know. I am down to ride any time," he said as he grabbed my hand.

"I know you are," I responded as he walked back around to the driver's side and climbed in. Laura took Sparrow by the arm and down the rainy street they wandered with Jay and Sahira, recounting the battle that they had all just survived.

Mike pulled away from the curb, going the other way with his cargo of newly freed scanners. It had all unfolded so fast that no one really had a chance to think about what they were doing. What we all expected to be a simple trap for the auburn-haired woman had almost become a death trap for Laura and Sparrow. The reality of the killing they had witnessed was just setting in as we saw an aide car pull up the hotel drive. We all just stood around in the gathering crowd as the EMTs exited the lobby with a stretcher covered with a sheet.

"What happened?" Sparrow asked one of the hotel workers who was standing outside in the crowd. "Some lady had a heart attack, I think," she replied.

Sparrow and Laura looked at each other for a moment before Laura finally said, Ok, let's go." Slowly we all wandered up the street. I was scanning just to be sure, but nothing. I picked up a few lightly gifted people who were, as yet, unaware as far as I could detect. The rain fell as we slowly simply disappeared into the throngs of regular people, coming and going--just cogs in the machine, unaware of anything outside the normal routine, unaware of the battle that had just transpired here, just another day like every other day under the gray sky in the rain city.

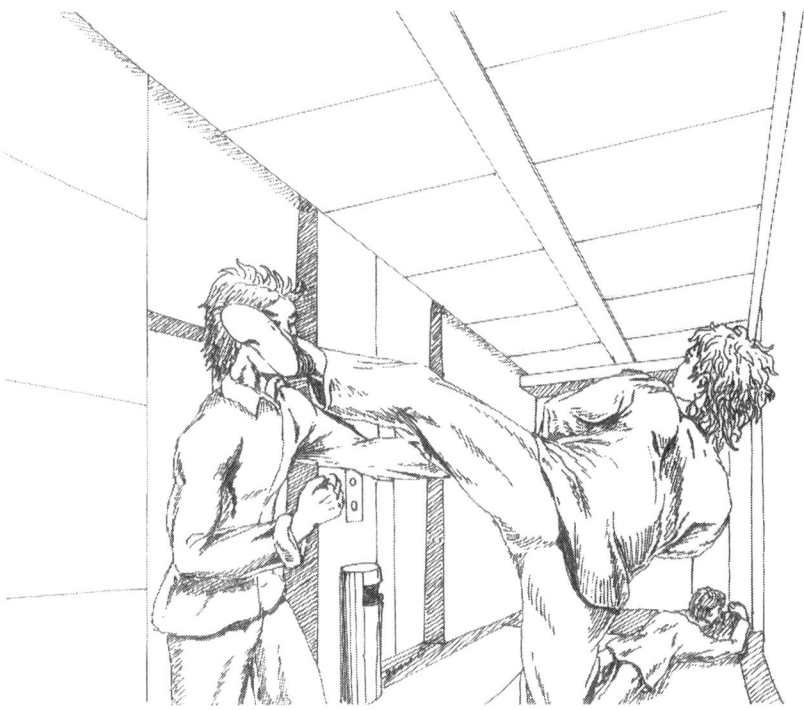

THE CHANGING TIDE:

WE ALL ENDED up back to the hotel room that Laura and Sparrow had been occupying for several days as they waited for what turned out to be an evil auburn-haired beauty. As soon as we got there, Laura walked straight to the mini bar and reached in, pulling out a small bottle. She then held a glass up to the light for a quick inspection before setting it on the counter and pouring herself a drink. She had taken a life today and that was something she did not take lightly. As she let herself fall softly backwards into a large chair, my attention was drawn back to the door.

I turned and opened the door with a degree of excitement. Looking down the hallway, I was just in time to see John jogging toward me. Behind him were several powerfully gifted, first nations elders that had come with him from his trip to Vancouver Island. They had hidden themselves from detection as they approached just in case. John grabbed me by the hand and then pulled me in close. He was clearly relieved to see me in one piece. John then pushed past me into the room, running over to Sparrow and throwing his arms around her. He hugged her tight for a moment before loosening his grip so he could look her in the face. John then turned to glance over at Laura. Laura raised her glass back in John's direction before taking another sip.

"I almost made the ferry boat captain crash us into the dock to get here as fast as they could go," John said. He then looked back at Sparrow with a look of intense relief before turning back to me. "I should have been here," he said with a note of regret in his voice. "But where are my manners?

Let me introduce everybody." John motioned his entourage into the room. "This is my friend and my daughter's teacher, Laura," John said as he motioned in her direction. Laura set her glass down and stood up giving the crowd a brief nod. She then walked over toward me. Pausing, she looked me up and down for a moment, studying me carefully before turning to John. "John, you were right about this one." She turned back to me, studying me again for a moment as if looking for something. "His power was amazing, particularly for someone who still doesn't know how to dress himself with any particular style yet--and speaking of style," Laura said as she turned back to John. John was clean shaven and had his hair pulled back into a neat pony tail. He was dressed in a black, collared shirt, under a black, mid-thigh length, leather jacket. He had on black jeans and black, cowboy style boots with trim that matched his belt. Laura looked him up and down with just a hint of a smirk. "Very nice," she said.

John fidgeted with the lapel of his jacket for a moment. Sparrow walked toward him with an ever-growing smile, "Yeah Pop, very nice," she said as she hugged him again.

Finally John turned to Jay and his sister. "You two OK?" John asked.

"Yes sir," Jay replied as he reached out to shake John's hand. "You must be some teacher," Sahira added, as she also reached out to shake his hand. "I have never witnessed someone as powerful as Alex was today, yet it is strange how his abilities seem to have grown so tremendously from when we first met, only a short time ago." Sahira turned back to me and looked me up and down slowly with an inquiring eye. She then lifted one hand with her palm facing me, making me just a bit nervous. She closed her eyes and spoke. "Stranger still, I see his power increasing as he learns to..," she stopped and opened her eyes. She looked at me and smiled, deciding not to finish her statement. "I'm impressed," she said.

"Well, I'm not *that* impressed," Sparrow interjected as she glanced briefly in my direction.

She strolled over and plopped down on the sofa next to Laura who was still nursing her drink. "You were pretty impressive yourself," Jay interrupted with a big grin. "I could not see it but I, you know, saw you, like bam and pow, that was sweet." Jay pantomimed a part of Sparrow's fight sequence.

Sparrow smiled a subdued smile and looked over at me, then back toward Laura. Laura just met her eyes momentarily then looked away to take another drink. "Yes, that's all well and good that we survived, what could, very well, have gone horribly wrong. Let's not forget that a life was taken today and that is never something to be taken lightly."

An awkward silence blanketed the room momentarily. "Laura is right," John interjected. He paused and looked over at Laura, "Even though in this case, Laura had no choice. That woman could have relented any time and saved her own life. She chose to go to the end. There was no alternative for you, Laura," John said as he contemplated all the scanners he had dispatched, scanners that today might have been saved.

"Let's hope we can avoid such events in the future," Laura said as she finished off her drink and cast a quick glance back in John's direction. Laura walked over to the minibar and reached for another drink. John quickly stepped over next to her, reaching in over her, grabbing a bottle of orange juice and handing it to her. Laura glanced at him for a moment. John just smiled and said, "Been there, done that. Trust me."

"So you have," Laura replied as she took the orange juice. "So you have."

John had observed Sahira as she studied me. He turned back toward her and said, "Excuse me Ms., but I could not help but notice. You have a unique aspect to your gift that is rare indeed. My people would call someone like you a seer. The gift is different for each of us but yours is quite special; tell me how it is for you?"

Sahira smiled, "I am not accustomed to speaking about the gift that we share so openly. Even my teacher back home was not familiar with my, um, uniqueness."

John took one of her hands, holding it between his two hands. "May I share something with you?" he asked. "There is someone I want you to meet."

Sahira nodded and John reached out across the water to his mother. He linked the two of them and a smile spread across Sahira's face. John released her hand and stepped back as Sahira remained connected for a few minutes before it was over.

"She is my mother and Sparrow's grandmother. She also has this facet to her gift, the gift of foresight," John said.

Sahira looked excitedly at her brother, then back at John. "Please tell me I might meet her," Sahira said.

"Of course," John said, "of course." John then turned back to me. "The person you faced today, do you know who it was, any idea at all?" John asked. "Anybody I might know?" he asked.

I just shook my head, "He was very careful to keep himself from me." I paused a beat. "He was very, very powerful."

John looked down, then back at me, "I could feel the waves of energy as your two wills collided even as I stood on the deck of the ferry coming here. I recognized your reflection in each wave. I thought for a moment I might have recognized your opponent as well, but I cannot be sure."

"Who is it, John?" I asked.

"I cannot say right now but we will know for sure soon enough," John replied. "Grandma has requested that all of those known to us, with the gift anywhere near this level, come to a potlatch. We will put this before everyone. Someone will know the person." John looked around the room. "Whoever he is, he will likely go into hiding now, he will not dare to show himself but still, we must stay together and be safe. Laura and Sparrow, I will ask you to take these elders to meet Mr. Rappaport as soon as you can and perhaps we can all meet back here later," John said before turning and walking toward the door.

"Alex, perhaps you would like to come with me; there is someone I want to invite personally," John looked one more time at his daughter. She smiled at him. "I'll be fine, Pop," she said.

"I know," John replied as he opened the door and turned away.

"See you all later," I said as I followed John out the door.

John and I stepped into the elevator and headed down to the lobby. We both concealed ourselves in the minds of others as the elevator doors opened and we walked through the lobby, invisible to those around us. As we stepped out onto the street the light rain hit us both like a caffeinated drink. Walking up the street, John turned and said, "Cyrus--we are going to invite him. You keep yourself hidden and lay back. Let me talk to him alone. As you know he is not very social so I will have a better chance if he thinks it is just me and if he decides to be antisocial. It is less likely to get out of hand if you let yourself be known, but only if it gets out of hand, Ok?"

"Yeah, Ok," I replied, "but what is his story anyway? What is his deal?

"Just hang back and stay low," John replied, "We can talk about him more later."

As we drew near the market I let John go on ahead of me as I paused to adjust my collar, take my baseball cap out of my pocket, and put it on. I could feel John reaching out to Cyrus, calling out to him as he walked. John stopped up on the corner at the end of the block waiting for a response. He did not have to wait long before he received a curt response. It was just the name of the newsstand at the front of the market facing the city. John went on and I waited. I ducked into a coffee shop and got one to go. When I stepped back outside, I looked up at the slate sky and let the rain wash over my face. I took off my cap and ran the water back through my hair with one hand before putting the cap back on and starting to work my way closer. I crossed the street focused on keeping myself closed and far enough away so as not to be seen. I stood under the awning across the street and up the block just as far away as I could and still see them both.

Cyrus appeared as tastefully dressed as ever. I could see him talking to John, but I could not tell what they were saying without risking giving myself away. Just then I spotted one of the guys from Cyrus' bar. He was doing the same thing I was. John had noticed him as well, along with another of Cyrus' employees. He just smiled at Cyrus and pointed them out. Cyrus smiled back and then turned and waved at me. I waved back at him but remained obscured and closed off until they shook hands and parted ways. I felt better as John started walking toward me. "Is he coming?" I asked.

"We'll see," John replied.

"So what is the deal with that guy?" I asked. "Do you think it was him, and how is he on to me? Can he sense me even when I am shut down?"

"No, I think he is like Sahira in that he can see things to some degree that have not yet happened or that happened some time ago. It is, as Grandma says, the hidden river of time that flows just beneath the surface. Some of us can see that aspect of the gift and I believe Cyrus is one of those," John said.

"Can we trust him?" I asked.

"Grandma seems to think so," John replied as we strolled down the street. We walked slowly, disappearing into the throngs of city people going about their lives, never realizing what was going on around them.

This was the price. I had been given this rare gift, this chance to be more than just another cog in the machine and this was the price. Like all good things that come your way in life, there is always someone or something that wants to take it from you. If I wanted to live to my fullest potential then I would need to fight for my life. Now I had a life worth fighting for.

I held out my hand and studied the small droplets of water as they collected in my outstretched palm. I marveled at the sensation that I received from the water against my skin.

"It never gets old kid, there is always more to learn--a new facet to realize in this relationship with the water," John said in a quiet voice as we walked along.

The tables had turned and now we were the hunters. Where would this take us? How would this end? Who was it that we were hunting and why had they initiated this campaign to control those like us?

We walked along as the rain fell all around us, just as it had always fallen before these streets were paved, before these buildings were built and before the first human set foot in this rain-sculpted land. I listened intently as the moisture seemed to fall in subtle waves all around us. I felt the impact of each little drop as it touched my skin, only now I welcomed each droplet. Now the rain gives me strength; it gives me comfort. The thunderheads above us, heavy with rain yet to fall, were now as welcome as the smell of fresh-baked bread and as reassuring as the soft comforting words of a mother to her child. We walked on, our shoes squishing against the sidewalk. I stopped and turned to John. I held out my hand to him and he looked at me with a quizzical look on his face before grasping my hand in a firm handshake.

"Thanks," I said as I looked him in the eye.

"I was just going to say the same to you," he replied. We both smiled and turned our faces directly into the rain.

CPSIA information can be obtained
at www.ICGtesting.com
Printed in the USA
FSOW02n2208110617
35120FS